TAKE MY WORD

OUT OF OFFICE SERIES
BOOK 2

DANI MCLEAN

TAKE MY WORD

www.danimclean.com

Cover Design by Ink & Laurel

Edited by Beth Lawson at VB Edits

Author photo by Rachael Munro Photography

CONTENT NOTES

Triggers

While this story is a light-hearted contemporary romance, there are elements which may be difficult for some readers.

The protection of your safety and mental health is absolutely crucial to me. Please do what you need to look after yourself. If that means skipping scenes or the entire book, I fully support that.

If you have any questions about this list, don't hesitate to contact me via social media.

- Explicit language
- Detailed sexual content, with the following featured on page: consensual role play scenarios, praise, spit as lube, brief anal play, dom/sub interactions
- Lying (on page); both characters lie or omit details of their life to others as part of the fake dating scenario

- Sex work (on page) in the form of audio erotica
- Discussion of sex work and derogatory comments of sex work by a side character
- Blackmail (on page)

Author's Note:

This story features a British MMC and an American FMC. While the majority of this book does use American spelling, his POV chapters will include exceptions (because I could not in good conscience let the man say ass instead of arse).

To Andy & Vonn,
Thank you for proving true love exists

Vonni, you're in our hearts forever x

CHAPTER 1
OH, LOOK, IT'S THE CONSEQUENCES OF MY ACTIONS

IVY

THE END

Life isn't a movie, with perfect lighting and mistakes hidden on the cutting room floor. It's theater. Chaotic and unpredictable, with no way to un-fuck a fuckup except to improvise and hope everyone rolls with it until you can throw yourself through a fake window and hope for death.

There are no fake windows tonight. Only the very real kind that won't be half as painful to go through as this awkward dinner party is.

The dining hall (which is as cold and vast as my college swimming pool) is dappled in candlelight. Darkness looms over the twenty of us forebodingly. Sondheim would be proud.

Yesterday, I sat here and smiled, my heart fed and full while the sun streamed in, flooding the room in its golden glow. Tonight, the thick curtains are drawn tighter than the knots in my stomach.

I can't believe it's come to this.

All I wanted was a bit of fun. A flight of fancy I could remember when I'm old and arthritic and no longer able to taste salt. Somewhere out there, Mom is shaking her head, asking if I'll ever learn.

(I won't.)

Of course the scene is set beautifully. My doom wouldn't be staged any other way.

Lincoln is as dashing as ever in a midnight blue suit, his dark blond hair brushed back in a charming swoop that is ruining my heart in three different ways. The birthday cake on my plate tastes better than any meal I've eaten in all twenty-seven years of my cake-loving life, and the past few days have been like something out of a fairy tale (complete with the dastardly villain).

And still, I'd rather puke all over the antique chair I'm sitting on than deal with the upcoming fallout of my big, beautiful mouth. Honestly, with the way my nerves are battling it out right now, there's a strong chance I might.

Astrid—one of the few people in this room I actually like—shuffles her seat closer to mine and catches my hand, telling me about the time she saw Christian Borle in *Falsettos*. "He's a fucking treasure," she whispers, earning a startled look from Darcy. "You must come with me to New York so we can see his next show."

My heart whimpers. "I'd love that," I force out.

Dammit, I'll miss her the most. After Lincoln, of course.

From the other end of the table I can make out the dark look in Kyle's eyes. They burn black as he stares me down. Even Lincoln's broad palm on my thigh isn't helping. Turning to him, I know I'm not the only one who's rattled. His expression is calm, but the low light dances over his newly shaven jaw every time it clenches.

Every bite of black forest goes down wrong, anxiety kicking and scratching in my gut like an angry toddler begging for attention. Damn Kyle and his fucking agenda. This cake is delicious, and he's ruined it.

Maybe when Lincoln's family kicks me out on my tap-dancing ass, I can sneak through the kitchen and take a piece for the road. It'll go well with my self-loathing.

Kyle clears his throat loudly enough to draw his father's frown from the head of the table. "I know it's customary on the last night for the birthday boy to make a speech," he says, pasting on his gummy smile. "But I'm hoping you won't mind if I say a few words instead."

Joe, who just turned ninety and does not look humored to be called a boy, waves his pale hand, looking as uncomfortable as I've seen him all weekend, which is really saying something. "I already said we don't need to bother with all that."

Oh, Joe. If only Kyle gave a shit.

Whenever I've imagined breaking a leg at a family gathering, it's always been in the "drama kid who forces their parents to watch their latest one-woman show to rave reviews" kind of way. Not the actual, literal kind.

Now, any joy I take in the way Kyle wobbles on his

sprained ankle as he pushes his chair back to stand is tainted. And yeah, okay, it's just a sprain, but come on. I'm posturing here. Go with it.

"Trust me, you want to hear this."

I swallow past the lump in my throat and grip Lincoln's hand, looking away from Kyle's beady little eyes, only to find Darcy watching me, concerned.

My time is up.

It won't matter that I'm completely head-over-heels, to-the-ends-of-the-universe-and-beyond in love with Lincoln, because at the end of the day, this is my fault.

My lies have touched every person I care about in this room, and now it's time to face my final curtain.

Beside me, Lincoln is doing his best night-before-the-full-moon werewolf impression, silently seething so loudly I'm shocked the whole room isn't shaking. At least king-of-the-assholes Kyle has the smarts to look a little cowed, carefully avoiding Lincoln's piercing stare.

It doesn't stop him, though.

"This weekend is supposed to be about commitment to this family, but someone here has done nothing but lie to every single one of us, and I'm here to set the record straight."

"Just get on with it already," Lincoln growls.

I didn't think it was possible, but Kyle's smile grows wider. Any more, and it'll split his face in two (a girl can dream).

"Lincoln, something you want to add? Or maybe your *girlfriend* does?" My spine ices itself when he looks at me. "Nothing? And you're normally so chatty."

Taking their cue, the rest of the table turns to stare at us. Well, *shit.*

It was good while it lasted.

CHAPTER 2
WHAT YOU NEED TO KNOW

IVY

I don't care; I'll say it. I love drama.

Plays, musicals, movies. Eighteen seasons of semi-scripted reality television that will become my entire personality until I can't have a single thought without quoting it.

Fabulous, give me fifteen more.

I mean, the last one's pretty bad for the mental health of contestants, but I can't stop watching them. The more ridiculous, the better.

It's all about the drama.

So when I find myself without a job or purpose, being asked to play the loving girlfriend on a weekend away at a mansion that rivals Pemberley? Where the family isn't mine and one man is currently embroiled in a scandal that threatens the reputation of his family's legacy?

Sign.

Me.

Up.

But I'm racing ahead.

It all started three months ago, when I got the call that ended my career…

CHAPTER 3
THIS SEASON IS CANCELED

IVY

THE BEGINNING

Waiting is the worst part.

When the redundancies were announced, management promised it would be over in two weeks, as if ten days of stomach-churning anxiety was a blessing.

It's not.

After six excruciating days, I'm pretty sure my stomach is eating itself.

"What if it's me?" Emma asks over lunch on day seven. "Maybe the leadership team has it out for me after what happened with Richards."

"It better not be you," I say, pitchfork at the ready. If it is Emma, I'll find that putrid rat bastard of an ex-boss she had and… well, I haven't gotten that far, but it'll be unpleasant.

Diana: The Musical unpleasant.

"If they call you, I'm marching in there and demanding they cut me instead."

Emma sighs, looking around the cafeteria where unease has turned everyone into zombies who shuffle awkwardly around each other. "I don't think it works like that."

"I know, but you've worked so hard for this."

"So have you," she says.

Honestly? I'm not sure I have. At least, not in the "I want this so much, it's all I live for" kind of way that Emma does. I've worked, and I've done my best, but at the end of the day, this is just a job.

Not my passion, not my purpose. A paycheck.

One I'd like to keep, sure, but nothing more.

Five percent of the workforce, they said. Seven hundred people. Just numbers casually listed. Not lives irrevocably changed.

Every minute of the day has become a waiting game, every phone call a jump scare. Going home isn't even a relief, because all I can think about is how much money I haven't saved and how long it's been since I've updated my résumé.

Oh god, I'll have to write a cover letter.

That's actually worse than being unemployed.

I haven't slept a wink all week, and sleep is my third favorite thing to do after kissing and reciting my villain monologue in the shower. I've heard the horror stories of the job market—hundreds of applications sent without a response, the terrible group interviews, the awful salary conditions. And to top it all off, I'll disappoint my mom.

When the phone call finally does come, bright and early on day eight, my stomach cannonballs up out of my throat. Doesn't leave a note, just "see ya, wouldn't want to be ya" as I listen to the instructions I'm given.

Come to room 1105. Don't pack up. Don't tell anyone where you're going.

It's enough to knock anyone on their ass.

My heart is pounding so fast, I might be dying. Is that toast I can smell? My left arm isn't tingling, but maybe that's an old wives' tale?

What do I have to show for it? All my years of clocking in, doing what I was told, following the rules… and for what?

In the end, it only takes a single phone call at nine a.m. on a Tuesday to drop the curtain on my time here at Helix.

Standing, I shoot a quick text off to Emma, because come on, "tell no one" clearly excludes my best friend.

What are they gonna do? Fire me harder? Please.

In some ways, it's a relief. For one, it's not Emma. Getting rid of the smartest person here is a bad decision even Helix would never make. But also, just between us, I've never really liked working here.

Document Control isn't my dream job or my calling. Not the way it is for Emma. It's the financial glue holding my life together, but isn't that what any job is?

The meeting is quick. Just me, the CIO, and HR in a room.

It takes five minutes. They say their spiel—"The company is in a difficult position; we wish there was another option; blah, blah, blah"—but all I can picture is every bill piling up, one on top of the other, until I'm run out of my apartment by collectors.

This was meant to be my safety job. The one you take for security. That's what mom said.

How do they sleep at night, affecting people's lives like this? It's not like profits are down. As we speak, it's just gone up by my whole salary.

Oddly it's the CIO who looks contrite. Mr. Fletcher, someone who must have had a part in this decision, still manages to sound like he means it when he says, "We're sorry to see you go."

Not sorry enough, apparently.

I sign the paperwork and walk out in a daze. As per instruction, I return my laptop and pack up my desk and get walked out of the building.

So, that's it. Eight years of my life… over.

As soon as I'm home, I throw myself face-first on my bed. I can't shake the feeling I should be in the office. That I'm slacking off. I didn't even have a chance to reply to Tanisha with the supplier template or cancel my meetings or set an out-of-office.

I roll over, stare up at the ceiling, and pull my phone out.

Me: busy?

Emma: Unfortunately.

Emma: I miss you, though! Hutchinson is on slide 67 of 108… Swap places with me?

Me: ughhhhhh ever since he discovered podcasts, he's become insufferable. I love you, but I'd rather gargle salt water.

Emma: So would I.

Emma: Wait

Emma: You're offline. Is everything okay?

Emma: Give me two minutes. I'll fake food poisoning and call you.

Me: no no no! I had to leave early. Will fill you in after work. Go get back to upstaging that airhead.

Emma: ILY. You're a shining glimmer of a person.

My phone lands with a thud beside me. Okay, so now what?

I could clean. Wash my sheets—which I almost never have the time to do—or tidy up. There's makeup scattered across my dresser from this morning and dishes in the sink from breakfast.

Really, I should be looking for another job. It's barely noon. I haven't updated my résumé in years, and there's about to be a flood of competition in the job market.

The thought of it makes me want to crawl under the covers. And actually, why not? I don't have anywhere to be.

I kick my shoes off, not caring where they land, and slip under the sheets while a wash of white noise settles in my ears. Reality lodged itself in my throat during that phone call, and now it's slowly sinking into my gut.

Shit. I'm unemployed.

I'm going to have to take back all the whining I did when Mom guilted me into putting money into savings. Without it, I'd be...

A chill crawls down my spine.

Yeah, let's not think about how bad it could have been. Heading up shit creek with one paddle is better than nothing.

I roll onto my side, listening to the way my eyelashes brush against the pillow with each blink. If Mom was here, she'd tell me not to get complacent. Get the ball rolling. Start applying now. The longer I wait, the more conspicuous the gap will look.

God… Eight years… Wrapped up in less time than an intermission.

Now I'm three years away from thirty — thirty! — and what do I have to show for it except a trauma response to spreadsheets?

At least I don't have to worry about rent. Since the new landlord arrived, the entire building has rolled back to prewar prices. Any cheaper, and it'd be free. No one in the building knows why, but it's been two years since the cuts, so we're gatekeeping our good luck lest some jack-in-office bill us for the rest.

But it's weird, right?

Who the hell buys a building and then lowers the rent for everybody?

A sucker is who. (Armando in 5F is convinced it's a tax write-off for some exotic billionaire, and I'm not saying I believe him, but I do make sure to smile at every well-dressed stranger in hopes of getting swept up in an international love triangle).

It could turn out to be Dracula diversifying his assets, and I wouldn't care. It saved Mrs. Moonsamy and her daughter from having to move across the country when she was between jobs last year, so whoever it was can't be all bad.

And the best part of new ownership is easily Manny and his bar downstairs.

In the past two years, the Dapper Scoundrel has been the set piece for all my life crises. When I go to ground, I mean it literally, because the Scoundrel is six floors below me. That alone would automatically make it the best bar in town, but then there's Manny, with his lilting English accent, model cheekbones, and goofy smiles, who pours the best French martini I've ever tasted.

It also helps that he lets me steal their Wi-Fi.

Borrow. I mean borrow.

———

On my first day of unemployment, Mom texts to ask how my week is going, and my gut twists so sharply with guilt that I can only manage a thumbs-up before I stuff my phone behind the sofa cushions and run to the bar. It takes two mojitos and a cosmo to untangle it again.

On day two, Emma comes over and makes me promise to use her as a work reference.

On day three, there's Lincoln.

CHAPTER 4
A SCOUNDREL, INDEED

LINCOLN

It's a Thursday afternoon when a goddess walks into the pub.

I've seen my fair share of beautiful women. It's impossible to find a woman who isn't beautiful, in my opinion. They're each spectacular in their own way.

But this woman…

This woman is phenomenal.

I knew the moment I met her that Ivy was special. Call it attraction or call it intuition; I'm not bothered. Something about her drew me in, and I'm not in the habit of denying my curiosity.

That she clearly doesn't immediately fall at my feet only makes the chase sweeter.

But it's best we begin with some context.

———

No matter how many times I return stateside, the sun is a welcome surprise. Rain is predictable. London rain, especially. Dependable, one might say. And if one was my brother, one definitely has. Reed cares about that sort of thing.

Reliability, I mean. Not the rain.

Although probably that too.

Dad's always said we're two sides of the same coin, approaching problems from opposite directions. Reed is regimented; I'm impulsive. Darcy, as the youngest and obviously the most perfect in our father's eyes, has thus far escaped clichéd metaphor.

"There he is," Manny calls out as I step through the painted double oak doors, his beaming smile greeting my own. If sun rays could take human form, they'd look like my cousin.

When he's finished washing out a cocktail shaker, he slaps his hand in mine, pulling me halfway across the counter into a hug. He's shaved his head and has let his goatee grow out. We're the same age, but he still manages to make thirty-three look like twenty-one, especially in the *Nightwing* T-shirt he's got on. Unlike my lily-white arse, Manny's blessed with his mum's brown skin and good humor, which makes him a triple threat.

I take my first full breath in twenty-four hours. Christ, I've missed the hell out of him. A year between visits is too long.

"How was the flight?" he asks. "I'm assuming you haven't unpacked yet, because you look like shit."

I flip him off, taking the second to last stool at the bar. It's worn, with a little wiggle that lets me rock when I position it right. "Thanks, mate. Your compliments always warm my heart."

Manny chuckles as he pours me a pint (a proper ale, not some pissy lager). I won't insult him by pretending he'll charge me for it. "Can't believe I finally convinced you to follow me here. Your dad owes me twenty quid."

"Well, I know how much you can't live without me," I joke. "Someone has to keep you honest."

"Fuck off," he laughs. He's practically glowing. I already knew he was thriving since making the move here, but seeing it in person is always a joy. "It's good to see you, man."

"You too." I raise my glass, and fuck, it's good. Jet lag has been kicking my arse since I landed six hours ago, and I haven't eaten since the dry sandwich I had on the plane, but sleep and food can wait. I've needed this.

Manny sets both hands on the wood and brass counter, one of the signature touches of the Scoundrel. I already know what's coming, but I'm going to put it off for as long as possible.

"You called Reed yet?"

Or not. "No."

He just shakes his head like he expected that answer, and I'm briefly saved any follow-ups when a customer steps up and orders two glasses of wine.

It gives me a chance to take a fresh look at the place.

Along the walls, green glass sconces cast a golden glow over the room, warming the deep forest walls and mismatched leather stools. The mission was to bring home here, and we damn well made sure to keep it on the right side of nostalgia without dipping into parody.

There are places where the paint extends too far, or a panel was cut an eighth too short, but sitting here, I can feel the care seeping in from the floor and extending to the ceiling. With the reclaimed wood trim and back bar, it's every bit a right proper pub.

"I see you haven't run this place into the ground yet," I say, when Manny makes his way back.

He wears his pride out in the open, as he absolutely should.

I'm proud of him. He's never been one to rest on his laurels, and it makes me want to be better. Disciplined.

Just as my brother wanted.

"It's gone better than I could have hoped," he replies, crossing his arms over his chest. "The whole building's embraced it."

Establishing a local had been a priority from day one. It's a relief to know it worked.

"You working today?" he asks.

"Just a bit," I say, attempting to wrangle my hair into order. It's grown longer than I usually let it. "I have to publish this week's audio, edit a few others, and set up the studio." It won't take long. Soundproofing the closet only requires a dozen panels, and I can run the mic through my laptop until I have the time to rig up something more permanent.

If I even need it. The permanent state of this move isn't guaranteed yet. "Then I'll sleep, I promise."

"Yeah, yeah. Just don't go running back to London on some post-nut epiphany. I only just got you here."

Manny is one of the few people who know I record audio erotica and the only member of my family I've trusted with the truth.

Ask them, and I'm lazy, irresponsible, and more likely to follow a skirt than a profit-and-loss statement. That's not who I am anymore, but I'd rather let them believe the lie than try to turn me into someone I'm not.

I'm not ashamed, but no amount of explaining that it's a creative exercise I enjoy will erase the sexual aspect if they don't respect the work.

Or if they don't respect me.

I slip my hand into my pocket and pull out the proverbial stone that's been weighing me down for the last week. It's probably not too late to change my mind, but then what was the point of getting on a plane in the first place?

This is what I wanted.

"What's that, then?" Manny asks, and I push the invite over to him. "Ah," he says, pushing it back to me. "You ready to see him?"

"It's what I'm here for, isn't it?" Mending fences is what brought me here, but this particular fence might want to stay broken. "Turns out Darce already put my name down. *With* a plus one. It appears her not so subtle hints that I need a girlfriend haven't been enough."

"Can you blame her? You've been avoiding anything serious for years." A customer calls out for a refill, and Manny nods, reaching for a fresh glass but keeping close. "Am I pulling my tux out, then?"

"I care about you too much to make you socialize with those toffs."

"I appreciate that." He steps away to close out the order, saying something that has them laughing as he hands back their credit card.

After I crashed my life into a veritable ditch, Manny let me bunk on his couch. He's never once let me lower the bar for myself, always holding me to my word.

He's my best mate, and it's really fucking good to see him again.

"Look," Manny says when he returns. "I know you want the whole deal, but a *for now* works while you wait, yeah?"

"I'm done with all that," I fire back. It's a new remix of an old song. He knows he can't change my mind about this. Why bother? I'm not interested in a sycophant hanging off my arm for a night. "I got enough of that in my twenties, and back then, I actually enjoyed it. Not anymore."

Now I want forever. A leg thrown over mine under the covers, a heartbeat to answer my own. Someone to spoil for the rest of my life, who won't judge me for the work I do.

"Hey, I hear you, but if you're going to go to that thing, you shouldn't do it alone. I'm serious, mate. Say the word, and I'm there." He would be too. Manny's good like that.

Silently, I stare down my decision, my brother's name in bold against the paper. I've already crossed an ocean. One more bridge shouldn't feel this impossible.

"I see you've dressed up for me," Manny says, and

in my periphery, a pair of gray joggers hops up on a seat farther down the bar. "Your usual?"

The old leather stool scrapes against the floor as the person pulls themself closer to the bar. Funny how much that sound reminds me of home. "Thanks. And keep them coming. Maybe if I get drunk enough, I'll forget my life is falling apart."

Then I see her.

Well, if she isn't a sight for these aching, greedy eyes.

"Hello, darling."

CHAPTER 5
WE MEET AGAIN

IVY

Even if I didn't recognize the accent, I'd never forget that face.

"You," I say calmly to the blond behemoth sitting a few stools away. Right now, my stomach is doing a Simone Biles impression, and I've learned to never let a man that looks this scorchingly hot know how nervous he makes me.

I try to douse the feeling with the G&T Manny serves me. It only half works.

"Ivy, you're as exquisite as I remember." His rich, rumbled English accent sends a shiver down my spine.

Ignoring him, I point at Manny, remembering why I came down in the first place. "I'm never letting you recommend a show again."

He rocks back with a hand to his chest, and though he's smiling (when is he not?), disagreeing with him always makes me feel terrible. "You didn't like it? The games were brilliant."

"Of course I liked it, but I'm traumatized. I cried myself to sleep last night."

He nods, like he's not the person who just emotionally ruined me. "Yeah, that was brutal."

Seriously.

I turn back to Lincoln. Yep, still as ridiculously handsome as I remember. He's wearing a short-sleeve white T-shirt over charcoal pants, looking like he's trying to cosplay as Business Casual but mostly just hitting equal parts casual and devastating.

"What are you doing here, anyway?" I ask. "Aren't you meant to be surfing or base jumping or something?" The tan lines he sported a year ago aren't there anymore, but with the way the stitching in his pants is fighting for its life around his thighs, I'm going to assume he spends at least forty hours a week pumping something.

Something I'm trying very hard not to imagine at this moment. I'm failing, but at least I'm trying.

Manny barks out a laugh like I've just said something ridiculous, and considering the guy always has a grin at the ready, it strikes me that he's more relaxed than I've ever seen him.

Honestly, calling the Scoundrel homely is like saying that Alex Newell can sing. Like, sure, *technically* it's true, but way to completely undersell it.

There are scuff marks on the floor where chairs have been moved and rearranged. Water marks on the countertop. The memories of gatherings linger in the furniture the way I remember Nonna's sofa sagging in the middle. It's as welcoming as Manny's smile, as joyous as his laugh.

Problems are nursed here.

Lincoln places his elbow on the bar, looking pleased. "Or something. Have you been checking up on me?"

Of course I have. The man plays at being mysterious so hard that my best friend has spent years attempting to guess his middle name.

"No."

Lincoln's smile deepens, his piercing gray eyes sparkling with interest, causing butterflies to skitter wildly in my chest.

His hair is longer. A dark blond lock is pushed behind one ear, and the rest curves and swoops over his head like artist's strokes, drawing softness around the strong lines of his face, and there's a day's worth of stubble making him look like the bad boy I've always been attracted to.

"I didn't realize you two were acquainted," Manny says, sounding excited by the prospect. I'm going to blame recent life-changing events for not putting two and two together until now. Of course they know each other. The accents really should have tipped me off.

Lincoln doesn't take his eyes off me. "I've only had the pleasure once before."

My face heats.

There was no pleasure, unless you count Lincoln's aggressive flirting (and also ignore how much I enjoyed it).

"Briefly," I say. "We're basically strangers."

Lincoln rises out of his seat in an easy glide and

carries his beer to the seat beside me. He smells like spice and sweat, and it's everything I like in a man.

"Let's change that, shall we?"

I would seriously love it if my insides could stop reacting to him. Even if he would be fun to sleep with — and, oh god, he'd probably be the best sex I'd ever have — I don't have time to wallow in heartbreak after he inevitably ghosts me. I'm too busy having a life crisis.

Lincoln will just need to take that chiseled jawline and those incredible shoulders and find someone else.

It won't be hard. His posture suggests he's a man who's been taught to push his way through the world, knowing it will move for him. Tall and broad shouldered, his strength is not a suggestion but a fact, present in his steely eyes, the curve of his biceps, the hug of his clothes.

I've dated his type before. Fast to desire and even quicker to disappear after they're satisfied.

The usual "hey, sweet thing. I've got just what you need." No hate to that vibe, but I like a little effort beforehand, you know? A little… pizzazz to my foreplay. And to me, everything is foreplay.

His T-shirt shifts as he lifts his glass, and bullseye — a tattoo. We have a tattoo. Oh god, I think my kneecaps just melted. Either that or I'm swooning. It's not just any tat, either. No, no. Lincoln Reginald Reeves (oh, nice alliteration) has a snake peeking out from under his shirt. How much of his chest is painted? Where does it go? Can I taste it? That's probably more of a second date question.

Christ, those thighs are obscene.

Come on, girl. He's blond, for heaven's sake. I should know better.

"Can you do something about him?" I ask Manny, whose only response is to chuckle from where he's mixing a cocktail for someone else. "Sorry, love. I know my cousin better than most, and he's a hopeless case."

Just as I suspected.

"Fine," I say. "Keep your secrets, Lincoln Lionel Reeves."

CHAPTER 6
SAY YES; I WANT TO SEE WHAT HAPPENS

LINCOLN

Manny's eyebrows take up residence near his hairline. "Lionel?" he says, "I'd say he's more of a Cecily." Great. What started as a guessing game I played with Darcy and Ivy's best friend when they were kids is now going to be Manny's latest way of taking the piss out of me.

"Choose your words carefully, Emmanuel Kofi."

He's still smiling, but he promptly shuts up.

Admittedly, the game is something I haven't thought about in years. Ivy's willingness to play only makes me surer of her curiosity about me.

A curiosity I intend to use.

"You like that I have secrets," I say, confident. I've a knack for knowing what women want, and I'd bet on being right. Despite her sharp edges, both now and last time, there's a reason she asked about me.

It's easy to hook my foot around the leg of her stool and pull her closer. Watch her eyes darken. "Does it make you want to peer into my dark corners? Strip me down until you know me?" It's what I'd like to do to her.

She swallows before speaking, and I wonder if she'd deny the blush on her cheeks if I pointed it out.

"I forgot you were like this," she says, breaking eye contact but not moving away from me.

It's clear she's at ease here, even without her current sartorial choices. The gray joggers and black T-shirt are a far cry from the cocktail dress and heels I remember her in, but as I imagine every piece of material gifted with gracing her body must do, it flatters her toned arms, the strong curve of her hips and arse, and the firm plain traversing the area between.

She looks grab-able. Like she can handle being tossed around. Like she'd like it.

Manny slides her a fresh drink, and as soon as it's within reach, Ivy downs half of it in one go. A classic case of "it's all gone tits up" if ever I saw one.

"All right, what's the story, then?" I ask. "The one that explains why a beautiful woman is trying to drown her sorrows."

"There's no story," Ivy says, but her gaze hasn't left the half-empty glass in front of her, the glass gripped tightly in her hand. "I got fired this week and wanted to soak my sorrows at the nearest bar. Since I live upstairs, you do the math."

Does she now? "Good to know."

Sharing a flat with the wanker for ten years means I can read everything Manny's not saying from a yard away. Right now, his expression says *don't mess around where you live*, and when I smile back, it's followed quickly by *fine, but you better not mess it up.*

"And I know there's a million more important things I should be doing," Ivy continues, unaware of our silent conversation. "Like updating the résumé I haven't opened since college, but I just… It wasn't supposed to be like this. Do you know I started working at Helix as an intern?" I shake my head. "Well, I did. I hadn't even graduated yet, but they offered me the position, and I thought, why not? It's just for a little while. Then one year led into the next, until eight years had gone by and now, I'm being booed off the stage." She pushes the empty glass away, frowning down at her hands.

"Why the rush to jump back in, then?" I ask. "You're allowed to take some time for yourself."

She looks incredulous. "Oh, you know how landlords are, always expecting the rent to be paid."

Farther down the bar, Manny coughs to hide his laugh, but he can keep his flappy ears to himself.

I change tack, turning on the stool to face her directly. "All right, then. Eight years. Why did you stay?"

Ivy rolls her shoulders, pulling her straight black hair up into a bun, exposing the bird tattoo that's been teasing me. Turtle doves. How sweet. Somewhere in there hides a romantic.

Then she's turning her big brown eyes on me, and the need to press my lips to her skin, to taste her, claim her, runs like a rapid in my veins. But I meant what I said to Manny. I want more than a night.

"I didn't survive years of my mother's exhaustive lectures to throw away a paycheck for no reason," she says. Ah, money. I should have guessed.

"Unhappiness is a reason."

Frustration twists Ivy's mouth, but I have the sense she's arguing with herself, not me. "Everyone's unhappy at work. What makes me so special?" She raises a finger at me. A tiny wrinkle dimples her nose as she pouts. It's adorable. "Don't answer that."

There's a story here. One she's practically tripping over herself to tell, even as she holds herself back. Beneath her soft clothes and natural suspicion, there's an ache for adventure.

Christ, I want to undo her.

"What am I saying?" She slides the empty glass away from her. "From what I've heard, you avoid work like the plague."

It's an old wound. One she cannot know is regularly poked at by my own kin. But it stings, nonetheless, knowing she sees me that way. On instinct, I find myself staring back down at the invitation I've been ignoring. "I know enough," I say. "What are you searching for?"

She bows out of whatever internal fight she's having, letting out a sigh. "Do you ever think about all the versions of yourself that you never became and wonder if they're out there somewhere?" she asks, twisting the glass this way and that under unadorned fingers. "All these lives unlived, unknown to us. What if I chose the wrong one? I just keep thinking about all the choices I didn't make. What if I'd never taken the job? Maybe I've spent eight years doing the wrong thing and I never realized it. Maybe I would have met the love of my life by now instead of living on autopilot and rationing my free time like a chipmunk during winter."

It's as clear to me as the dove tattoo on her shoulder that Ivy is yearning to take flight. Here is a woman who has grown used to reining herself in, and that, I cannot accept. The good news is I'm inclined to help her.

"If you can't find yourself inside of work, find yourself outside of it. You wouldn't be the first person who suffered for a paycheck. What matters is that you have free will to make the life of your choosing, so choose wisely."

"I know that," she huffs, then pauses, closing her eyes and taking a deep breath. When she exhales, the fight leaves her, softening her posture and the crease of her mouth. "I guess I'm just feeling lost, is all."

"Ivy, stop second guessing yourself. You're driven, but you're bored, because what you've been doing hasn't been enough. It's exhausting but not rewarding. And you want more. You should go for it."

"That's some party trick."

I shrug. "A lucky guess," I say, but it doesn't look like she believes me.

When she looks at me, the longing in her brown eyes threatens to tilt my reality. "Sometimes I want to stop being *Sensible Me* and try someone else on for a night."

There's so much hope — in her eyes, in her voice — I'd be a fool to not move mountains for her.

"Sorry," she quickly adds. "I talk a lot. I'm working on it."

"Don't," I demand, ready to find and correct anyone who has ever said differently. "I enjoy listening to you."

Perhaps it's arrogant, but when I know what I want, I'm not easily distracted. It made me reckless in my youth, enough to make awful choices that Reed still won't let me live down, but it also helped me rebuild my life into one I'm proud of.

"What's that?" she asks.

I follow her gaze to the invitation. Ah.

I slide it toward her. "A disaster, most likely."

The light in her eyes intensifies, as if I've said the magic word. That's got her attention. "Tell me more."

"I'll do you one better. Are you free Saturday night?"

"Hmm, I'm pretty sure that's the night I'm having an existential panic about how I'll spend the next fifty years stuck in a career that will suck the life out of me before I get to retire. But I can probably push that to Sunday."

I laugh. Christ, she's a surprise. I want to spend a week doing nothing but getting to the bottom of her. Discovering what makes her tick.

Ivy picks the card up, reading the details. "A masquerade, huh?"

"My brother hosts an annual fundraiser to support the arts college. Invite only, student exhibit, with a silent auction for the pieces on display."

Like a hound caught on a scent, she reads the invite

again. "That sounds amazing. Why don't you want to go?"

Manny cuts in, sliding two fresh drinks in front of us. "He's being a coward."

Sod off, I say, silently, but it works.

Ivy traces the gilded lettering with reverence, and I throw out my original intentions to go alone. "Join me. A room full of strangers, a mask; you're free to be anyone you like." I shift closer, trailing my fingers around the curve of her elbow. "It'll be fun."

Fun is a word that's never been used to describe Reed, but for Ivy, I'll make sure of it.

"Oh, I'm sure it would be. That's the problem."

She's beautiful, from her thick eyebrows to the straight slope of her nose and pillowed lips that are currently set in a wicked pout that I'm aching to see in all manner of positions.

"What's wrong with fun?" I ask. "It's the bar all other experiences must live up to. Life doesn't mean more because it hurts. Fun is as important as anything else. Don't run from it. Chase it." Brushing my fingers along the tail of the doves on her shoulder, I watch the goose bumps rush to her skin. "Soak in it."

She lets out a shaky breath. Licks her lips. She's so close to saying yes, I can taste it.

"Will you let me show you?" I ask.

Her eyes lift, catching mine.

"One night," I promise. "Say yes."

I swear her eyes glimmer as she smiles, and I scold my heart for picking up its pace. She hasn't agreed yet.

It attempts a weak protest as she makes me wait,

picking up her glass and taking a slow sip, teasing me with the elegant line of her throat. The long drag of her tongue across her bottom lip is akin to torture.

I really need her to say yes.

Her breath hitches. "Now?"

"Now, later, *always*… take your pick."

The fill of her lips calls to me. All I want is to reach up and discover them. Their warmth, the way her breath would catch if I slipped my thumb between them. My tongue.

"Say yes, Ivy. Leave the rest up to me."

CHAPTER 7
MASKS ON

Arranging for a bespoke mask to be overnighted from Venice isn't cheap, but it's well worth it when Ivy slips it on, the sculpted wool paper hugging the round curve of her cheekbones and coating more than half of her face in black. A gold streak parts the valley between her chestnut eyes, highlighting her crimson lips.

My breath catches in my throat as she steps out of her apartment and into the hall.

Her floor-length gown takes that red and paints her body in it. The barely there straps are bravely holding up a length of free-flowing velvet dotted in sequins, with a neckline so deep, magic tape has to be keeping it in place. Her dark hair is carefully plaited in a French braid and tied with a ribbon.

There's no two ways about it—she's phenomenal.

I take my time securing her mask, savoring the hitch in her breath as our chests touch.

It's obvious there's a craving in her that's gone

unfulfilled for too long. If tonight goes as planned, I'll be able to show her exactly how well versed I've become in satisfying desire.

The way she waits, hands at her sides, while I stretch the moment out, is a good sign. "Thank you," she says softly.

"My pleasure."

As I pull back, I drag the tips of my fingers gently across her jaw. The soft sound of pleasure Ivy makes is only audible because we're standing so close, and I can't help but dip my gaze down to her lips.

"Did you know there is a history and meaning behind every mask?"

There's a gentle shake of her head, and her eyes remain closed.

Not kissing her is torture, but I endure it. All the better for later.

"They were worn during festivals, which encouraged freedom and theatrics. It was a chance to become anyone you wished. It made for mischief."

She licks her lips. Unadulterated want roars in my chest, filling the cavern there and reverberating like an echo. Christ, she's so perfect it's a physical ache.

"This," I say, passing my thumb along her cheek where the mask sits, "is a Colombina, historically worn by women and inspired by early Italian theatre. Mine," I say, referring to the white mask covering everything but my mouth and jaw, "is a play on the Bauta mask, and is rumored to be what Casanova wore."

The curl of her smile is incredibly satisfying.

"Venice had some very interesting laws regarding masks," I continue. "Including one which stated that by wearing a mask, you needed to become a mask, or more accurately, play the role. Something I believe you will be able to appreciate tonight."

Ivy blinks her eyes open, clears her throat, and steps back, pulling her door closed with a soft click. "How do you know all of that?"

"In fear of ruining your good opinion of me, I was a horny young sod trying to impress a date."

Her soft laughter settles warm under my skin. "Did it work?"

I lean in. "You tell me."

Her gaze dips down to my mouth and back again. "The jury is hung. I think you need to try harder."

She's going to fucking kill me. I may be the one laying the trap, so to speak, but she's definitely not going to make it easy on me.

Tenor House is beautiful. It's good to see it put to use after years of lying dormant in our family holdings. I'll try not to look too deeply into the kinship that is churning in my gut. It is not a night for doubt.

The eclectic heritage-listed Victorian was built back in the 1850s, boasts three floors, a grand staircase, six fireplaces, pocket doors, and oak flooring. It's magnificent and not a little foreboding, which is rather fitting tonight.

Before I can impress this knowledge upon Ivy, she beats me to it.

"I couldn't help myself," she explains, and it's an impulse I fear she's held back for a long time. There won't be any holding back this evening. "I did some research on this place. I mean, Emma told me your grandfather was Deacon Bradbury, but I hadn't realized he was the original owner. It didn't say what it had been used for before your brother donated it, though. Was your family always interested in art?"

She stuns in the moonlight as our invitation is checked and confirmed at the door. I'll have a hard time finding my brother because I can't take my eyes off her.

The entryway is narrow, the crowd moving slowly through the dimly lit hallways. It allows me to stay close to Ivy, one hand on her back, leaning in to speak quietly in her ear.

"Not exactly. Deacon's interest only extended as far as his profits. My father is the only painter in the family. Nothing creative, only residential." She smells of jasmine. It's divine. "He's always joked that he never had the patience for anything more."

It's not true. He's nothing if not patient. Soft, where the rest of us are harsh.

Jaded.

"But I suppose you could say we were all raised with an appreciation for the arts," I say. I only wish Reed's appreciation didn't mirror our grandfathers so directly.

"That's really sweet," she says. I'm glad to be standing behind her so she can't see the tightness in my jaw. "That must be why every cent raised from tonight goes into art scholarships and mentor programs."

"I didn't know that," I push out. It's been a long time since I spoke to my brother for longer than a meal, and guilt sinks, uneasy, into my gut, layered over the building anticipation of this evening.

As if called forth by lady luck herself, Reed appears ahead of us, tall and slim, cutting a fine line in a plain black suit and mask, escorting who I assume to be Mum up the central staircase.

Diverting course, I steer Ivy into a side parlor, where a couple is silently analyzing a series of sketches. Soon, every room will be full of socialites and wealthy business associates attempting to impress my brother and each other with their "generosity." For now, they gravitate to the bar in the main room down the hall and upstairs, where Reed is no doubt holding court. It'll be impossible to talk to him tonight, let alone have a reasonable conversation.

Perhaps this was a terrible idea.

I return my attention to Ivy, who manages to shine under the glow of the carefully dimmed sconces. At least this evening won't be a complete waste.

She stares up at me, her eyes narrowed, scrutinizing. "You don't get along with him, do you? That's what Manny meant when he called you a coward, right? What's that all about?"

Christ, she's observant. It's impressive, even if it's a topic I don't enjoy talking about, especially when I'm meant to be the one plumbing her depths, not the other way around. "My brother and I haven't gotten along in a while, and I'd rather not ruin a perfectly good evening."

But she's undeterred. It's a trait I admire, when it's aimed at more pleasurable pursuits than my familial wounds. "So you could have moved to anywhere in the world, but you chose to come here where your brother is, only to avoid him?"

She certainly doesn't mince her words. Dad would love her. Manny would be having a right old time if he were here.

"It's complicated," I say, with enough edge that anyone would know I mean to end the conversation.

The thing I'm rapidly learning is that Ivy isn't just anyone. "I'll get it out of you."

"We'll see."

Trusting that Reed will stay upstairs, I lead Ivy to the bar in the main room. Shadows crowd each room of the house. They linger in the corners, under the staircase, draping every surface in mischief and mystery. It's a night for secrets. A night for truths.

Ever want to know a person's real character?

Give them anonymity. Let them show themselves.

Unfortunately, once we have our drinks, I discover a new problem. Cursing under my breath, I'm hoping the din of conversation covers my slip, but ever vigilant, Ivy catches it.

"What is it? Is he here?" she asks, looking past me.

"No," I say, pressing my hand to her waist to keep her back to him. "It's Kyle. He's a cousin on my mother's side." A Bradbury through and through, and thus, utterly awful. There's only one reason Kyle does anything, so for him to be here… "He must be after something."

Chauvinistic and opportunistic (an unfortunately common combination), Kyle has only ever spoken in declarative sentences while holding neither intelligence nor wit. It leaves arrogance in its wake, which he has in abundance, along with the mildly greasy residue of having been slobbered all over.

Ivy darts her eyes across the crowd, searching eagerly. "How can you tell it's him?"

"I'd recognize the twat anywhere." Hard not to, since he's doing little to hide his appearance tonight. Kyle's calling card is his surname. It's the only connection to greatness he's ever achieved, and it wasn't due to any effort on his part (his favorite way to achieve anything, in my experience). "The last time I saw him, he tried to pry a cool fifty thousand from me."

"What did he want with fifty G's?"

"With him, it's as much about what he can get as it is about proving what he can take from you."

It's only mostly his fault; entitlement is as much a part of Deacon's legacy as the business is.

I will never understand why Reed looked up to our grandfather. He spent every summer soaking up Deacon's lessons like sermons and nodding along like he knew he'd be quizzed on it someday.

Deacon naming Reed as his successor wasn't a surprise to me, but apparently it hit the rest of the family like a ton of bricks. Kyle's dad, Richard, as the eldest, threw a shit fit of epic proportions according to

Darcy, huffing and puffing and threatening to blow the whole empire down.

Three decades spent as Deacon's head of operations, and it wasn't enough. But that's Deacon for you. Reed had been smart enough to fire our uncle before he could follow through, but it's been icy cold around that side of the family since.

Ivy's eyes burn bright, lit up from within. "Point him out to me. I want to talk to this guy."

I pause. I'm not used to anyone wanting to fight my battles with me.

"Please?" she whispers, and like magic, I know I'll give her anything she wants. "It's a night of mischief; you said so yourself. I'm only taking your direction." Before the night ends, she'll take more than that, and I'm looking forward to it.

I raise my hand to her shoulder, tracing the outline of her tattoo. Every piece of her speaks, sings, moves me. She's art itself. "Ivy, you are as delightfully surprising as you are beautiful. We're going to have a lot of fun together."

"Is that a promise?"

I smile. It's a guarantee.

Kyle has made it his personal mission to extract as many dividends as our lingering guilt might provide. If Ivy wants to have a go at him, he deserves it. I'll enjoy watching him get eaten alive.

"All right. See the jackass in the bright red smoking jacket and transparent mask?"

She zeroes in on him immediately. I'll wager she's

cocking a brow under that mask. "The one that defeats the entire purpose of a masquerade?"

"The very same."

She hums, staring after him as he struts out of the room, her lips pursed to one side. "You're right. He is a twat."

Christ, I want to kiss her.

He's also a complication. Getting my brother alone is looking like an impossibility now. Time to refocus.

"See all these people?" I ask Ivy after we've settled in the darkest corner with drinks in hand. "They're going to be your audience tonight. They don't know who you are, and you're never going to see them again. All the versions of yourself that you sometimes wish you could be? Try them on. See how they feel."

Low stakes, no consequences. A few white lies here and there, but no one will get hurt.

"You're giving me permission to lie to everyone here, including your family. Isn't that a little weird?"

"I'm going to let you in on a little secret. I've spent time bringing people's fantasies to life. And do you know what I've learned?" I step so close I know she can feel my breath against her skin. "You can't be good until you've first been a little bad."

I hear the exact moment her breath catches in her throat, and while I long to follow its path, coax it to the surface with my lips, I don't. There'll be time for that later.

There's power in wanting.

"Tonight is for you and you alone," I tell her. "Don't

hold yourself back, and promise me one thing." I allow myself a single touch, slowly trailing my fingers from her shoulder to her wrist. She shivers. "Say anything you like to the people in this room, but we don't lie to each other."

She nods. "Okay. I promise."

"Good." I raise her hand to my lips, an indulgence I can't ignore. "Tonight," I whisper against her skin, "I'm the only one who knows you."

CHAPTER 8
PICKING A PART
TO PLAY

IVY

I try to catch my breath as I look around the room.

The crowd is thicker now, strangers shifting and pausing at each piece on the walls. Shadows pool in the spaces between, rolling like mercury and calling to me.

Putting on the mask earlier had sparked a trickle of excitement in my chest, but now, the thrill of what is possible—anything, everything—is like lightning in my veins.

The last time I wore a mask I was eleven, collecting candy dressed as Bo Peep's sheep with socks on my hands as hoofs.

This? This is so not that.

Jumping from the pan into the fire? More like jumping from training wheels to the high wire on a unicycle.

As we ascend the staircase of my dreams, I'm so busy admiring the needlework curtains that I completely miss the next step and have to grab on to

Lincoln's arm to steady myself before I fall face-first into the ornate oak railing.

"Let me," he says, lowering himself to his knees to rescue my shoe from the last step. He takes it in one hand and my ankle in the other, and wow, I couldn't feel more like Cinderella if I tried.

When he looks up at me and places a gentle kiss over my knee, my heart stops.

The all-black ensemble he's wearing tonight will be my undoing. I just know it. His dress shirt is basically painted on, clinging to his broad shoulders and chest like an aspiration (read: *my* aspiration). Its open collar teases me with that damn tattoo and a promise of the most delicious of bad choices.

Then there's the white mask and slicked back hair.

Prince Charming, eat your heart out. (Wait, was Prince Charming the one from *Cinderella*? You know what? It's not important right now).

Emma's going to have to come and collect my ashes if he gets any hotter. I might light that funeral pyre myself if it means finding out where that snake leads to, and if it has any friends hiding under there.

However, when we reach the second floor, Lincoln pulls away. "Wait." I reach out, catching him by the hand. We just got here. The thought of losing him to the dark sea of the masked crowd is both scary and exciting.

"Where are you going?" The question is out before I can stop it, my stomach twisting at how needy it sounds. I've never been good at showing my soft, vulnerable underbelly to anyone new.

"Don't worry. I'll be keeping an eye on you," he says, his voice warm and thrilling as he leans in. "I only need to look for the most beautiful woman in the room."

My breath catches in my throat.

"How will I find you?" I ask, even though I can't imagine a room he could enter where I don't immediately lose track of everyone else.

"Would you allow me a small request?" he asks, his devilish smile peeking out from under the white mask.

I nod, my heartbeat racing.

He turns his face, pointing to where the mask covers his cheek. "A kiss, to mark me as yours for the evening. So you'll never have to wonder who I am."

Normally, I live for wonder, for curiosity. I hope I never know enough to stop. I always want to be surprised. But right now? I want this more.

Lifting onto my toes, I hold his jaw in my hand, loving the rough feel of his trimmed beard against my palm. Gently, I pull him toward me, and the butterflies thrash in a whirlwind when my lips meet the smooth surface of his mask.

I pull away to admire my handiwork, and oh, boy, am I in trouble now.

The dark red stain of my lips on his cheek makes my pulse spike. The realization that everyone he talks to will see my brand on him, a claim and a warning, well… it turns out I'm one possessive bitch.

I really am learning about myself tonight.

"Time to play," Lincoln whispers. His voice is a deep rumble in my ear, and I can't stop a shiver as his lips graze my skin. "I'll be watching." His sleeve brushes my hand, followed by the lightest touch of his fingers. A promise.

The second Lincoln steps away, the rest of the world rushes back in.

I take a long, deep breath, fighting the nerves racing under my skin. It's the high of those seconds behind the curtain, knowing one step will take me across the threshold and under the bright lights of the stage. Adrenaline fills me up, rushing like rapids in my veins, the same buzz I get after sparring—sweaty and strong and ready for anything.

I have to pinch my thigh to make sure I'm not dreaming. *Ow.* Okay, definitely not dreaming. But now my leg hurts, so there's that.

Every time I make eye contact with someone, I have to remind myself I'm wearing a mask. No one here knows me, and they wouldn't even if I wasn't wearing it. But the thrill persists.

I'm anyone tonight. Anyone and no one.

The possibilities are *endless*, and I've never felt so alive.

Regular life doesn't exist here.

I take a deep breath, releasing it slowly as my smile spreads.

It's time to have some fun.

———

I let the art guide me, since it's the whole reason for this party and so few people are paying attention to it. I hate that. What's the point of supporting an art school but ignoring the artwork?

There's a woman staring intently at an oil painting in the corner, head tilted, a glass of sparkling wine held aloft in her bejeweled hand. I move confidently, coming to a stop beside her.

Her mask is charcoal and silver, framed by her matching hair. The wrinkles around her mouth remind me of my mother and years of pursed disappointment. Even in the dim light, I can see her eyes are narrowed.

"It's a beautiful painting," I say. The striking image of a lone woman bracing herself on a crumbling wall, her head hanging low, expression hidden, is heartbreaking in its simplicity. There's so much being said without words. So much pain bleeding through the canvas. It's incredible.

"Debatable," comes the response, the woman's tone as flat as my chest. "It's hardly surprising, is it? There's no imagination, and the brush pattern is too flat."

As an art layman, I'm 90 percent sure she's making that term up, but tonight is all about the bluff, right?

Following her lead, I cross my arms and nod once, slow and considering. "I agree." *I don't.* "It's so nice to know I'm not the only one who"—how had Lincoln put it?—"Appreciates the arts."

I gesture to the next piece, which has given me the creeps since I stepped into the room. The weird melted bird-bag-*thing* doesn't even have eyes, but I know it's watching me. "What are your thoughts on this one?"

Her eyes widen comically, but she keeps an impressively straight face.

"It's certainly…" she trails off. I can only imagine she's struggling to find a word that could encompass the eyesore we're looking at.

Honestly, I don't think there's a word good enough to do it justice. I'm kind of in love with it.

"Interesting" is what she settles on, and I stifle the laugh that's threatening to escape, my left eye twitching with the effort.

"It is, isn't it?" I say, faking enthusiasm. "Don't tell anyone I told you this," I start, and she almost gives herself whiplash with how quickly she snaps her attention to me. "But I have it on good authority the painter is related to a certain famous street artist, if you know what I mean. Apparently, they're keeping the connection under wraps, but a few years from now, this will be worth a fortune."

She's hanging off my every word. Damn, I've missed having a captivated audience.

"And it's perfect timing," I say, touching her arm like we're girlfriends.

I'm really getting into the flow of the role now. Maybe in another life I left college to travel, met a billionaire, and never knew what a Teams notification sounded like. "I've been looking for a piece for my yacht," I tell her. "You wouldn't believe how difficult it's been. None of my dealers in Morocco have been any help."

Hearing the lies roll off my tongue is an out-of-body experience. If asked, I couldn't say where it came from. I'm not even drunk.

Just inspired.

"I know just what you mean," she says, turning back to our golem friend with a new glint in her eye.

Now that my nerves have disappeared, the floodgates open.

To a graying gentleman in an ill-fitting suit, I'm an aeronautic carpenter (a job I made up, but wish was real) who is currently designing cabinetry that can withstand Mach 10. A story so patently ridiculous, the effort of keeping a straight face should earn me a medal.

The fact that he believes me makes me so giddy I almost have to excuse myself.

No doubt he's regretting the conversation when I point out the small framed watercolor of a white archway leading nowhere, especially when I start waxing poetic about buttresses. It only takes sixty seconds of nodding before he bids on it and pretends someone is calling him.

It feels like a win.

Then, to a group of girls wearing see-through lace masks, I'm the secret lover of a movie star whose name I tease but never give up, no matter how many times they pry. It starts a bidding war over a hand sculpture I've convinced them is "true to life."

One by one, I try on as many faces as I can.

The inventor of a hands-free ceiling vacuum.

A struggling ballet dancer.

An influencer famous for sneaking into parties uninvited. That one earns me a raised eyebrow. I'm especially proud of that.

Lincoln appears in glimpses, a looming presence at my back, under my skin, his eyes sharp as they follow me.

Where I move, he follows. When I look, I find his eyes already on me. Dark. Eager. Interested. It's the smallest audience I've ever commanded, but it could be a stadium of people, and I wouldn't feel as captivated as I do right now.

I'm the one holding his attention and yet it's me who feels under his spell.

When Kyle's red jacket enters my periphery, it's hatred on sight.

I don't have to be rich to have met guys like Kyle before — a-holes don't need money to exist; they just blow their cover faster when they have it. It's obvious from his wing tips to his dental caps that Kyle likes to throw his money in your face.

Jesus, his arrogance might as well be a blinking neon sign hanging over the big top.

As he stalks toward me, he's smiling like we're sharing a secret and sidles up so close I have to take a step back, stopping when my back hits the wall. "I didn't realize the artwork was allowed to wander around."

Seriously? He's so gross.

Kyle makes a show out of checking me out, and I have to look away before his face starts to look like a good landing spot for my right hook.

"I don't think we've met yet, and that's a damn shame." His American accent throws me until I remember half of Lincoln's life was spent here. It must be strange being split between two continents. Maybe I'm not the only one who is playing a version of themselves. "You might have to make it up to me."

Hmm. The fuckery is strong in this one. But I've been on a roll tonight. Maybe I can mind-trick him. *This isn't the pussy you're looking for. Move along.*

My first girlfriend was in college (I'm so cliché sometimes it hurts). Once, I took her on a date to a jazz festival. The whole night went great. My flirting game was top-notch, but then an asshole at the bar started leering, asking us if we wanted a third for the night, telling us he could "fix us right up."

It's men like these who make me sorry for straight women. I don't always dislike being attracted to men, but being bi, I have options at least.

"How flattering," I say, and slip into the role of someone who isn't five seconds away from kneeing him in the groin. It's my toughest act yet.

"I have excellent taste," he drawls, his hot breath singeing my ear. "And you look better than a ten-course meal."

Fucking hell, I'm going to be sick all over his shoes.

Lincoln better be a fantastic kisser, or else spending time with his cousin will not be worth it. "It's so refreshing to meet a man who doesn't let a lack of height impact his confidence." He's easily six feet tall, but that's what makes it hurt.

There's a split second where I can tell Kyle grinds his teeth. But his smile holds firm. "You know, the problem with having a sense of humor is that it can't keep you warm at night."

Must be why he doesn't have one.

I fake a laugh, taking a sip of champagne to cover the fact that I'm screaming internally. "Luckily, I'm covered either way."

"Only if you say please," he says with a grin.

Yep, I'm definitely going to puke on his shoes.

His mouth bothers me. It's thin and reedy. Like someone typed "human smile" into an AI generator and then gave life to the nightmare fuel that came out.

Maybe I'm being too harsh. Even walking dumpster fires have rights.

"Are you enjoying the exhibit?" I ask.

"I'm certainly enjoying the view." Oh god, someone look up insufferable in the dictionary, because I have the perfect mascot for it. "That's why I put this party together. All this artsy stuff is a real passion of mine. I owe it all to my grandfather, of course. Brilliant busi-nessman. The man taught me everything I know."

This lying liar.

"Wow," I say, feigning interest. "The man of the hour. How lucky am I?"

This facsimile of a man preens, as I knew he would. No one on earth likes boasting about themselves as much as trust fund guys. He probably played lacrosse and still talks about how he "could have gone pro."

Kyle strikes me as one friend short of a podcast, cruel and boastful and completely unaware of how vile he is.

I know better than to touch him (who knows where those hands have been?) but I lean in and whisper, "That's such a relief. For a second there I thought you were someone else in the family. I overhead some women talking earlier, and they had some *very* interesting things to say about his hair plugs."

It's too dark to tell if he pales, but he doesn't act fast enough to hide his frozen expression. Oh, what a shame he didn't wear a mask tonight. I fear that might have helped.

Pride too wounded to recover, Kyle finally drops the facade, his grin turning sharp enough to cut. "Actually, there's really nothing special about you at all." He throws back the last of his glass in one gulp, stepping back. "But maybe if you're lucky, I'll give you a second chance."

Yeah, right. I never plan on seeing that man again.

Shaking off the grime meeting Kyle left on me, I search out a fresh glass of bubbly and make my way to the largest painting in the room. Abstract splashes of yellow and blue clash across most of the canvas in tiny explosions of color. All but one are kept separate, the colors fighting beside each other, angry and opposite. There's only one spot, right in the center, where the teal coupling meets in a gentle sway.

Like a dance.

"What do you like about it?" Lincoln asks, his breath brushing my ear as he steps closer. I lean into him, pulled by his gravity.

For the first time tonight, I have no words. I shrug, unable to pull myself away from staring at the art.

I don't know why it speaks to me, only that it does. In the same mystical way I find myself drawn to certain people. It interests me. It makes me think.

It makes me *feel.*

"Would you like it?" he asks.

I whip around to face him. "You can't buy this for me." It's huge, for one. Where would I even put it? It would look fabulous on that empty wall next to the door that I've been wanting to wallpaper, but it's too much.

I couldn't.

Could I?

"I think you'll find I can do a lot of things," Lincoln says, kissing my cheek. "As can you, if the rumors are to be believed. You certainly have a lot of people talking tonight. Are you enjoying yourself?"

A flush creeps up my neck.

As I take in the crowd now — a server gliding through the room with a tray of entrées, four bored men in the corner probably discussing interest rates, the group of twenty-year-olds who are more interested in who's here than the auction, and everyone in between — I see the possibilities. What I'd say, who I could be to pique their interest or their curiosity (a confused ingenue, a self-assured mean girl). Anyone but myself.

"I am," I say, finally, because how could I possibly explain why this means so much to someone I just met? This is only a game for him. "I'm surprised you need to ask. You're the one watching me."

"You're worth watching," he says as his smile curls under his mask. "Although I'm looking forward to getting you all to myself soon."

Later, when I look back on tonight, I'll remember

how incredible Lincoln smells—deep and dark, like sinking to the ocean floor.

I'll think of the weight of his gaze, a heavy cloak trailing after me down hallways and dimly lit rooms.

I'll taste the thrill of electricity on my tongue, a sharp, acidic burn that speeds up my heart and makes me hot all over.

When I look back, I'll forget the faces of the crowd, the exact shade of green in the wallpaper, and how long we were there. None of it matters.

Everything, I'll learn, pales in comparison to Lincoln. Fading to precisely the right frequency to be forgotten.

———

I wait for Lincoln downstairs in what must have been a reception room when the home was still lived in.

A low murmur of conversation fills in the gaps between silences, harmonized to the cellist hidden in the corner. Nobody bats an eye. I doubt anyone here has even noticed her. It pains me to think of her talent going unnoticed, serving as background music while a hundred strangers debate art they don't appreciate.

Fuck that.

I admire artists. Their bravery is evident in each stroke of paint, each smudge of charcoal.

Does it feel different to live a life distilled into art? Is it easier to contain your emotions, to name them, when you can transfer them onto a canvas and make them tangible? Let them bleed out for all the world to see?

"I adore Dvorak's cello concerto. If only everyone would pipe down long enough for me to hear it." The words are articulated perfectly, though the accent is something not quite home grown, like it's traveled so much it can't quite remember how to sound, but it's also soaked in good humor, and that's what causes me to turn around.

The woman beside me is easily twice my age, maybe more, with fine silver hair that I'd guess used to be blond. It's down but pinned back behind her ears, softly framing her face. The mask she's holding makes it easier to see her features, giving me glimpses of delicate cheeks, an upturned nose, sharp sea glass eyes.

"What a beautiful shade of lipstick you're wearing," she says.

"Oh, thank you," I reply. "It's my favorite."

Amusement slowly transforms her smile into something deep and intimate as she tilts her chin over to where Lincoln is standing on the other side of the room. She looks over to him and back to me, her eyes sparkling. "I believe I've seen a young man tonight wearing a similar color."

I can't help it. I laugh.

I don't know who she is, but I like her a lot.

"I'm Ivy," I say, giving out my real name for the first time tonight.

"Astrid. A pleasure to meet you, Ivy. Though perhaps not as much of a pleasure as it was for him."

"The night is still young," I joke, and my cheeks already hurt from smiling. Astrid is the first person I've met tonight who seems like a real, genuine person. Like

I've been holding my breath against a bad smell, and she's my first breath of fresh air.

Astrid's mask dips away from her face as she lets out a light bubble of laughter, filled to the brim with surprise. Maybe she wasn't expecting to enjoy anything about tonight. "As flattered as I am, it couldn't ever work between us."

"The good ones are always taken," I tease, delighted when she lights up. It softens the lines of her face and reminds me of how tense Lincoln was when we arrived.

"What brings you here tonight, Ivy? Are you a fan of the arts? Or do you simply enjoy leaving impressions on strangers?"

Lincoln was right. My reputation is getting around. It's a good thing we're leaving soon, or I might really get myself in some trouble.

As I draw in a deep breath, the truth collects on my tongue. All of it. Losing my job, worrying about my future. The panic I feel every time my mom calls and not knowing what to tell her.

The promise Lincoln made to me a few nights ago, while I drank gin and tonic and enacted my confession.

Why am I here tonight? Lincoln flirted over chasing fun, but if that's all I'm after, I could have spent the night eating barbeque pork bites on Emma's couch rewatching *High Society*.

"I was hoping for adventure," I admit. "Although the art is lovely." Golems included. "And the house…" I sigh. "It's like stepping into a fairy tale."

"It's Victorian, you know."

I do. Astrid would probably laugh if she knew I'd

gone down the rabbit hole of the owner's history while lying in bed. "From the eighteenth century. It's a beautiful restoration."

"It is." She looks impressed. I really want to tell her about the rumor of how Deacon Bradbury almost lost the deed in a card game, but I can hear my mother's voice in my head saying not to bombard new friends with enthusiasm, so I don't.

"Are you a fan of history?" she asks.

"Not really, to be honest," I say. "But I'm in a bit of a rut in my real life, so I guess I've been ruminating on the past a lot more than usual. Hindsight, you know?"

From the way her gaze sharpens as she nods, it's obvious she knows hindsight intimately, and I bet there are a million interesting stories hiding behind it. I want to ask her about it. I get the strongest feeling she'd tell me, too, like we're old friends who have been waiting to see each other again so we can catch each other up on our lives.

Astrid hands off her glass to a passing server, clasping her free hand around her sequin clutch. "It's funny you should mention that. I've been quite nostalgic myself lately. Sometimes it's easier to reflect on the problems of the past than face the uncertainty of the future, even if it's painful."

God, I can't even imagine what it must be like to look back in your sixties. My issues are probably ridiculous by comparison. As if reading my thoughts, she adds, "There is no measuring stick for regret, except the one you keep for yourself. I find it helps to focus on the things you care for."

Heat prickles at my eyes. If I'd known I was going to cry tonight, I would have packed tissues. Or worn a better mascara.

Embarrassingly, I'm overcome with the need to hug her. Or to ask her to adopt me. It's as if she knew exactly what I needed to hear at the exact time I needed to hear it. No guilt, no pressure.

"I'll try to remember that," I croak out.

"Will you be leaving your calling card with anyone else tonight?" she asks, once again sparing a glance over my shoulder.

I follow her gaze to find Lincoln's eyes on me, warm and intense. Always watching. A thrill runs through me.

Maybe that's why I say what I do.

"No, only him. I mean, when your boyfriend is as wonderful as he is, you want to make sure you can find him again."

I haven't turned away from him as I talk, our eyes locked through the gaps in the crowd. Even as Lincoln pushes off the wall and starts to cross the room, his eyes don't leave mine.

"It doesn't look like you need to worry about losing him," Astrid says, and I watch, breathless, as Lincoln cuts through the room, imposing and determined.

I try to douse my racing heart with the last of my drink.

When he's close enough to touch, he looks to my left, and ice drips down my spine as Lincoln straightens beside me.

"Evening, Mum."

Astrid leans in to kiss his cheek, and I don't get time to take a breath before she says, "Lincoln, your girlfriend is delightful."

They turn in unison to face me.

Oh no.

CHAPTER 9

ROLLING WITH THE PUNCHES (EVEN THOUGH THEY HURT)

LINCOLN

My what, now?

"Sorry," Ivy rushes out, her eyes wide as she stares apologetically up at me. Not planned, then. "It just slipped out."

Christ, they only talked for a few minutes.

It's been incredible to watch Ivy work, weaving magic through the crowd as she caught their attention and then kept it. Slowly, I've watched her bloom, shedding the confines of her cocoon and stretching her wings, utterly captivating me at every turn.

Had I been able to take my eyes off Ivy sooner, perhaps we could have avoided this. But it's too late for that now.

I kiss Ivy's cheek, slipping my arm around her waist. Ivy isn't the only one playing her role tonight. Dutiful son, adoring brother. It's all an act, and one I am an old hand in. What's one more? "There's no need to apologize. I was hoping to introduce you."

Mum's astute eyes are watching us, her mouth

pinched. If I'm not mistaken, I'd say she's protective of Ivy. "This is either very new or very secret, Lincoln, since you've only been back for a few days."

How did she…? "Did Darcy tell you?"

"Your father and I are capable of speaking with each other."

Ah. I should have known.

Mum's eyes dart over my shoulder, and then there's an arm brushing my sleeve as the person I've been avoiding joins us.

"I called the car for you, Mum. It'll be downstairs in fifteen minutes."

"Thank you, dear. Would you look who I bumped into."

I turn to face my brother.

The last time we spoke — he spoke, I yelled — I wondered if I'd finally spent the last of his good will. It's been years since he saw me as anything other than a problem to be solved, another cog to set in line.

"Lincoln," he says. "I'm surprised. Darcy mentioned that you'd accepted, but I didn't quite believe it until now." His shoulders are set back, claiming the inch of height he has over me. As kids, we'd never noticed the difference. Now Reed takes the high ground whenever we're in the same room.

"It was a last-minute decision."

"Your favorite kind," he says, and I clench my jaw and stuff my fury down.

My brother has always had a clear head for responsibility. No recklessness, no scandals. Nothing like me.

Reed is the dependable one. How could he not be? His name's Reed Reeves. He's a fucking superhero.

"Reed, this is Ivy. Lincoln's *girlfriend.*" Mum is overly pleased. I know I've never introduced anyone to them before, but she's acting as though I've never dated before.

His surprise is there and gone in a blink, only a flicker of his gaze to me, before he presents Ivy with his best welcoming smile. "Lovely to meet you. Have you settled in all right?"

Ivy answers quickly. "Oh, no, I'm a local. But, uh, obviously I'm very happy to have Lincoln within reach now." And to prove it, she presses herself to me. It's oddly fortifying.

His eyes meet mine, challenging. "You never mentioned you were seeing someone."

"Perhaps I wanted to avoid the inevitable speculation," I say, holding his stare, not interested in backing down.

He frowns.

"Honestly, it's my fault," Ivy says. There's a mole by her ear, half hidden by her hair. I want to reach out, feel the skin under my fingers. Touch it with my lips. Would she shiver? Sigh? Melt deliciously under me the way I want her to? "Lincoln wanted to tell you, but I didn't want to rush anything, especially since we lived so far apart."

She's good at this.

"I remember thinking the same thing when I met your father," Mum graciously offers, smiling approvingly at us both. It punches at a deep need I wasn't aware of until now.

"It must be in the genes," Ivy offers, looking up at me with so much naked adoration I want to believe the lie.

Everything else falls away — the crowd, the bull-shit — until it's only us. Two strangers, searching for meaning, caught in the same storm. My heart picks up speed, hammering against my ribs.

It must be the illusion. The evening. Being in front of my family again.

Nothing more.

Tonight was only meant to be a seduction. Pure fantasy. Ivy isn't meant to see my mess, the cracks in my facade, the grime beneath.

It was never supposed to be about anything real, and yet here she is, defending me to my own brother. And I haven't even had the pleasure of kissing her.

As Mum pulls Ivy into conversation, I shake the feelings off. Reed has me unsettled, that's all.

"Where's Darcy?" I haven't seen her once tonight, and it's unlike her to skip an event she planned.

"She's a little under the weather tonight, so we're managing it." My blood runs cold. Darcy being sick is news to me.

"What is it? Is she all right?"

"She's fine. Nothing to worry about."

Like hell it is. They said the same thing a decade ago when she was rushed to the emergency room, only deigning to tell me days later that we almost lost her.

I pull my phone out of my pocket, typing rapidly. If

it's bad, Darcy might not be able to respond, but I can't do anything else right now, and I won't be able to breathe without knowing she's okay.

Her response is quick and as acerbic as ever.

Darcy: Don't get your knickers in a knot. FFS it's just the flu.

The relief is immeasurable.

Me: You better be resting. That means actual vegetables and water.

Darcy: Sure, doc. Would you also like an update when I hit the loo next?

I roll my eyes. She's definitely okay.

Darcy: Call me tomorrow during daylight hours. And be nice to Reed.

At this, I lock my phone and pocket it again. Even though she's the youngest, Darcy's become the glue holding Reed and me together.

It wasn't always this way. Growing up, we were thick as thieves. But when the divorce happened, he chose Deacon, and I chose dad, and we've never been the same since.

"So," he says, his voice flat, his eyes coasting over my shoulder, the very picture of unbothered. "You've moved." Reed's accent is polished and clipped to perfection. It grates against the badly healed wound of our relationship.

Nothing's changed. We are who we've always been. Reed, exemplary and reliable. Lincoln, the perennial fuckup.

"I have."

Titillating conversation, this is. So glad I traveled over an ocean so we could have this little chinwag.

"Does this mean we'll be seeing you in the office come Monday?" His disappointment is a wider gulf than any ocean could fill.

"Why the hell would I do that?"

"I'm not sure, Lincoln," he says, his tone sharp with sarcasm. "Perhaps to help someone other than yourself?"

I ball my free hand into a fist at my side. Unbelievable. "I'm not another employee you can boss around. Just because you dragged Mum and Darcy into it—"

"Grow up," he interrupts, low and controlled. "Everything I've worked for has been to protect our family, and they understand that. Excuse me for thinking that, as part of that family, you would be willing to do more than swan about, wasting your inheritance."

"Reed," Mum warns quietly.

Ivy steps between us, her hand clenched into my jacket, her chin raised, looking seconds away from challenging my brother to a duel in my honor. "If family is really that important to you, you wouldn't be so quick to insult your own brother."

Bloody hell, she's sexy.

The Reed I remember almost had an asthma attack before asking a girl out. He drew comics in the margins of his textbooks and was annoyingly pedantic about the merits of pouring milk first in a cup of tea, like a heathen.

But he's also the same guy who lectures me regularly about throwing my life away. Who called me when Deacon passed and said not to waste my inheritance because it was "the last handout" I'd ever get. That if I was hard up, the best he could give me was a job. I called him a cunt and hung up on him.

That was five years ago.

"Just tell me what you want me to do," I sigh.

"What I want..." he says, then deflates, huffing out the anger and returning to his robotic self. "Just show up. If Mum or Darcy ask you for something, you're there, all right?"

As if I'd ever turn them down.

"All right?" he presses, and if we weren't in public, I'd have some choice words to throw at him.

"Yes, of course."

Jesus.

"If that's all," I say, maintaining as much calm as I can. "We'll say good night."

Reed nods his dismissal, but Mum comes in for a hug, saying, "We'll see each other soon, I'm sure."

CHAPTER 10
CATCH AND RELEASE
IVY

Of all the people to say the wrong thing to, I had to go and call Lincoln my boyfriend to *his own mother*.

Great work, me. Perfect aim. Ten out of ten. Might just want to work on the whole "think before shooting" thing next time.

Oh god. I *flirted with her*. At least I can say I have impeccable taste.

He hasn't let go of me since his brother appeared. That must be a good sign, right? But as he leads me by the hand to the hallway, I can't judge his expression, and I'm spiraling a little.

I just need to know how badly I screwed up so I can start planning my apology meal. Frustrated? Caponata. Pissed? Gorgonzola gnocchi. Disappointed and turned off forever?

My nonna's sfinciuni made from scratch, with all the cannoli he can stomach.

God, tonight was going so well until now.

"Lincoln—"

"Hang on," he says.

So I do, my stomach clenched until we're past the party and out the door, where the cool night air kisses my skin.

It's quiet on the porch, everything muted, like sinking under water, leaving nothing to distract me from the running monologue in my head.

Pulling Lincoln to a stop, I let my thoughts spill free. "I'm so sorry. If I'd known she was your mom, I never would have said… But she's great, by the way. Even if your brother is a bit stiff."

Lincoln's mouth curls at the edges like he's holding back a laugh.

"You were doing what I asked. Nothing more. I only hope they didn't make you uncomfortable."

The gentle stroke of his thumb on my skin means I don't immediately understand what he's just said. But when I do, I'm confused. He's worried about me being uncomfortable? The person who created this mess?

"What? No."

Relief appears to loosen his smile, and it unfurls to its full, devastating effect. My bones forget how to be a solid.

"There's something I'd like from you." His voice is low, a secret being traded in the darkness, one I'm desperate to follow down the rabbit hole. Of course he does. He hasn't been subtle. Neither have I. "Do you trust me?"

Trust is complicated. Do I? I'm not sure yet, but I think I'd like to.

I like a man more when he can take charge. If he can

take care of himself, I know he can take care of me. And I need a lot of looking after. Just ask my mom.

It's a rare quality, sadly. I once dated a guy who would eat on the couch (not the crime, stay with me) and when he was done, put his plates on the floor by his feet. They'd sit there for hours. Sometimes days.

The real kicker was if I brought it up, he'd simply say, "If it bothers you, you can clean it." As if he was doing me a favor by letting me wash up after him.

I didn't date a single man for a year after that.

Then I binge watched *Narcos* and… Let's just say Pedro Pascal has a lot to answer for.

I know that, come morning, this infatuation will be over. So why not go all in? The ultimate "yes, and…" Let's see what he can really do. "I'm in your" — strong, sexy, extremely capable — "hands."

He caresses the inside of my wrist. "No follow-up questions? Or perhaps it's the surprise that excites you."

I lick my lips. He's right. It's like I'm glass. My every desire laid out before him. That'll make this interesting.

"If you're as good as I think you are," I say, my pulse tripping over itself when his eyes darken, "I won't have anything to worry about. And if you're not, I'll say *mask off*, and you'll stop."

I've played enough to know my way around safe words and a traffic light system, and the confidence in Lincoln's shoulders as they roll back tells me he has too.

"You have my word."

Nerves I never knew existed are sparking to life, jolted into hunger with each whispered tease.

Obviously, he's gorgeous, with the exact ratio of height-biceps-waist that is my personal catnip. Don't even get me started on the accent. It should be registered as a weapon.

Goose bumps blossom to life all over my body as he brushes his fingers up the line of my neck.

"Can I be anyone?" I ask, because tonight gave me a taste of excitement I'm not ready to give up yet. *Maybe it'll be easier to walk away tomorrow if I'm not myself.*

He tucks a stray hair behind my ear, then traces his thumb along my jaw. "Of course. Set the scene, and I'll do the rest."

Okay.

I'm transfixed by the pull of Lincoln's shirt over his pecs. I've never seen a button fight for its life the way this one is. It probably wouldn't take much for it to give way. Maybe a quick pull of teeth, and it'd be undone.

I wonder if it's smooth underneath, or if his nipples are dusted with the same dark hair that shades his forearms. I like a bit of hair. Can definitely get on board if Lincoln's sporting some. Or maybe he keeps it tidy, lets the tattoos take the spotlight. I lick my lips. I can almost taste it.

"Tell me, Ivy." His eyes are black. I'm momentarily speechless.

A thrill runs down my spine at the lead he's giving me. I can take this anywhere I want. Who am I tonight? Who is he?

Lincoln presses in close, until I'm taking a step back, until I'm pressed to the wall and he's surrounding me in every way. Until nothing exists but him.

"I'm someone…" My eyes flutter closed as Lincoln trails two fingertips across my collarbone. "Powerful."

He hums his understanding. "Even powerful people need protecting."

"I can take care of myself."

"Yes, but it's my job to protect you, isn't it?"

God, how did he know? *Yes, please, protect me.* I don't care if it isn't real.

"Only inside the castle walls," I whisper, silently begging him to play along. I've never done this before, but all of a sudden, I want to see how far he'll go. Will he surprise me? Or will I scare him off, like all the others?

He ducks his head, placing a gentle kiss on my shoulder. "That's where you're wrong, princess." Fire sparks to life under my skin. It thrills me that he's playing along. Oh, this is going to be good. "You're lucky your sharp tongue kept everyone from guessing who you truly are, but you can't fool me."

No, I can't, can I? "What happens now?"

Time has frozen while we breathe, his lips so close I swear I can feel them against mine. Even with the mask, I feel exposed. Bared to his eyes only. As though he knows everything I can't ask for.

"Now," he says, the word gliding down my spine like a caress, "I'm going to take you home, and you're going to do as you're told. Isn't that right?"

I nod, my pulse hammering in my throat.

His smile is absolutely sinful. "Good girl."

———

I've always liked the dark. The mystery, the possibility, the drama. It's things that go bump in the night, a waiting stage, a blanket of shadow to hide misdeeds under.

It's always thrilled me.

Walking down the hallway to my door, I can feel the pressure of him at my back, even from a distance. It's in the silent way he stalks me, only a few feet away. The weight of his gaze on my back, heavy as any caress, sends tingles down my spine.

It's in the chasm of the unknown ahead of me. Each step brings me closer to danger.

I keep walking.

There's a heavy heat between my thighs, where I'm wet with anticipation. What happens when I reach my door? Will he drop the charade? Kiss me good night and leave?

He was right. I want this. I want him.

When I pull out my keys, he stops me, his palm warm as he slides it around my neck, this thumb tipping my head back. I'm caught by his eyes, staring into mine, our breaths in sync. We stay like that. In, out. The ends of his lashes glow golden in the hall light.

My heart is pounding.

He dips down, stopping just as his lips catch mine. "This kiss is mine. No games. Just you and me."

I go breathless as he closes the gap, slotting our mouths together so perfectly I lose all sense of anything that isn't us.

Finally.

Lincoln wastes no time. He sweeps his tongue into

my mouth, swallowing each sigh I make. Every move he makes is sure, firm. Dancing his fingers along my neck. The little scrapes of teeth as he sucks on my lower lip. The soothing touch of his thumb afterward.

It's everything a first kiss should be.

When he straightens, I can tell we're back to the game. It's in the wicked gleam in his eyes.

I nod, and it's the green light he's waiting for.

He fits himself to my back, stilling my hand where I'm holding my keys. Goose bumps rise along the stretch of my neck when he dips his head, his voice a husky whisper in my ear.

"You say the word and it stops. Do you understand?" He takes a step forward, pressing me against the door. Anyone could find us like this. My pulse races. "Answer me."

He thrusts his thigh roughly between mine, biting down on my ear, pulling a gasp from me. I can feel my body responding, my thighs clenching around him. I want him so much it hurts. "Yes."

"Good."

Lincoln pulls my hand up to the lock, opens the door, and slowly leads me inside. "Stop," he says, then when I do, adds, "Eyes forward." Fireworks are detonating below my belly button.

He closes the door and steps up behind me, taking my keys and purse out of my hands and putting them somewhere I can't see.

The lights in my apartment are out, moonlight glinting off the handheld mirror I left on the coffee table next to my makeup; a half-finished glass of water beside it. The pair of heels I'd decided against lying on the floor.

Plastering himself to my back, he teases his fingertips from my hands to my shoulders, then curls his hand around my neck, guiding my head back. Holding me there.

Every nerve in my body is on fire.

"Do you know how easy it would have been to hurt you tonight?" he asks. I hope it's a rhetorical question, because I'm so turned on I don't think I can speak. "You're lucky I found you before anyone else did."

Yes, I am.

My heart is going rabid under his palm. Jesus. He wouldn't even need to use those insane biceps; he could crack me open with his jaw. "I should punish you for disobedience. Maybe then you'll listen to me."

My knees buckle. *Please.* His hand flexes. Not enough to hurt, but to show he could if I wanted him to.

"You've been too reckless with your own life, princess, but I won't be."

With my throat still cradled in one hand, he uses the other to slowly pull down the strap of my dress. It falls down my arm, and my nipple hardens in the cold air.

Goose bumps flood my skin. "Did you really think you could hide from me? I've been tasked with your protection, and I take my vow very seriously."

Fucking hell. I'm a puddle.

"This is what you wanted, wasn't it? Teasing me all night. Begging to be caught. To be put in your place. Chasing danger and wanting to find it."

My hands lay limp at my sides, waiting for his next move. I'm desperate for him to touch me. Anywhere.

"Always so responsible, taking on everyone else's issues. It's all right. I'm strong enough, princess. That's why you picked me. I'll look after you." He keeps his whispered promise, dragging his fingertips along my breast and circling my nipple. One touch, and it peaks, striking a chord that goes straight to my throbbing clit.

He circles, pinches, teases it, holding me against his chest with intent and his palm.

Please, I want to say.

Take care of me. Prove you're someone who cares. Prove I'm worth caring for.

The words stick in my throat, coming out as a pleading moan that Lincoln must understand, because he tightens his grip, sliding his palm up until his thumb and forefinger frame my jaw, tilting my head back until my mouth falls open. My breathing is ragged, loud in my ears.

My hand comes up, sliding through his hair as he licks the pleasure from my lips. Making me pant as he pinches my nipple again.

He breaks the kiss. "Take it off. I don't want anything in my way."

Quickly, I shake off the other strap of my dress and let gravity help slip it to the floor. It pools at my feet, and Lincoln plucks at the waistband of my black underwear. "All of it."

Fuck. Is it possible to see heaven without dying? Because I may find out tonight. I pull them off, and then I'm standing naked in the middle of my living room, a fully dressed Lincoln pressed to my back, with only my heels and a mask left to hide behind.

Without removing his hand from my throat, he dips his head, kissing my shoulder. "Christ, look at you. You're beautiful."

My clit is tingling, and he hasn't even touched it yet. And then he is, and holy fucking shit. Oh my god oh my god oh my god, *his fingers.*

"No one knows that this is who is hiding underneath all those pretty clothes, do they? Maybe I should keep you like this. Safe and secure."

I squirm as he touches me, hearing myself whine as he circles my clit, dragging his fingers down my pussy, playing with my wetness, dipping one finger, then two, in, out.

"Look at how wet you are," he says. "Fucking perfect."

Fuck, I need him inside me already. It's not enough, but oh, I don't want him to stop.

"Please—" I bite back his name just in time. "More."

"Uh-uh, this is all you're getting for now. Come on, ride my fingers. Show me how much you want my cock inside you."

The scratch of his belt on my back turns my blood red hot. He's still fucking dressed, growling filthy lines in my ear while his fingers work me over, deeper and deeper.

"Fuck, you love it, don't you? I could slide right in. You're sucking my fingers in, darling."

Oh, god. I can feel it. His thick fingers pumping into

me, slick, moving easily inside me. And it's so good. All I can do is hold on. Be good.

"Is that what you were after tonight? Did you get sick of life locked away in your castle? You needed to get a taste of excitement? A bit of danger?"

"Yes," I breathe.

"No, that's not it. Not completely." He curls his fingers around my throat, grip loose, weighted. A shiver rolls through me. "Trapped inside all the time, yearning to be free. Always so good." My pulse hammers under his palm. "Trying so hard to make everyone else happy. But what about you? Who is taking care of what you need?"

He is.

Lincoln pulls my jaw down, opening my mouth wider, licking his way inside. Owning the kiss without hesitation. If he stepped back, I'm sure I'd fall. I'm not aware of anything that isn't his lips on mine, the pressure of his thumb digging into the soft skin under my jaw.

"Please," I gasp when I can breathe again.

"Please, what?" He circles my clit faster now, heat building under my skin, my orgasm so close he must be able to taste it. "Always in control. Wanting someone to take care of you. Anyone can adore you, but what you really want is to let go. Maybe it's time you followed orders for a change."

Oh, god. Yes.

"Come on, princess. It's my job to take care of you, so let me."

Another swipe of his thumb, and I'm shaking all

over, pulsing around his fingers as he makes me come. It explodes everywhere, all at once, overwhelming in the best way.

"That's it."

It goes and goes and goes, and all I can do is let it, arching against Lincoln. He never stops holding me, rock solid at my back, his arm a steel bar across my chest. Steady. Sure.

Letting me let go.

My mouth is dry from panting, my hands cramped and sweaty from gripping his arm, his hair. Lincoln kisses a damp trail along my cheek as I come down, never letting me go.

"Beautiful," he breathes against my skin. "Do you need more?"

I nod, still floating.

He guides me over to the couch, the friction of his clothes lighting sparks along my skin. My knees wobble, weak from coming. Weak from him. When my calves hit the sofa, he cradles my jaw and turns me for a filthy kiss. I let him take whatever he wants, and he does.

"Up you get," he directs. "Hands and knees. Let me look at you."

I follow his order, clutching the back of the sofa, my heart knocking against my chest. His hand never leaves me, gently touching my hip as I get into position, then stroking a firm line down my spine once I'm settled.

Every touch is a relief.

"Beautiful," he says, then steps closer to touch the ribbon at the back of my head. The feel of his pants against my sensitive pussy sends a shiver all the way to my toes. "Do you want this off?"

"No." Definitely not. This is too good. I'm not ready for real. "Please."

"It's all right," he soothes. "I've got you."

Then he falls to his knees, his hands splayed on my thighs, encouraging them wider, and I slide them apart. "That's it, good."

Lincoln drags his hands up my thighs slowly, palms hot on my ass, holding me open with his thumbs. "Look at this greedy little clit." My knees shake when he breathes a hot gust over my clit.

"Come on, princess. Show me how sweet you can be."

I jolt at the first touch of his tongue, still sensitive from my orgasm, but — oh, fuck — needing so much more. Each drag of his mouth against my clit makes me hotter, wetter, needier.

Lincoln pulls off with a little suck, his fingers digging deliciously into my hips. "My fucking god. I could spend all night here. Christ."

Yes, do that. Please.

I whine, breathless, as he stands. But the sound of his belt is a relief. I close my eyes, clenching against the cool air, listening as it hits the ground and the zipper of his pants is dragged down.

Then the heat of Lincoln's palm is back on my skin, gently brushing my damp hair away from my back, over my shoulder.

"What would they say if they could see you like this? Begging me to fill you? Their sweet, wholesome princess bent over so easily? One look at this greedy cunt of yours, and they'd know who you really are."

He rubs soothing circles into my skin as the sound of a wrapper hits my ears, feel his hand leave me briefly as he must roll it on. I wish I could see him, but I don't think I can move.

"You're not invincible, princess. You need protecting. I'm going to show you."

I press my forehead harder against the cushion, my pussy clenching, pleading.

He must know how much I need it. Has to. I feel it screaming from every pore. *Touch me, take me, have me.* He has to know.

"Say it."

"*Please*, fuck me."

"Such pretty words you're filled with. I'd love to see what else these beautiful lips can fit."

"Lincoln," I whine. He curses, dark and low, when he finally slides inside me, like it's punched out of him. "You're perfect, darling."

CHAPTER 11
SWEET DREAMS
LINCOLN

I've watched her all night, weaving her spell, entrancing more than only me. When she spoke of losing her job, of being lost and seeking adventure, I falsely expected her to shrink tonight. To use the cover of the mask to hide.

But it was the opposite. And I couldn't look away.

Learning how to get what you want without asking is a skill not many have, and watching Ivy flaunt it effortlessly was quite possibly the hottest thing I've seen in a long time.

But nothing compares to the way she's come apart under my fingers tonight, or the way she's taking my cock so beautifully right now.

Christ. I could dedicate my life to her lips. Thighs. The swell of her arse. I pull her cheeks apart, watching as I slide in and out of her wet heat.

She pants and whines, sweeter than I had hoped.

Collecting spit on my tongue, I slow down, letting it

fall from my lips directly into her crack, where it rolls down from her ass to her pussy. Ivy moans.

I tease my thumb in it, rubbing it into her hole as she pushes back against me, wordlessly begging for more.

She's fucking perfect.

"Please," she finally begs.

I abandon my teasing to fuck into her hard; fast, deep strokes that slap and sting and earn every hungry plea for more.

"Yes, that's it. You feel amazing. Let me give you what you want."

Her arms are shaking where they hold her up. Sinewy, strong arms, defined by years of dedication. I have no doubt she could knock me out if she wanted, which makes her submission all the sweeter.

Christ, she's been deprived. It's a fucking shame. But no more.

By now, I've abandoned the game we started, too wrapped up in the reality of her. There's nothing but her supple skin gripped under my palms, the droplets of sweat collecting along her spine, the sway of her hair as she arches and bucks against me.

"Let go. You don't have to worry about anything right now. Everything else can wait."

She doesn't last long. She's sensitive and worked up from already coming, and soon she's pulsing and clenching hard around me, triggering my own release.

Ivy all but collapses when I pull out, falling onto her side with her eyes closed. If she wasn't still making little whimpers under her breath, I'd swear she was asleep.

Stripping quickly out of my clothes and both of our masks, I gather her up in my arms, kissing the sweat off her shoulder as I deposit her in her bed.

"Do you need anything?" I whisper.

The shake of her head is slow with exhaustion, and I know in that moment I'm going to stay. I don't want to leave her with answers she won't remember in the morning or the fear that she isn't wanted.

So I slip under the covers, wrapping her up tight, and follow her into sleep.

I thought tonight would be enough.

Just a taste to soothe the ache of another lonely year.

But as she clenches and comes again, crying loud enough that the neighbors are likely waking up to the show, I know once could never be enough.

CHAPTER 12
WAKE UP, PRINCESS; WELCOME BACK TO REALITY

IVY

There's a welcome ache between my thighs and an unwelcome one in my chest. I know before I've opened my eyes that I'm in trouble.

This is always how it starts.

Lincoln is still here, sleeping soundly beside me. I wiggle out from under the weight of his arm across my waist, stare up at my incredibly boring beige ceiling (I wonder if our mysterious landlord would let me paint it), and start practicing my lines. *Thanks for last night. It was fun. See you around.*

Anything that says *I like you and the sex was amazing and I want to see you again, but I don't want to seem too eager in case it puts you off,* but, like, in an effortlessly cool way.

I turn my face completely into the pillow and release a long sigh.

Last night was a dream that is going to be stamped on my soul for the rest of my life.

Practiced and careful (two words I never imagined

calling myself), I roll out of bed and get dressed, throwing on a black sports bra and leggings before throwing my hair into a ponytail.

It doesn't matter how many times I've run this scene — men, women, prefer not to say — I've been here before.

See, I have a worrying habit of forming a crush and running faster than an Olympic medalist. Going from like to monogrammed towels overnight. Which is why I keep things casual. As soon as I get too attached, it's time to bow out, find the understudy.

I'm no nurse, but I've patched up enough of my own heartbreak that I should have an honorary degree in cardiology.

Stretching, I check the time. Six a.m. That's what I get for being an early riser. It's not like my body cares that I was up late getting fucked so well I think Lincoln's dick has added a few years to my lifespan.

He's even more gorgeous in broad daylight. The lingering buzz of last night's Prosecco does nothing to dull the curve of his pecs, the V of his hips, the thick presence of his dick.

I hadn't realized how much of his body was covered in tattoos. Pieces connecting over his chest, stomach, *those thighs*. A map. The snake I admired so much last night, smoke, vines, a glorious replication of The Kiss. My mouth waters as I follow the lines of each illustration where they wrap over the muscle and under his cock.

I lick my lips.

"Breakfast?" a low, rough voice asks, cementing

Lincoln as the hottest fucking being I've ever laid eyes on. "Or is there something else you're hungry for?"

Oops.

I clear my throat and look away. "I think you fed me enough last night," I lie, picking up the pieces of his outfit off the floor. I doubt I could ever have my fill of him, and that's exactly why I'm going to stop.

He sits up, stretching out his arms and shoulders, not caring how naked he is, daring me to look. *To want.*

I thrust his clothes at his chest, a full stop to his unspoken sentence.

It's not because I didn't enjoy having (insanely good) sex with him. It's because last night was the most *me* I've felt in a very long time, despite not being myself for most of it.

Lincoln saw me, somehow knew exactly what I needed and then gave it to me. And no matter how much I want to crawl back into bed and lick my way down those incredible tattoos, it would be all too easy to let his smile lead me down the path to heartbreak.

Somewhere out there, there's a different version of this morning, where I give in to the urge to kiss him awake and spend the rest of the day discovering every way we might fit together.

It's a different Ivy who gets to enjoy that. The one who imagines last night as the start of a wonderful love story.

The Ivy who is going to get her heart trampled on.

All I'm doing is protecting her.

"Come here," he says, his biceps bulging and his legs splayed open like an invitation I very much want to RSVP to. Discarding his clothes on the bed beside him, he takes my hand and pulls me between his thighs (oh god, those tattoos might actually kill me). He's gentle as he turns my palm over and kisses it.

"Sure I can't change your mind?"

When he looks up at me, I have to tip my head back against the sparks zipping along my skin.

Am I sure? Of course not.

I step back, and he drops his hands to his thighs. *Seriously, Ivy, stop looking.* "Maybe next time," he says with a smile, finally gathering his clothes and getting dressed.

There's nothing special about the apartment on its own. Every right angle and perfectly uniform light fixture makes me mad if I notice it for too long. I like it a little messy. I fit with messy. When everything's put away just right, it feels like I can't touch anything.

But messy isn't a good habit for dating.

The history of my love life could read as a warning label. *CAUTION: Prone to falling fast into unrequited love.*

It reminds me of those safety warnings on appliances that make no sense. Like "please don't lick the hairdryer," as though someone out there hurt themselves and then complained that there was no strict instruction against it.

It's good to know my heart is on the same level as dryer-licking guy.

It's just that, when I like someone, my hopes tend to rise like Lazarus. It's not Lincoln's fault, just like it wasn't Hannah's or Elijah's. They want a bit of no-strings-attached fun, and for a night, I can give it to them.

Any longer than that is dangerous for me.

"Hey, uh," I say, shoving one foot into a sneaker and looking around for its mate. I should probably clean now that I've got all this extra time on my hands, but I could probably spend a day organizing, and it would just look like chaos again before noon. "I know I already said it, but I'm really sorry about calling myself your girlfriend last night. If I'd known I was talking to your mom, well… Anyway, I'm sure you can come up with a reason for us to break up."

"No apologies necessary, Ivy. I'll take care of it," he says. I can't place the odd note in his tone, but when I turn, he's smiling softly and holding out my other shoe.

"Thanks."

I've gotta say, my foot hasn't gotten any tastier than when I was a kid. I really have to stop putting that thing in my mouth.

But afterward… oh.

It was more intense than any one-night stand I've ever had, which is really going to make dating complicated. Because I already want more, and I really didn't need to be *more* of an odd duck.

"Do you do that a lot?" I ask him while I lace up. Which is a ridiculous question now that I think about it, because of course he does. Why would I think I'm the first? Just because he reached into my soul and made my deepest desires come true doesn't mean it was anything special to him.

I need to get a grip.

When he doesn't answer, I look up at him and add, "The role play?"

He finishes the last button on his shirt, the sleeves rolled up to his elbows, his collar leaving a tantalizing peek at the black lines I know run all over the heavy muscle. His jacket sits draped over the back of my couch.

I thought having clothes on would make me want him less. Yeah, and Caillou is a sweet kid.

"There's a longer answer, but to keep things simple, you're the first person I've been able to enjoy it with."

I have zero clue how to interpret that.

"You were amazing," I admit, before remembering that's something the other Ivy would say. I'm the one who needs to reel things back. "Kind of felt like the best naughty dream I've ever had, times ten."

"I appreciate the feedback," he teases, the cocky bastard.

I find my keys on the coffee table, zip them into the hidden pocket in my leggings. "Yeah, okay. Don't let it go to your head. I'm pretty sure you know how good it was."

"A little positive reinforcement never hurts," he says, backing me up against the front door.

How is it even possible that he still smells incredible? Probably better than last night. Like sleep and sex and rebellion.

"For example," he says, voice a low rumble against my cheek. "You were gorgeous last night. Working the room as though you owned it before giving yourself over to me so beautifully. I've never seen anything like it." I shiver as he brushes a kiss along my shoulder. "You're a revelation."

It's disarming.

He's disarming, as though he's not only seen this show before, but he's working off his own notes from the margins, steering me onto my mark with a firm hand and a lazy smile.

I close my eyes, my heart rabbiting in my chest.

Damn, do I want to follow.

"It's almost a shame we have to break up," I whisper, the only allowance I'll make to wishing for something more.

"Hmm, it is."

There's a moment where my eyes are still closed and the heat of his body blankets mine and I'm sure he's going to kiss me. One for the road. A memory to hold on to.

But it never comes.

Instead, I blink my eyes open as he steps away, smiling softly with a promise I have to ignore if I want to keep my resolve.

The elevator ride downstairs borders on awkward, and, ah, there is the tension I remember from every other morning after. Everything in me is screaming to not let him leave, to make a move, ask for his number, anything.

Maybe he's expecting it. Or maybe he isn't. Maybe I'm the only one left off balance by last night. My heart is already skipping ahead down the road of romance toward date nights and home-cooked meals and text messages that leave me giddy.

Who the hell am I kidding? Of course he isn't.

They never are.

At least I have last night. For a few hours, I was another Ivy. The one who's lived a hundred different lives and had a devoted boyfriend.

It was a fun role to play.

"Hey," he says, like a man without a care in the world. He's leaning on the wall of the elevator, close enough that our elbows brush and no less attractive for being unwashed and in last night's clothes. Maybe it's time I raise my standards. "I have to know. What did you say to Mrs. Vanderweide? I heard she offered triple the price for *The Totem*."

The creepy eyeless golem comes rushing back to me, and I light up, grabbing Lincoln's arm. "She actually bought it?"

"Wouldn't take no for an answer. She was insistent that it was the perfect piece for her boat."

"That bitch," I whisper, but I can't help smiling. Not only did she buy my art, she stole my line.

When we finally get to the ground floor, Lincoln holds the doors open for me but doesn't follow. I stop in the middle of the foyer, confused. "What are you doing?"

He pulls his hand out of his pocket to swipe a keycard on a scanner I've never noticed before. Wait, what? "I'm going up to my apartment."

"Upstairs?" I squeak. Avoiding him just got a hundred times harder.

Don't lie. You're not upset about that.

"Ivy, I want to be honest with you, but you might be mad."

The elevator chimes, but we ignore it. "Well, that's a sure-fire way to get me there."

He steps back, cocking a smile. "I own the building."

The doors close.

The shock doesn't wear off until a mile into my run, when I have to stop to laugh so hard it scares off a woman with a stroller who was jogging behind me.

He owns the building. Fuck. Of course he does.

CHAPTER 13
WHAT BEST FRIENDS ARE FOR

IVY

For the record, this whole job search thing? It really, really sucks.

Look, I'm not sticking my head in the sand. I know I can't keep putting it off, but can anyone blame me for not wanting to run with open arms toward a nine-to-five desk job that I'll be stuck in until I'm seventy? (Probably eighty, at this rate).

I like working (well, I like having a paycheck), and I know how to work my (absolutely juicy) ass off. But every day and every week was nothing but routine. Bland, boiled chicken. No seasoning. No flavor.

Life should be more exciting than a one-woman show on health reform.

I used to have hobbies. I used to be interesting.

Then I turned into someone who woke up on a Monday morning, already counting down until the weekend.

But what other choice do I have? We're all out here

making the most of the time we have. Well. Other people are.

I don't think I've made the most of anything in years.

Every time Mom calls, I want to cry. I haven't updated my résumé. I can't bring myself to open it, even though I need to. Time's a-wasting, and my savings won't last forever. Then I remember the emails, and endless pressure, and I have to ask, is this it? Is this all I'll be for the rest of my life?

When I got offered the internship, I said yes immediately. I'd heard the horror stories about the job market. How hard it was to find anything in my field — or even out of my field. The hundreds of applications that went rejected or unanswered. The long, complicated interview process.

Even the lucky ones who got hired talked about the shitty work conditions. Being judged for a terrible work ethic if you didn't devote every second of your life outside of your working hours to the job or had the audacity to not come in early because you had — gasp — personal obligations.

I knew I was being offered a privilege few had. So I took it. And the permanent job offer that followed. I thought I was making a mature decision.

I thought I'd be happier.

———

"I can't believe it's been a week already," Emma pouts prettily, her long legs curled up under her where she's draped elegantly on the end of my olive two-seater. Usually, after Pilates, we lunch, but until I get another job, the only reservations I'll be making are at *Chez Ivy*.

Emma clasps her hands together, stretching them above her head. "I hate not seeing you in the office. First Charlie, and now you. It's awful not seeing my favorite people every day."

It really is. Working with my best friend made even the worst days better. "If I ever get another job—"

"When," Emma stresses.

Always the optimist. I smile from where I'm sprawled out on the floor with the pile of laundry I've been ignoring. "Maybe you can come work with me. Get the gang back together."

I can't imagine Emma ever being without a job. She's the most capable person I've ever met (even though she would never brag), but that's not why I love her. It's the giant heart underneath, the same one that I worried for when she was still pining over her piece-of-shit ex, before she and Charlie sorted themselves out.

"I'd follow you to the ends of the earth," she says.

I haven't been to church since I hit puberty, but if there's a god, the proof is in how lucky I am to have Emma in my life. "Have you spoken with your mom yet?"

"No," I say, throwing myself back on the pillows I pulled off the sofa, sinking into them like they can protect me from the oncoming train that is going to be my mother's disappointment. "And it's getting harder not to tell her. I can't lie to her, but if I tell her before I have a job worked out, I'll wake up tomorrow to fifty news articles she's sent me about the decline of the economy and how ungrateful and irresponsible our generation is."

Either that, or I'll get an email the length of a small novel that I'll inevitably have to call my therapist about, and I was sort of hoping to talk about something new for a change. My therapist has been through enough.

No. It's better this way, even though it's slowly eating away at my insides. There's enough on her plate right now with Ciara and the baby, and I certainly don't need any help with freaking out over my current situation.

I'm managing that just fine on my own.

"Surely she'd understand if you explained wanting a break," Emma says.

Maybe. I throw the striped blouse I'm holding on to the clean pile without folding it. What's the point in ironing anything when I've spent the past two weeks exclusively in gym gear?

"In my senior year of high school, this local news-paper came by to do a piece on our end-of-year-show. Nothing special. A photo of the cast and some sweet stuff about how enthusiastic we all were." A total puff piece, but nothing beat how cool it felt to see my face in the paper. "I stuck it up above my bed, and when it came time to choose a college, she sat me down, looked at it, and said, 'I know you're going to miss it, but you need to think about your future.'"

I inspect a pair of jeans for stains and find none,

rolling them into a ball and putting them on top of the clean pile. I get that it's my mother's job to protect me and all, but wow, dagger straight to the heart.

Emma slides off the couch to tackle me into a hug. "I want you to know I support you, 100 percent, no matter what you do. Also, we're missing two very important things right now."

I squeeze her back, blinking away the heat prickling my eyes. "Those two things better be tacos and booze."

"Great minds think alike," Emma says with glee, standing and grabbing her phone. "I'll order, and you can tell me all about your date with Lincoln."

That sly, sexy bitch. Where the hell do I even begin?

I give up on folding a camp T-shirt, throwing it back on the dirty pile to stretch my legs out. "I don't know what you want me to say. It was good, and weird, and completely unpredictable." I haven't been able to stop thinking about it.

"All your favorite things."

"I know," I groan. "First dates will be doomed after this. And the sex… Record making. Scale broken. Tens across the board. I'd let that show run into the ground just for one more season."

The tip of Emma's button nose scrunches. "While I'm happy for you, it's a little strange to think of him like that. All I know of him are glimpses of the cocky kid who used to walk his sister to my house and swim in my pool every summer. We weren't close. Back then he was too cool for everyone." She finishes typing and places her phone to the side.

"He's still like that," I say. But boy, does it turn me on. I've always been a sucker for a guy who had enough of his shit together to not be bothered with petty crap.

Emma smooths out her hair, which is barely damp. Meanwhile I look like I ran face-first into a hurricane. "And the masquerade? I know you were looking forward to it."

I pause, because this is Emma — gorgeous, smart, looks incredible in a pantsuit, got her shit together, Emma — and I may have oopsied a little too close to the sun this time.

I bury my face in a blue sundress. "I accidentally told his mom we were dating."

Silence. I open a single eye to find her staring at me, fighting a smile with her jaw dropped.

"It wasn't on purpose!" I clarify.

"I gathered that from the accidentally," Emma says. Through the ceiling come the harsh stabs of piano keys that mark Hania's weekly lessons. "What happened?"

I abandon the pile to slide into the seat next to her. "I told him that I was wondering who I would have been if I'd made different choices in life, and he said to be whoever I wanted because no one would know the difference. In my defense, I had no idea it was his mom until after I said it."

She's eyeing me knowingly. "It's interesting that in one of the roles, you wanted to be was girlfriend."

"Don't think I haven't been deconstructing *that* for the past twenty-four hours." Crap. I really was going to have to call my therapist, wasn't I? "What's the deal with his family?"

Emma crosses her legs and shrugs one shoulder. "I only met his grandfather a few times. He was a very severe man, the type who talks to children as if they're business associates. Nana always said he wasn't worth the air it would take to curse him, but I remember Lincoln's dad being down-to-earth. Always smiling, always friendly. I don't know much about the split, only that his mom moved back here with Reed and Darcy, and Lincoln stayed in the UK with his dad. After that, I barely saw him, not until the party last year."

God, I have so many questions. Reed had been equal parts welcoming and cold, and while Astrid had been a delight, there was a clear distance between her and Lincoln I wanted to understand.

I hate the thought that I'll never see her again.

A knock at my door gets me off the couch, signaling treats have arrived.

When I answer it, I'm not at all surprised to find Charlie there, bags in hand. "Oh, cute," I joke over my shoulder. "You got a new personal assistant." Although it might as well be true. They started out slinging insults to each other, but eventually they became a team.

I want that. I've always wanted it. Deeply, with every fiber.

"Jealous?" Charlie winks.

"Not in a million years." Except I am. A little. Not about Charlie — *God, no* — but having someone rock up when I need them? Yeah, I'll take some of that.

I take the treasure out of his hands, ushering him inside. "Hey, you quit without having anything lined up. Weren't you worried?"

I leave him the spot beside Emma on the sofa, sinking back onto the floor, leaning against the TV unit opposite them. He slots in perfectly beside her, his worn dark jeans beside her candy pink leggings, their edges clicking into place.

There's gray under his trimmed nails, stubborn oil that won't be scrubbed off. Last week he almost floated out of his bones when I asked about the 1978 Datsun he was rebuilding at work.

What I would give to have purpose like that.

Charlie shakes his head. "Not really."

"That's not entirely true." Emma nudges his knee with her foot, which he catches and starts rubbing. I split the food between us, piling extra cheese on my plate.

"Okay," he admits. "I was a little worried, but I've always found my feet. You got a payout, right?"

"A small one," I confirm.

He nods. "Yeah, that helps. So maybe take some time, if you can. I know what it's like to keep going, rain or shine. Starts to feel like if you stop—"

"Everything'll fall apart," I finish for him.

"Exactly, but if you don't stop now, when will you?"

It's a good point.

Above us, Hania stops, starts again. It's getting better. Now there are at least two and a half blind mice. I should take her some hand cream tomorrow; her fingers will be aching.

Charlie picked well. The food smells and tastes delicious, and a comfortable silence settles as we all eat, Hania's practice serving as background music.

Back in college, it was all about moving out. Getting my own place. Then a car, covering my student loans, eating better, finding a good hairdresser, and being able to make appointments *in advance*. Seeing a dentist more than once a decade.

Now it's like there are more downsides than ups. Working until I'm exhausted, followed by an ocean of guilt if I'm not making the most of every spare minute. Check in with my mom, pay my bills, be a good friend, eventually read a non-fiction book instead of doom scrolling first thing in the morning. Take my vitamins.

Sometimes life feels like free labor.

"Every time I think of going back to doc control, it's like I've eaten bad sushi. I can't tell if that's because I'm over it all or because I can't stomach jumping back in so fast. I know I was decent at it. Maybe not as fabulous as you two—"

"You're brilliant," Emma cuts in. "Don't you dare suggest otherwise."

And okay, I am. I just like hearing her say it sometimes, with all the indignant fury she carries. It's nice. Charlie is smiling like he knows exactly how I feel, and yeah, he would.

"I just keep thinking, maybe I've hitched my wagon to the wrong horse. I won't ever be able to do anything else."

"Nah, that shit's transferable," Charlie says. "The way you handle the toughest of customers without breaking a sweat? You've got skills not everyone can learn, and the rest, you're smart enough to pick up. I wouldn't be worried. Anyone would be lucky to have you."

Well, damn. Here I was thinking Emma's compliments were the only kind that could knock me over, but it turns out Charlie's got a mean right hook when he wants to.

Gratitude warms me from the inside out. The one love I have never shied away from is this — friendship.

"I've been meaning to ask," Charlie says, his grin stretching out, and I know the tender moment is over. "How was your night of mystery with Mr. Moneybags?"

I flush at the memory of every touch, every whisper in my ear, every filthy promise.

Emma turns to him. "Be nice. That's her boyfriend you're talking about."

I groan into my hands as Emma laughs.

"Already?" Charlie asks. "Damn Ivy, you work fast. Should we RSVP to the wedding now, or...?"

I drop my hands to give him the finger. "You can keep your RSVP because we've broken up, and I'm never going to see him again."

What I don't say is that I keep hoping to bump into him in the elevator, or that every time a man sits beside me at the bar, my heart jumps until I realize it isn't him.

In senior year, I won the lead role in our production of some show I can't even remember the name of now. It wasn't a sign of my skill, because I truly cannot undersell how average an actor I was, but it didn't matter, because lead meant playing lover to Jake.

My crush on him had lasted two years, kept alive by my own naivety and his manipulation. Not that I'd learned that until after graduation.

But the day casting had been announced, my heart had soared. Straight to the clouds, where my head has always been, lighter than air.

There was a kiss on page twelve.

I dreamed of that kiss every night. It would be our first. Maybe then he'd finally see me as someone other than his friend.

Our lips would meet — and they had to; it was scripted — and the agony of my unrequited love would finally come to an end. Good or bad, I didn't care.

I just wanted that kiss.

We skipped over it in rehearsals. I'd been too nervous to attempt it at the time, and Mr. Thomas was too focused on staging to care. As long as we hit our marks on the night, he said.

Still, I played it out in my head every night.

By the night of the performance, we'd kissed a dozen times, if only in my imagination. Jake's strong hands cupping my face, his lips soft under mine, but not hesitant.

Never hesitant.

The moment came, and…

No kiss.

The cue was his, and he missed it. Said his line and walked off stage just as he was supposed to. But no kiss.

I kept going — the show must go on, always — but

it stayed with me. The regret of inaction. Of longing. Of dragging someone else into my fantasies.

And a month later, when he sat next to me in the stairwell, whispering how I treated him better than his girlfriend, keeping his hooks in me even as he said we couldn't be anything but friends…

I decided I'd never lie to myself again.

CHAPTER 14

MOM'S THE WORD (OR IT WOULD BE, IF I COULD KEEP MY MOUTH SHUT)

IVY

If a situation calls for it, I can keep a secret. I once took the fall when Ciara broke the garbage disposal because she wanted to turn the sink into a fish tank, but I am not Fort-Knox, okay?

Of course I'm going to fold. The guilt is killing me. I can't take it any longer.

My updated résumé (yes, I finally updated it) sits finished on my laptop, glaring at me every time I log in. There are multiple tabs open for recruiters, five job searches, and in one early morning bout of ideas, post-grad college options. I've done nothing with any of them.

After an hour of scrolling through movies I've already seen, I turn off the TV, determined to think of something more productive to do with my time, only to stare into space for twenty minutes, where the only sound I hear is the building's air steadily humming.

There's an itch under my skin, one I can't seem to scratch, insistently tapping at my brain. I hadn't realized how much I like being busy. Lincoln's right. I'm searching for something; I just wish I knew what it was.

"Gigi?" Mom says when she answers my call, her tone halfway between worried and stern (it's a permanent setting; I'm used to it now). "Is everything okay?"

She's the only one who still calls me that, instead of my middle name like everyone else, and I let her, because she named me after herself, so I get why she clings to it.

"Of course, why?"

There's an odd pause. "You never call me in the middle of a workday. Are you sick?"

Fuck. I'd completely forgotten.

"No, I'm fine," I scramble, guilt threatening to make my breakfast stage a comeback. "I wanted to see how the baby was."

Lucky for me, the diversion works. When in doubt, ask about the grandchildren.

"Oh, she's gorgeous. Of course, she's not sleeping at all at the moment. But the nurse is confident it's nothing serious, and I keep reminding your sister it's just a phase. They all go through it. One day you might discover that yourself."

Right. I squeeze the phone between my shoulder and my ear and start drying this morning's dishes. It's just a bowl and a spoon, but I have so much spare time on my hands now, it's weird to leave them in the sink for long.

"Of course, Ciara keeps saying she doesn't need me to come around every day. Something about wanting some alone time with the baby. But she's barely remembering to feed herself at the moment. If I wasn't there, none of the chores would get done."

It's the same old argument they've been having since the baby was born. I'm half convinced Mom doesn't know what to do with herself when she's not hovering over them.

"I read about your office's layoffs," she says, and that's when I crack.

"I didn't want to keep it from you," I stress, and it's the truth. "But I didn't want you to worry."

"Of course I'm worried, Gigi. I wish you'd told me. When did it happen?"

"Two weeks ago."

"Gianna."

I wince. Mom never uses my middle name, but to go full first name? Not a good sign. "I'm sorry I didn't tell you sooner, but I've already updated my résumé, and I'll start applying for jobs soon. It's okay. I've been saving like we talked about, and they gave me some money when they let me go, so…"

"You need to be responsible, Gigi. Look at your sister—"

I close my eyes. I could write a thesis on what my mother says I need.

She's only ever wanted me to be one thing, but I'll never be as clever or accomplished as my baby sister, never have it together like she does, with a PhD and a husband and a baby.

"Not everyone can be as perfect as Ciara."

My sister came out of the womb knowing what she wanted.

And I'm proud of her. So, so proud. No one cheered louder than me when she graduated. She was always destined to do great things, and she deserves every win she's achieved.

I accepted early on that my little sister would shine bright. It was nice to move aside and help make that happen.

By contrast, my job was just a job. Clock in, clock out. Pay the bills. Sleep.

"You need a job, Ivy, whether you like it or not. You can't pretend that work doesn't matter."

"I'm not," I say, tossing the towel on the counter. "Of course it matters. It's all I've been thinking about since it happened, but I haven't done anything else since I graduated, and I don't even know if I'm happy anymore. If I'm going to spend the rest of my life working, shouldn't it be something I enjoy?"

The sigh she heaves is so laden with feeling I'm shocked the phone doesn't drop out of my hand from the weight. "Not everyone gets a choice, Gigi. If you need to find yourself, you can do it when you can keep a roof over your head. It's only going to be harder if you wait. You know that. A big gap in your work history isn't going to look good to future employers, and what are you going to tell them when they ask?"

"That I haven't had a break in eight years."

"Take this seriously, please."

She isn't listening. All I've done for past eight years is be serious. That's the problem.

Somewhere along the line, life sped up while I wasn't paying attention, or perhaps I've been willfully fast forwarding. "I don't want to wake up one day and be too old to enjoy life."

"Gigi, you have plenty of time for life later," she huffs, and then there are cries in the background. "And now the baby's awake. We can talk about this later."

Of course it doesn't stop Mom's points from dangling in the air long after we've hung up. Needling at my resolve, unspooling my anxiety, thread by thread.

I hang my head in my hands, my hair falling around my face like a closing curtain. Not even my hair escaped her attempts to polish me into someone proper. Straightening out the curls, keeping it long.

Orderly. Responsible. Lifeless.

CHAPTER 15
FLY AWAY WITH ME
LINCOLN

I enjoy my job, take pleasure in the delivery of other people's desires, but I haven't been this invested since I started. Each word spoken to one person in particular.

One night with Ivy has reinvigorated my work. Suddenly I can't write ideas down fast enough. I've been jumping on audio prompts faster than I can find them.

The more inventive, the better.

When I originally auditioned for Pulse, I never intended to make narrating erotica a full-time job. But the team at the app has been nothing short of wonderful, and what started as a lark has become a passion.

The fact is, between planning, recording, and edits, it's a hell of a lot more work than anyone would expect. The heavy breathing alone is hell on my vocal cords.

I've been careful not to mix business and pleasure, but it's different this time. The simple fact is, I can't stop thinking about Ivy.

Did I expect to be here when I left London? Absolutely not.

Am I complaining? Not even a little.

I want to see her again. I need to know what makes her different. Why she's having such an effect on me.

I won't stop until I know. Hell, I haven't even gotten around to telling anyone about our fake breakup.

On paper, Ivy feels like the opposite of what I should want. The untamed energy of my youth paired with a propensity to say what's she's thinking at all times.

Naked honesty? I can barely imagine it.

If I started saying what I really thought, the universe might collapse on itself.

Delving into my relationship history is a short, uninteresting tread. There are carparks with more fanfare. I'd liken it to an abandoned Olympic Park: once a beacon of great enthusiasm and promise, now a rusted obstruction, home to more failures than successes.

I'm better at the short term, at wining and dining and athletic morning sex that stretches out to lazy dessert sex. Perhaps it's not in my nature to do anything by half measures. If I want something, I don't deny myself.

I may not have much practice, but I'm determined and not easily distracted. If Ivy shoots me down, so be it. But I have to try.

———

I've spent so many years giving away my wealth that I'd almost forgotten how disgustingly rich Deacon was. He always used it as a weapon, forcing people to his will. Dick gave him thirty years of servitude, my parents lost their marriage, and complete knobs like Kyle tried to copy and paste themselves in his image.

After the split, he used it as emotional warfare, paying my ticket to Oxford and sending endless amounts of money that I was too much of a muppet to throw back in his face.

Back then, I lapped it up. Thought I was invincible, until I chased a girl to Bruges — it's always fucking Bruges — and lost it all. Shit story short, it was my fault, then Reed bailed me out, and he's never let me forget it.

I've worked really fucking hard for fourteen years to become a better man, using every cent Deacon tried to bribe me with to help someone else. Dad's mortgage is paid, Manny got his bar, and every cent I earn from tenants goes back into making this building better for the people living here.

I have no use for titles or status, but I think I can be forgiven for enjoying the benefits, just this once.

It's for a good cause, after all.

It only takes a quick call to the hangar to prep the family plane — and some convincing that Reed approved it and the trip is for family business.

Now, I need to understand why Ivy is having an argument with herself in the hallway.

"Hey." I hasten my approach, catching her elbow in

my palm. Even in scuffed sneakers and jeans, she's stunning, enough of her hair falling out of where it's tied up that she's clearly been attacking it in frustration. "Careful there. How about we try a full breath?"

I'm pleased as she follows my advice, her chest rising and dropping slowly. Relaxing in small doses. "Much better," I say. "Tell me how I can help."

I don't like to flaunt it, but the truth is, there isn't much money or influence can't solve.

She huffs a laugh. "Convince my mother I'm not making a terrible mistake?"

Except that. "If she knows you, she's already aware of that," I say, ducking to catch her gaze. Long lashes frame her wide brown eyes, but at least her breathing is slowing down.

When she notices I'm still holding her, she slips slowly out of my grasp, not meeting my eye. "To what do I owe the pleasure of this visit? Or is this part of a new landlord outreach program I'm not aware of?"

"Perhaps I simply wanted to see if my memory had captured your beauty adequately."

"And?" The morning light glows around her, and it's not a stretch to say she's the most beautiful woman I've ever laid eyes on.

I sigh theatrically, enjoying the tug of a smile I can tell she's holding back. "Sadly, it doesn't hold a candle to the real thing. You defy belief."

For a moment she doesn't say anything, her gaze sliding to her feet. But unless the crack in the linoleum (must get that fixed) is fascinating to her, I'd say I've found Ivy's shy spot. I'm expecting the door to close, but it doesn't, and her next words are soft, small.

"Why are you here, Lincoln?"

"We have an appointment."

She meets my eyes finally. "Do we?" There's a lash on her cheek, and she turns into my touch when I reach out to brush it off.

"Yes. You're minutes away from being very charmed by me."

There's a shine to her eyes, a spark, asking me to lead the way. It's a request I'll gladly answer as many times as she asks. "That was last week. I don't remember booking a repeat."

"I took the liberty."

"You do that a lot."

"Well, would you look at that," I say as I lean in, kissing her cheek. She smells divine, freshly washed and skin warm. "Right on time."

"Lincoln…" She fades off. I know what comes next, but I'm not finished.

"I'm also here to take you out," I say, sliding one hand into my pants pocket and holding the other out for her. "And I'm not taking no for an answer."

She leans on the doorframe and crosses her arms, and I remember exactly how good it felt when all that toned muscle slackened under my touch. "Do I need to change?"

"Never. I want you just as you are."

Her smile is electric, a torment and a pleasure.

———

As we board, our pilot, Roger, lets us know it's the perfect day for an impromptu flight. "Low cloud cover and wind today, so we'll get you there in a jiff."

There are eight recliners to choose from in the private Bradbury jet, four singles and two doubles framing a table. I let Ivy take her pick first, curious to see whether she's a window or an aisle. True compatibility arises in the smaller things, I find.

She's been wide-eyed and quiet since we arrived at the airstrip, and it's so unlike what I've come to know about her that I'm hoping it's a matter of awe and not discomfort.

I'm not sure I could forgive myself if it's the latter.

It pleases me when she slips into a double by the window, beckoning me over to take the seat beside her.

With the engines on, crew onboard, and the two of us buckled in, I'm surprised to find the aircraft door still open. Flagging down the attendant, I ask, "Is there a problem?"

"No sir," he confirms. "We're just waiting on two more."

Bollocks.

"Sorry, love," Darcy calls out, sounding anything but as her voice floats into the cabin. "We left as soon as Roger called, but traffic's been a nightmare."

Within seconds, my little sister appears, polished in wide-leg pants and an asymmetrical shirt. Mum follows her onboard, looking far more relaxed in jeans and a hopeful smile.

A family outing isn't exactly the romantic

atmosphere I was going for, but I can at least be grateful that Reed isn't here.

"Hello, Darce."

"Hello, you," she says, ducking down to kiss me on both cheeks. She looks well, which always eases my mind, her honey blond hair cut to her shoulders. She waits as Mum sits across the table from Ivy, then glides elegantly in beside her.

"What a surprise," I say. It's exceedingly interesting that the person who has been too busy to see me in the last week is free suddenly. "I would have thought you'd be working."

"I am working," she retorts, but the gleam in her eye says that's a big, fat lie. "I've been meaning to visit the factory, and it's the perfect day for it." Her gaze lands to where my hand is holding Ivy's before jumping back to my own. She looks a little too eager to have caught us together. "Don't mind us interrupting your romantic interlude. You'll barely notice we're here."

I doubt that.

It's cheeky as fuck, but that's Darcy for you.

Suddenly, Ivy is pressed as close as she can be, holding her hand out to my sister. "You must be the wonderful sister I've heard so much about. Hi, I'm Ivy."

"Lovely to meet you," comes the pleased response, and they shake hands. "Sorry we didn't know you existed, a small oversight on my brother's part." So, it's going to be that sort of a visit, then. "I adore your necklace."

Ivy touches the black leather cord that's tied at her

neck and the two pendants hanging from it. "Thank you so much. I broke the bracelet I originally had these on while sparring with my friend Fil, and actually, the leather is an offcut from a dress he was making, which was perfect, because I haven't taken these off since I bought them."

"What do they mean?" Darcy asks.

"The heart is my mom and the seahorse is my sister, Ciara. She's a marine biologist and obsessed with them."

"That's beautiful. Nothing for Lincoln yet? My, my. You're slipping, brother."

Ivy laughs, but this is starting to feel too much like an interrogation for my liking. "Don't be cheeky," I chide gently, with a pointed look to add: *Be nice. I like this one.*

I need this to go well.

Darcy softens.

"Oh, there's plenty, I promise you," Ivy lies smoothly, saving me once again. There's a freckle caught in her hairline that I haven't noticed before, one of many hidden gems I'm keen to discover. "Before Lincoln, the most I ever got from a date was a complex."

Well, that's just unacceptable. She doesn't know it yet, but I'm going to make sure she has any and every-thing she desires.

With her gaze firmly on where our hands are linked, Ivy speaks softly. I'm too enamored with the pink dusting her cheeks that it takes a moment before her words land. But when they do, they knock my heart around. "I can honestly say I've never met anyone like him before."

Mum and Darcy share a look I can't interpret. Behind us, the attendant locks the door, shutting me in with the two most important women in my life and one I'll be lucky to have, if I can manage not to fuck this up.

CHAPTER 16
TIME TO IMPROVISE

It gets *real* quiet during take-off. I might be digging my nails into Lincoln's arm right now, but it's hard to tell because I'm trying to listen to the safety instructions over the sound of my heart pounding in my throat.

How am I supposed to play this? When Lincoln showed up at my door and asked me out, I'd hoped that maybe… but now his family is here, and he obviously never told them we broke up (boy, would that make this three times more awkward), so… what is this? A date? An audition? Payback?

It's my fault he has to pretend to date me, after all.

Lincoln, looking unbelievably sexy in dark denim and a buttery soft T-shirt, covers my hand with his, but doesn't pry it off like I'm expecting. Instead, he leans over and kisses my forehead. It's so sweet, so comforting, that no, I can't picture him planning this as petty revenge.

I wasn't the only one surprised to see Darcy and Astrid onboard.

It's just, this was so much easier at the masquerade when I was playing someone else. Less chance of getting hurt.

"So, Ivy," Darcy says, leaning forward and pinning me with the sharp stare I now recognize as a family trait. No wonder their family is formidable. Her hair is darker than Lincoln's, flicking out in a thick wave, but it's the black nail polish that surprises me. "Tell me everything. How did you two meet?"

"You remember Emma," Lincoln says, and Darcy lights up.

"Of course! Oh, I've been meaning to get in touch since I heard about her parents selling the house. How is she? It's been ages."

Emma's a topic that requires no falsifying. I'm lucky to have a friend like her. "She's great. Kicking ass at work, and it's a long story, but she's completely in love. It's almost disgusting."

Darcy flashes me a wry smile. "She probably says the same thing about you two."

"Anyway," I say, breezing on past that land mine. I should stop the charade. I'm not sure why Lincoln never told them the truth, but is it really even my life if I'm not embroiled in a deeply one-sided fantasy relationship? I might as well enjoy the perks while they last. "Lincoln surprised us at her parents' farewell party and left an impression." All true. "He's not shy about going after what he wants, and what can I say? He's a hard man to resist, but also surprisingly sweet when he wants to be. After that, it was easy to fall for him."

"Yes, he's always been that way," Darcy says, and I feel Lincoln tense under my palm.

Perhaps making up a whole backstory for us is making it worse, but then, he's not exactly setting anyone straight.

Hoping he'll feel the apology in it, I thread our fingers together. "Oh, trust me, I thought for sure he'd get bored with me at some point—"

"Impossible," he says, and the blush that rushes to my cheeks is 100 percent real. "It's me who has to worry about keeping you entertained."

"You won't have to try hard. There's nothing about you I don't like," I admit.

Darcy pulls a camera out of her bag, a brick of a thing that means serious business. There's easily a couple grand in her manicured hands, and then I remember I'm sitting on a private plane. So silly of me to forget.

"You two are adorable. I have to get a photo."

"Darcy," Lincoln says again, a whole sentence distilled into one word. He's good at that.

"Just one kiss. It'll be great. You've had her to yourself for a whole year, Lincoln. Don't be greedy."

She's smiling knowingly. I can't tell if she's buying this or not, so even though I know my heart is going to read all the wrong things into this, I curl my hand around his jaw and pull Lincoln in for a kiss.

I only mean for to be short and sweet, a simple meeting of lips. Demure. Safe for familial consumption. But the moment he presses his mouth to mine, once, then again, a little firmer, lightning shoots through me, all the way to my toes.

It's so tender, my heart aches. Like he can't get enough. Like there's no one he'd ever want to kiss but me. It's overwhelming in all the best ways, and I already know no other kiss will live up to it.

It can't be more than a few seconds, but it leaves me off balance, and when he playfully nudges my nose with his as he pulls away, I have to duck my head and remember to breathe.

These are dangerous waters.

But it's not real. He's playing it up for his family, and I can't let myself fall into the trap of believing this is anything other than an immersive improvisation.

———

The view before we land steals my breath. Buildings dot along the coast, weathered but unshakable, as though they sprouted from the very ground, unearthed by the lapping waters.

A car is already waiting for us when we land, and when we arrive at the factory, I find the people, too, are durable, chipped from the stone that surrounds us.

It's impressive.

The Bradbury name looms large in wrought iron, a stamp on the building, and I dare say, the town. The building stands firm at its center, bearing the marks of a long history. Apparently, it functions as shelter when storms hit.

Makes sense. It's probably older than the sea.

Most people who pass us know Astrid and Darcy, although it surprises me when they're greeted like old friends and not corporate overlords. It's a nice change. Only a few people recognize Lincoln, but it's always with the same exclamation — something akin to "you're so grown" — before telling him to send their love to his dad.

I guess this town bears the history of the Reeveses too.

As good as the tour is, what I really want is to get a moment with Lincoln alone. Maybe then he can tell me what the plan is. Should we stage a fight and break up before we fly back?

Wait, bad idea. Who will hold my hand during take-off?

I could always pick a fight after we land — *something, something, I never want to see you again* — A quick scroll through my old Tinder messages should help me come up with something.

I'll hate every second, but if it's what he wants, I'll do it.

Before I can pull him aside, Darcy links her arm in his and insists on getting some shots of him inside, even as he grumbles that "I don't work for you. Or Reed."

She looks to me, but I get the feeling that once Lincoln sets his mind on something, there's no changing it. There's a relief in knowing he can't be moved easily, as steadfast as the building she's attempting to persuade him into.

But for her sake, I try. "You should go." Stretching up to my toes, I kiss his cheek. "Come find me after."

There's too much to read in his gaze and no chance to ask while his family is here, but he eventually nods.

As Lincoln and Darcy walk away, Astrid waves me onward. "Come on, I'm going to take you over to Octavia's."

CHAPTER 17
MY SOFT SPOTS (ARE SHOWING)

LINCOLN

"I like her," Darcy says as she corrals me into position, the heavy presence of Deacon's name at my back, generations of judgment hanging over me like a guillotine.

It's putting my teeth on edge.

Darcy must catch it through her viewfinder, because she sighs, but nonetheless takes the shot. Her first camera was a garish block of plastic, barely capable of more than a grainy smudge, but somehow, Darce knew how to turn the blurriest of shots into something meaningful.

She could have any job she wanted. Magazines, advertising, broadcasting. They've all tried to poach her. She's certainly been offered enough to tempt even the most discerning person away from the family business. But if there's one thing we Reeveses have in common, it's our stubborn streak.

What Reed has done to earn her loyalty when he's been so quick to dismiss me, I'll never know.

She's assessing the results as she says, "You could have told me, you know. I would have been happy for you."

"I know."

She looks up at me, her brow furrowed with a tenderness that makes her look ten years younger. "You and Reed, always with your secrets." She shakes her head. "Our family needs a new trade."

"As though you don't keep things to yourself. When were you going to mention being sick?"

"It was nothing, a simple cold. And I didn't mention specifically because I know how you get."

She's right. She's impossible, but she's right. God, I love her.

"You need to tell me next time, Darcy. I mean it. I don't care what it is. An earache, a sprained ankle, anything. I can't help if I don't know."

I can't be in the dark again. Not after last time.

"I promise to tell you if it's serious," she says. That's probably the best I can hope for. "And you better promise not to propose without warning me first. I need time to plan."

I pull her into a hug. Darcy still fits under my arm, still prefers shampoo that smells like Fruit Roll-Ups, and still clears her throat obnoxiously loudly when she's trying to be conspicuous.

It killed me to be on the other side of the ocean when we almost lost her. Darcy might be able to wave off a burst appendix, but I will never forget the bone-chilling terror of almost losing her and being an ocean away. Every painstaking second waiting for updates from Reed as she went through surgery. The fucking gall he had to tell me to focus on exams while our sister lay cut open on some operating table. As if Uni mattered more than her life.

But she's here and she's healthy, and that's all I care about.

If I cling to her a little too much, she doesn't mention it.

"You're still satisfied with all this?" I ask. "No regret about turning down the Vox job?"

Darcy nods against my chest. "There are more important things than money," she says, repeating something I've said too many times to count. "I'm exactly where I want to be."

I should let it be, even if I don't understand it.

Eventually, Darcy steps back, raising the camera again and ignoring my eye roll as she prods me to stand beside an assembly line. It smells of glue and throws me back about two decades.

"Ivy isn't like the others," she says, mid-shot. It isn't a question, and I'm not surprised that she can see through me.

"I'm out of my depth," I admit, rubbing the back of my neck.

She stops and looks up. "Of course you are, but you haven't messed it up yet. She wouldn't be here otherwise."

Christ, I hope so. "I want to do this right. Ivy deserves that."

"So do you," Darcy says, firmly. "As long as you don't go overboard, it'll be fine."

As though it's a crime to want to take care of someone. To spoil them. Well, if it is, I'm surely fucked. "When have I ever gone overboard?"

She raises a single brow, and okay, fair point.

"You'll get wrinkles if you keep frowning like that," she teases. "Besides, you've always been good at winging it."

"Some would call that a character flaw," I say, following her past a row of stations where filament is being hand sorted. We both know who that someone would be.

Darcy bumps our shoulders together. "Don't start."

It's been decades since I was last here. It's remained the same, while I am leagues from who I used to be. Now I feel stretched thin, torn between two separate worlds. Never knowing where I fit.

I've never regretted choosing Dad. It was the right decision, even though I hated not being able to watch over Darcy. I couldn't have it both ways, but it's never stopped me from wanting it.

"How is he?"

Darcy's my only hope of getting the true answer, but it seems she's done playing middle woman. "Now that you're here, you could ask him yourself. You have to learn to talk to each other eventually."

"Debatable," I say.

I follow her around, allow her to position me as she wants, take her photos. People recognize and thank her as we go, treating her more like a friend than their employee. Things have certainly changed a lot since Deacon's time.

"Do you think we'll ever escape him?"

She doesn't answer right away, looking out at the factory floor from the mezzanine we're on. There are as many people as machines, laughter echoing above the din. From the look of it, it's a great working environment. Full of life. It's a long shot from the drudgery I remember as a child.

Darcy sets her camera down, her expression fond as a loud cheer goes up in the corner. "Of course. It's up to us who we choose to be and how we impact the world. Deacon was all about himself. Reed cares about community, which is why he made sure every employee has equal share of the company. Including us."

"What?" This is the first I'm hearing it.

She turns to face me, crossing her arms. I feel a lecture coming on. "You heard me. Reed might have the title, but every single one of these people has a stake. He's changed things, Linc. It's not like it was when Deacon ran it. He's dialed back expansion and kept things local. Increased benefits, increased flexibility. We all look after each other, and we all succeed."

"Why would he do that?" It doesn't make sense. When he cut the rest of the family out of the estate, it seemed like Reed was on track to be the perfect successor to Deacon, putting profits above all. But sharing ownership with the company flies in the face of that.

But why?

"You should ask him," Darcy retorts.

My grandfather was a lot of things, not all of them

good, in my opinion. If anything, I'm proud that Reed has become a better man than he was.

She reaches out, placing her hand on my arm. "He's missed you. We all have. He's just shithouse at showing it, which is why it has to be you who goes first. I promise you, if you can let your guard down, he will listen."

Unlikely.

"Are we done here?" I ask when I see Darcy lowering her camera away finally. I'm itching to get back.

"Why? Are you worried about what Mum is telling Ivy, or what Ivy is telling Mum?"

Christ. "Both now, and thank you for that."

So much for whisking Ivy away on a romantic date.

CHAPTER 18
A LITTLE ADVICE

IVY

The main street is wonderfully devoid of franchises, instead lined with local shops with handwritten signs outside. A leather shop promises that "all our cows are vegan." Another hanging outside a small jeweler notes the "husband drop-off point." It's all so quaint. All that's missing is the city girl who is out of her depth.

Oh shit, it's me, isn't it?

We keep walking, past soap stores that smell divine and a jewelry maker. "It's really beautiful here," I say.

Astrid nods. "It is. After Simon and I got married, we lived here for a while. Found this gorgeous little house that had been left to rot. I almost wept when I saw the state of the cast-iron fireplace upstairs. But oh," she touches her heart, "the potential. We signed immediately and got to work fixing it up." Her eyes have a faraway look in them like Mom gets when she talks about dad. "Simon's work took us back to London while I was still pregnant with Reed, but as soon as he was able, he had a replica made for me." She smiles, as delicate as a bluebird, and I just know there's a story there worth hearing. "A piece of advice? Marry a romantic."

I swallow down my reaction at the M-word, hiding my flush while I enter the little boutique Astrid's led me to. It's bursting with wall-to-wall color. Crocheted rainbow socks, sand-casted gold jewelry, beaded phone holders, artisanal hats with brims Carmen Sandiego would kill for, what I can only describe as the cuntiest sunglasses I've ever seen, and… the list goes on. "I'm not sure I'll ever marry, but thank you."

"I can honestly say I don't blame you," she says while trying on a pair of thick tortoise-shell sunglasses. "The piece of paper isn't as important as the love you feel, and between you and me, it's a huge pain in the ass to get rid of."

Surprised laughter explodes out of me. I had no idea Astrid could swear.

"But," she says, dragging out the word with a light tone that clashes with the very direct look she's giving me. "You don't always need a ring. You could always, say, leave your mark another way."

Damn. Her memory is a steel trap.

"Yes, well…" I clear my throat, picking up a pair of octopus studs that Ciara would love. "I don't even know how serious Lincoln and I are yet." Mostly because we're not really a couple and haven't gotten our stories straight.

"Ivy, he moved here, which I never thought he'd do, and with the way he looks at you, I don't think you have anything to worry about."

Guilt drags the contents of my breakfast down into the center of the earth. Great, now his family thinks the only reason he came back is me, when I had nothing to do with it. "It really wasn't me that he moved for. Family means a lot to him."

I don't need to know him to see that.

"That's sweet, but you don't have to save my feelings. I know how Lincoln feels about us." Astrid sounds so defeated my heart cracks like thin ice under the weight of it.

Now would be the time to own up to the lie. If I wasn't so afraid to make things worse. "What was he like as a kid?" I ask instead.

She smiles, soft and fond. "Much the same, only smaller."

I can barely imagine it. I just assumed he'd exited the womb as a mini-Viking.

"He's always been more willing to throw himself into the unknown," she adds, putting the sunglasses down and moving down the aisle. The owner, Benson (no relation to the titular Octavia, apparently), smiles as we pass him. "It's admirable, and a lesson I've tried hard to learn myself in the last few years. Risks haven't always come easy for me, but Lincoln reminds me they're worth it."

"He's a good man." I know in my gut I'm right, which only makes me feel worse about the situation I've put him in.

My heart burns in my chest. I'm the reason he's lying to her.

There's a long pause. "He is. Though I'm not sure he

sees it. I've missed him dearly, but I understand why he chose to stay. He and his father have always been very close."

I hear what she isn't saying. "When I was a kid, I couldn't relate to people who were best friends with their parents. It seemed so strange. Then Ciara started middle school, and every day, she'd make me walk her to the bus stop so we could meet Mom after work. The whole way home, they'd talk. About their days, Ciara's classes, Mom's coworkers, all kinds of stuff."

"It's difficult to be the odd one out."

I shrug. "They have more in common, so it's okay."

Astrid smiles knowingly. "Have you ever talked to them about it?"

"Have you?"

"Touché," she says. "Simon and I worked very hard to ensure that the kids stayed close. My siblings and I don't see eye to eye, you see, and things really took a turn when my father passed. It hurts me to see the boys as distant as they are."

I pause at a display of beaded bracelets in a combination of colors that each represent a queer flag, all beautifully handmade. "They were different when they were younger, I'm guessing?"

"Very." She holds up a pair of earrings, admires them with a tilt of her head. "You'll see in June. They have a way of bringing it out of each other."

June? I can't imagine Lincoln will still want to keep up this charade in two months' time, but I just have to know. "What's in June?"

Astrid blinks. "The big birthday reunion," she states

like a known fact. Because of course Lincoln's real girl-friend would know that. "You'll come, of course."

Shit.

"Wouldn't miss it for the world," I say, forcing a smile, because what the hell else am I supposed to say? *Sorry, two months is a long time to lie to my fake boyfriend's family, and he'll definitely have a new girlfriend by then?*

Lincoln can cross that bridge himself. That is, if he hasn't thrown me out of the plane on the way back.

Astrid moves to the back of the store where there's a small shoe rack of boots on sale. She takes a seat on a footstool and taps the one beside it. "It's lucky that you were off today."

Right. The job that I definitely still have. I really should stop forgetting about that. It would have come in real handy sixty seconds ago to explain why I can't go to the reunion. Sitting beside her, I fake a cough. "If anyone asks, I'm sick."

She chuckles, toeing off her flats to try on a pair of tan ankle boots. "Well, then, I'd say the fresh air is doing you a world of good."

I wonder what all this lying is doing to me.

"So," I say. "I know Lincoln's dad is a painter, but I'm sad to say I don't know what you do for work."

"I'm long retired, even though I indulge Reed on occasion. But when I did work, I was an environmental lawyer."

My eyebrows shoot up. Wow, I would never have guessed.

She hands me a pair of black slouchy boots, miracu-lously in my size. There's embossed detailing and a sturdy gold zipper. I hope they're uncomfortable as shit because they're so gorgeous I want to cry, and I'm too stressed about money right now to let myself buy them.

Astrid slips her ballet flats back on. "I can't tell you how many times Simon had to talk me out of quitting in a rage."

"I know the feeling. There's a shower argument I've been winning for three years running." My boss at the time refused me a raise on the basis that I "didn't present professionally enough." So I did what any over-dramatic, petty person does. I turned it up to eleven.

In hindsight, the redundancy may have been justified.

"Arguments are best had in the car," Astrid says. "Never waste the acoustics of a bathroom when there are songs to be sung."

"I don't think my neighbors need to be subjected to me ruining 'At the End of the Day' any more frequently than they already do," I joke, and Astrid laughs loud enough to startle Benson.

"If high notes don't scare you, you should try 'Think of Me.' It's my personal favorite."

I slip the boots on. Dammit, they're a perfect fit.

"Oh, they suit you perfectly," she says. I walk over to the mirror to see she's right. It's a shame I can never own them. "Have you always been a fan of the theater?"

"Always. When I was nine, I wanted to be a fly operator. I got a library card solely to borrow Stella Adler's *Art of Acting*. One Christmas, Ciara and I got Barbies, and I made her wait a week to play with them so I could 'get their backstories in order.' She still brings it up."

Astrid laughs. "Gosh, I haven't thought about Stella in years. Uncle Val, my mother's brother, worked in the theater. Did Lincoln tell you that?"

I shake my head.

She smiles down at her hands. "He took me backstage once, put a headset on me, let me watch from the wings." Her mouth twists at one side. "I miss him a lot."

"What happened?"

Astrid clears her throat. "It was a heart attack, which came as a surprise because he was very particular about what he ate. I was twenty-two, if you can believe it." She touches her fingers to the pendant on her necklace, and suddenly, she looks very small.

Heartbroken.

"Simon was with me when I got the news," she says. "It was our second date. Simon had taken me to this beautiful restaurant that he'd saved up three weeks' pay for, and when the mains arrived, I burst into tears all over my monkfish."

My eyes burn hot.

The music changes in the store, something pop-y I don't recognize. It clashes with the moment, but I can't exactly go over and ask them to change it. I've tried that once before, and they did not appreciate it.

Astrid moves slowly along the table, eyes lowered to the earring display, but the faraway lilt in her voice tells me she's not really seeing them. I keep close, not wanting to miss a single word.

"He stayed up with me all night," Astrid says. "Asked me all about him. Didn't say a word when I ruined his best shirt with my mascara." She smiles. "I think I fell in love with him in that moment."

As soon as the boots are off my feet, Astrid walks them over to Benson. "Add these to my bill."

"Astrid, I can't let you—"

She places her hand on my arm, her smile filled with a pleading that makes my heart squeeze. "Please let me. I've already crashed your date, and I've enjoyed getting to spend some time with you. Accept it as my thank-you for entertaining me."

My mouth flaps uselessly until it's obvious I'm going to give in. I nod. "Thank you."

She hands me the boots. "It's my pleasure."

I'm speechless. Without hesitating, I step forward and wrap my arms around her.

Astrid startles. "Oh, you're so sweet." I wonder how often she gets hugged. Even at my maddest, I never went to bed without kissing my mother good night. Slowly, Astrid hugs back. "Thank you, Ivy. I'm so happy my son brought you into our lives."

Guilt sours on my tongue, and I slip out of her hold. I really hate lying to her.

CHAPTER 19
GRASPING FOR SOMETHING OUT OF REACH

IVY

Lincoln and Darcy catch up with us along the water. The plane is refueling, apparently, and they've elected to wait here rather than at the airstrip.

Darcy pulls Astrid into a hushed conversation a few shops away, their hands clasped around matching teas, and I finally get to steal a moment to have Lincoln to myself.

Aware that they can still see us, I slip my hand in his. "Did you have fun?"

Lincoln catches me around the waist and pulls me in until I can smell his soapy cleanness under the brisk air. God damn, does he smell good. "I am now." I soak in the comforting quiet he provides.

His hair has been knocked loose by the breeze, tumbling over his forehead like a dashing hero. "I'm sorry today didn't turn out as we'd hoped," he says.

"I'm not. It's been great." Sure, I'd hoped for more. No one has ever done anything remotely romantic for me, so it's no surprise my heart swan-dived when we arrived at the airport earlier. But I think I understand now.

Family isn't always easy, and if I can help him bridge the obvious gap between them, I'm happy to do it.

A slight turn of my head shows Astrid watching us with a smile. I hug him a little tighter. "You plan a good date, Lincoln Filbert Reeves."

He chuckles into my hair. "Nice try."

The lookout we're on frames the city in a distant ode, like the backdrop of a faraway dream. My real life feels like a memory. I wonder if that's why Lincoln brought me here.

I take a deep breath of fresh air. "All this for some paintbrushes, huh? I knew I was in the wrong business. I guess it makes sense now that your mom fell for a painter."

He breathes out a hum, or maybe it's a sigh. Either way, it rumbles through his chest and makes me flush.

It's a really beautiful day, the spring air full of promise. The water lays still across the bay, as calm as the man holding me, a far cry from the riot I can feel in my chest.

"I was fighting with my mom when you found me earlier." I keep my eyes on the horizon, the buzz of the airfield, the trees in the distance. "She wants me to be someone I'm not." I wish she was easier to talk to. "But I didn't grow up knowing I was going to publish a noteworthy thesis on pigmentation bias in squids like Ciara. All I cared about was convincing my high school drama teacher to stage *Chicago* because I'd spent all summer learning 'Cell Block Tango,' or whether I could pull off Uggs and a miniskirt."

Ciara has everything Mom wants for us — success in her field, a loving husband, a family. It's a lot to live up to. "She was so happy when I was offered the job at Helix, and I thought *I've finally done something to make Mom proud.* I wish she could trust that I can make my own choices."

Lincoln rubs my back, his fingers drawing up and down my spine in a soothing distraction. For a fake boyfriend, he's really good at this. "Do you have that trust in yourself?"

Heat stings my eyes. How does he always know where to find my soft spots?

"May I offer a suggestion?" he asks.

Please. Maybe I shouldn't be so eager for his opinion, but also, why the hell shouldn't I? The guy has lived all over the world and had a first-class education. Even if we were raised as opposite as two people can be, I'm not gonna turn away a suggestion.

I mean, I've liked everything he's done with me so far.

"Sure, hit me with it."

"It's okay to feel this way, to not know what comes next, to stumble through until you find your way. You aren't doing it alone." My head hits his chest with a soft thump, my tears spilling over while Lincoln rubs my back. "You haven't failed anyone, and you certainly don't need anyone's permission."

Yes, I have. Tears sting my eyes. Is it really so hard for me to believe?

Yes.

"How do you always know exactly what to say?"

He pulls back, cupping my face and raising it until our eyes meet. "You could say I've had a lot of practice."

I rest my chin on his chest, looking up at him. "I'm the older sister. It was supposed to be me who had her shit together first, me who set the example." Instead, I'm two steps behind. "There's so much I haven't done yet."

"Such as?"

"Silly things. Go on a road trip, dance in the moonlight, fall in love."

"None of that is silly," he says, his palm warm on my cheek. "Everyone wants to fall in love." The way he says it surprises me, sounding too close to my own yearning to be true.

"Surely you've come close, though, with your dating history."

"Sadly, no. I'm still searching."

If Lincoln can't find it, then what hope do I have? "Is that all you're searching for?"

It takes a while — where there's only salt in the air and the quiet symphony of life in the background — before he responds.

"No, I'm still trying to find home, I suppose. It's difficult to settle down when parts of your life are scattered in different places, and I've spent a lot of time keeping my distance from certain things." He takes a slow, measured breath. "I'm trying to change that now.

That's partly why I'm here, to clear the air before it's too late."

And here I am, planting myself right in the middle of it all.

If it is going to end, *when* it ends, I hope he remembers that. From the little I've seen, he's hiding a big heart, and he deserves to be happy. "I think if you told your family what you just told me, they'd not only understand, but they'd be proud of you."

His eyes are so bright and sincere it's like staring at the stars. "I've never met anyone like you, Ivy. You're enchanting." No one's ever used that word to describe me before. "I hope you don't mind, but I think I'm going to keep you. Something tells me you're about to change my life."

He must have been lab tested to make my knees weak. Or maybe it's the rush of sea air. It's hard to tell when my heart is melting in my chest.

"All right, you two," Darcy calls, pulling me back to reality. "You can cuddle later; Roger's ready to go."

CHAPTER 20
FAMILY MATTERS

LINCOLN

I'd hoped my allotment of surprises had already been used up, but there's a black town car parked on the tarmac when we step off the plane and a frown in an ash gray suit waiting beside it.

Christ. What now?

The unannounced appearance of my brother is suspicious and unwelcome. Darcy, at least, made some kind of sense, because she's Darcy, and her untamed glee at meeting Ivy has been apparent from the second she bounced onto the plane.

My brother is another story.

"Reed, you remember Ivy."

Mum and Darcy make their way over to him. Me? I'm trying to hold on to what Darcy said earlier today, but I don't like the way he's looking at her, with narrowed eyes and a cold distance.

"I do, although it's nice to see your face this time."

"And yours," Ivy says. "Now I have a face to put to the judgmental tone."

Over Reed's shoulder, Darcy hides a smile behind her palm.

His expression twitches briefly, the frown disappearing before he looks back up at me, and it returns in full force. "I'm calling a family meeting," he says. "Ivy, can you get home from here?"

What the fuck? "I'll take her home."

"No, we need to talk, and it can't wait. All of us." One sweep of his hand, and Mum and Darcy are already getting into the car. But I'm not a lapdog and no one treats Ivy this way.

"You don't get to order either of us around."

"It's okay," Ivy says, tugging on my arm. "I'm a big girl. You should go."

I trust her to get herself home, but I don't like being treated like my brother's underling. I have half a mind to leave, but there's something desperate in his eyes that I've never seen before.

Fear.

Reed holds the car door open. "Thank you, Ivy. Lincoln, you've got two minutes." With that, he walks to the driver's side, the door closing like a gavel.

I kiss Ivy goodbye. "Be safe."

She pokes my ribs, the adorable wrinkle on her nose calling out to me. "Don't worry about me. I can take care of myself."

"Of that, I have no doubt. But do it anyway. For me."

She's beautiful when she blushes. One thing is certain: I need to keep her in my life. "Go. I don't want to annoy your brother any more than I already have."

Directly ignoring Reed's two-minute deadline, I wait until Ivy is safely away before I return to the car. In protest, I refuse to say a word the entire drive back to the house, spending the time in a state of barely contained rage.

Reed and I have always been different. He's a thinker, I'm a doer. He likes work, I like fun.

My brother has never understood that I won't wait. For anything. He needs graphs, research, to tell him how to feel, when to act. He's never understood any explanation I've given him because they aren't led by numbers.

None of my decisions have ever made sense on paper. So he tuned me out and called me selfish.

He was right. For a while. I didn't see it until it was too late, but what hurt was that he was so busy being worried about the family — sounding every bit like Deacon that I could see his hand puppeteering Reed's mouth — that he never asked me how I felt.

It was always blame, blame, blame. Keep Lincoln contained, keep him in line. I'd hoped we'd grown out of it, but clearly, I was wrong.

The house hasn't changed since I last visited. A modest two-story Victorian with a warm red finish on the outside and an open floor plan. When we arrive, I tear into the living room ahead of him. "Are you going to explain that bullshit you just pulled?"

Reed folds his gangly body into an armchair, crossing one leg over the other. He's lost the jacket but is still holding himself like this is a business meeting. "Sure. You can start by telling me why you thought you could use family property for a joyride without permission."

Fucking permission? "Since when have I needed your permission to do anything?"

"Of course. What was I thinking? You merely swan about, doing whatever the fuck you want, with no care for the consequences."

"Boys, please. Can we not do this right now?" Mum says.

I turn away from Reed to shove the anger down.

"At least explain the whole cloak and dagger act, Reed," Darcy says.

"Someone attempted to access the trust account last night. Security notified me while you were gone. They didn't get in, but we're reviewing our current security measures." He looks at me, and I know what's coming before it leaves his mouth. "If you needed money, you could have just asked."

Darcy is out of her seat first. "Reed!"

"You bastard," I spit out, voice low. "How dare you?"

"Reed, you don't really think your brother had anything to do with this, do you?" Mum asks.

He hasn't taken his eyes off me since we entered the room. "Didn't you?"

"No, you fucking asshole. I make my own money. I don't want any of yours."

His shoulders sag, and it's just so fucking *him* to be relieved after he accuses me of stealing. "What about Ivy?" he asks.

My teeth grind together. "What about her?"

"How well do you know her, anyway? Do you even know that Ivy is her middle name?"

I don't even blink. "Of course I do," I bluff, because what does it matter? It's still her name. "She could choose a different name each day of the week, and I wouldn't care. What is this really about? Are you seriously implying she's only after my money? That's insulting, even for you."

"I'm not accusing her—"

I loom over him, fuming. "You damn well better not be. Ivy has nothing to do with this."

Reed leans his head back, his expression serious. "But it wouldn't be the first time you've been led astray by a pretty face."

Blowing out a breath, I step away from him before I do something I'll regret. "Unbelievable. Always getting one more hit in… You're never going to let that go," I say, shaking my head. I turn back to face him, hearing the menace thickening my voice almost into a growl. "Ivy is my girlfriend; you should show her some respect."

Like he's been cut off his strings, Reed's expression crumbles, and he lands back in his chair with a thump. My hands are shaking with frustration, but at the sight of him slumped over in defeat, my pulse calms.

"You're right, you're right," he says, rubbing both hands over his face. "Fuck, I'm sorry. If you trust her—"

"I absolutely trust her," I insist. There's not a doubt in my mind.

Reed backs off, nodding, pained. "Then I believe you. It's not her."

"Jesus, Reed. And you wonder why I never told you about her," I huff. I need a drink.

"Christ, Reed. I love you," Darcy says from her perch. "But you really can be such an arsehole."

As I walk over to where I know he keeps his whiskey, Darcy throws me a nod, and I figure *why the hell not?* and pour us all one.

"I'm aware," Reed replies, thumb and forefinger digging into the corners of his eyes with one hand as he takes the offered drink from me with the other. It's a big sign that he's not as pulled together as he'd like everyone to believe. "I shouldn't have accused you. Or Ivy."

"Thanks, love." Mum says when I pass her a glass. Then she shocks me by throwing two fingers of aged scotch back like its water. "Reed, you better get this nonsense out of your system before the reunion. I don't want you making Ivy feel unwelcome."

I can practically hear the record scratch in the room.

Fuck.

It's not that I forgot about it. It's impossible to in our family. Deacon never let us miss an occasion to celebrate his birthday, and now that he's passed, Joe's been bullied into carrying on the tradition for him and his long-gone twin.

But I didn't account for Mum inviting Ivy, and I should have.

Shit. The last thing she needs is to be dragged farther into the depths of our drama.

"Of course I won't. What do you take me for?" he

says, to a resounding silence from the rest of us. "Yes, yes, all right. Arsehole, I know. I'll apologize."

"You damn well will," I stress, knowing it's the first thing I need to do when I get out of here, because dammit, I have so much more to say sorry for.

Namely, the disaster of today.

"It's these fucking tariffs that have me on edge. Bloody two-faced politicians trying to force us to cut our benefits. That's not an excuse." He holds a hand up, stopping my argument before I can start it. "And now this breach." He leans his elbows on his knees. "I'm sorry I accused you. It's my responsibility to look after this family, and I take it very seriously." Yes, and water is wet. "If there's anything I need to know, tell me now. I can't do anything if I don't know."

Darcy pins me with a challenging look. "Now where have I heard that today?"

I throw back my drink. Coming back here was meant to be complicated, not a complete disaster.

CHAPTER 21
ROSES ARE RED

IVY

When I blink awake the next morning, I'm convinced I'm still dreaming.

When I was twenty-one, a guy started our date by telling me he didn't believe in buying a girl flowers. Our server looked me right in the eye and said, "I really hope there isn't a second date."

There wasn't.

So waking up to find a bouquet of red roses on my bedside table is confusing but nice. Then I realize I'm surrounded by them.

I shoot up in bed and stare. There's got to be at least three dozen of them here. Scratch that, four.

"What the fuck?" I whisper.

How did they get in here?

It must have taken a few guys to move this much stuff, and I didn't hear a thing. Oh god, a group of strangers was in my apartment, and I never even woke up.

What the fuck?

Seconds flow past, liquid and smooth, as I stare in awe around my room. My lungs soak in the smell — clean, subtle, fresh. I've never lain in a meadow, but I imagine it must be like this. I can practically feel the sun kiss my skin the way it does in my dreams, bathing me in warmth, holding me close.

I fling the sheets off, ready to run. Maybe I should check with Lincoln, ask him if there are cameras in the hallways. And if there are, does he have access to them? Because then we could at least find out who the hell did this.

My spiraling ends when my hand hits a note.

I'm prepared for some magazine clipped message foretelling my imminent death — which on second thought, I shouldn't be in such a rush to read — but what I find steals my breath in a different way.

For yesterday, and all the dates who came before me, L x

That sexy, mysterious, British son of a... wonderful person. (Sorry, Astrid).

Throwing the note back onto the bed, I squeeze my way through the field of flowers. Oh god, they're so beautiful. I want to *hate him*. How will I ever like anyone normal after this? I grab my keys and phone, and the first thing I can find to throw on, jumping into a pair of mustard-colored overalls, before sending a quick video to Emma.

Me: woke up to this! what is my life?

Fil is stepping out of his apartment as I lock up (not that it does anything to stop roving English would-be Don Juans). "What's the rush?"

I'm already at the elevator. "I'm just going to murder our landlord."

"Oh, cool," he calls before the doors close. "Can you tell him my oven's busted again while you're there? Nice flowers, by the way."

"Thanks," I grit out. Because they are nice flowers. Really nice. All seven thousand of them. But they're also trespassing in my apartment, because my lovely not-actually-my-boyfriend thought it would be romantic to traumatize me.

And the worst part?

I actually fucking love it.

It's ridiculous and over-the-top and probably a massive violation of his authority, but it's also the single most romantic event of my whole life, and I don't even know how to contact the asshole to thank him for them.

Because, of course, he doesn't have a problem sending me more roses than a closing performance of *Phantom of the Opera*, but he couldn't *possibly* do something as simple as tell me his phone number.

I'm either going to rip his dick off or blow him. I won't know which until I find him.

So I start with the one person I know can help me.

"Tell me where your cousin is, or I'm never coming here again," I say to Manny after I've thrown open the door to the bar. "Wait. Why are you here so early? It's, like, eight in the morning."

"They're called deliveries, and I'm having a great day, thanks for asking. Now what is it you want with my cousin?"

"He saw fit to let himself into my apartment so he

could leave a nursery's worth of flowers in my bedroom."

"He did what?"

A thumping knock comes at the side entrance, and Manny calls out a greeting, pulling a wad of keys from his pockets to open it. A slip of a man is waiting on the other side with a keg. "Just pop in the back. Thanks, mate."

"Sure thing." The guy nods, a short, sharp thing that reminds me of my uncle. "You should know, there's a truck blocking me in. Says they're delivering some art to the owner? I told 'em to talk to you."

Manny sighs. "Yeah, all right. I'll fix it."

Curious, I follow him outside, stopping in shock as the "art" in question is practically airlifted out of the truck. The two guys carrying it aren't lightweights, either.

"What the hell?" Manny asks, and we look at each other in confusion. "He doesn't do anything by halves, does he?"

I'm getting that impression.

"Look, I have to stay here to mind the bar. If I key the code into the goods lift, can you take these guys up to the penthouse? Lincoln should be home, and you can have your chat."

"Yeah, yes, of course." I wave them through, eager to move before he changes his mind.

As they squeeze into the elevator behind me, I feel as though I've stepped into a heist film. Ever since Lincoln came into my life, it's been one wild ride after another.

Manny tries to shield the keypad, but he's distracted and doesn't seem to realize that being short gives me a perfectly good vantage point, so I hold my breath and memorize as he types *1-1-0-5-2-0*.

I'd feel bad, but I have about 200 reasons not to, all wafting their scent into my flannel sheets.

It's kind of nice being sneaky. Maybe this is why Lincoln does it.

The elevator opens right into the apartment, which explains the key code, and I'm too busy being blown away by the size of it to do anything but stand and stare.

I knew it'd be big, but damn, he could stage a *Newsies* revival in here.

One of the delivery guys clears his throat, and I step out of the way, standing awkwardly by as they shuffle the crate they're holding out of the elevator.

"Hello?"

I'm pointing my finger at Lincoln as soon as he steps into the hallway. "You."

He stops short. "Ivy? What are you—oh, hey." He nods to the guys behind me and waves us all in. "Thanks, lads. You can leave that over here."

They lower it to the ground with matching groans, then the shorter of the two walks over. "If you could sign this," he says, handing over a clipboard. "We'll unpack it quick and be out of your hair."

"Thanks." Lincoln signs and turns back to me.

I know I came up here for a reason, but all of a sudden, it's escaping me. Because Lincoln isn't wearing a shirt.

His body is unfair. Who even has a six-pack in real life? And those tattoos… How dare they live permanently on his skin, touching him all the time when I can't?

Jesus, the valley between this man's pecs could be classified as low ground. Small armies have been conquered there. My fabulous ass certainly has no chance of survival.

Body building? More like world building.

Light-wash jeans hang low on his hips like a tease. Fuck, one little tug would probably have them on the floor. Then there'd be nothing left between me and those thighs…

Side note: who would I have to petition to get shirts permanently banned?

"We have company," he reminds me, my gaze jumping up to meet his, where he's smiling with a mix of hunger and amusement.

"Put some clothes on so I can yell at you," I say, because I can't think while his muscles are out.

He chuckles, but leaves without a word.

I stride over to the windows, taking in the open plan room. Stained wood flooring with coordinated dark wood furniture, a patterned red rug that could cover my apartment spread out from a tan leather sofa. It's warm and inviting, with the same careful curation of colors as the bar, the same commanding presence that says, "Stay, I'll look after you."

There are touches of him everywhere, a book opened face down on the counter, a few cushions pushed to the floor by the sofa, an enormous water bottle drying by the sink next to a pot that's starting to rattle. There's a faded palm print in the handle where time and use have left a mark. This isn't a new item. He must have traveled here with it. It makes me indescribably fond. This is where he spends his time, a little piece of who he is, the man he couldn't leave behind.

The delivery guys really do work quick, and they even take the crate back with them, leaving the canvas propped up against the wall. I don't even hear them leave, struck silent for a second time as I finally see what Lincoln bought.

A familiar clash of blue and yellow stares back. Holy shit. This is…

"It's yours," Lincoln says, appearing beside me, now in a pale blue button-down.

"I…" I don't have any words. It's too much. I don't know what to think. I don't know what to say. "You can't…"

"Only I decide what I can and can't do, darling."

This isn't fair. I came up here to yell at him. Or kiss him.

And now…

"If it's too much," he says. "I can hold on to it for you. Until you decide what you want to do with it."

I don't even know what I'm going to do with Lincoln, let alone a painting that cost him—god, I'm not sure I want to know how much.

I spin around to face him, my hands landing on my hips so I can make this point without jumping him like my body wants to. Priorities. "We're gonna circle back around to," I gesture behind me, "all that. What I want to start with is, what the hell?"

His smile widens. "You don't like the roses?"

He's kidding, right? "What I didn't like was waking up alone to a scrap of paper and half my salary worth of a botanic garden. You didn't think about maybe, I don't know, sticking around? Not making me think I'd been the victim of the weirdest crime in history?"

"I wanted it to be a surprise."

My heart dips and dives in my chest, and for a moment, everything feels too big to contain. I have to get a grip.

The giddiness translates to a laugh that bubbles out of me, and the brightness in his eyes is about to be my undoing. I push past him to address the room. "A surprise, he says. Yeah, you surprised me right into almost calling a lawyer."

The room is no help. It's like a crystal ball sent me to my dream home. I turn back to face him. He's still watching me with open appreciation.

"Stop smiling at me like that. It makes me want to kiss you."

He steps close enough that I can smell his body wash. It's disgusting. Which is what I would say if I was a liar. Of course it's delicious. What else would it be?

"That's a good instinct; you should follow that." He smiles as he hooks a finger in the pocket of my overalls, pulling me closer.

"Stop it," I say, but I'm smiling too much to sell it. Damn his steel-gray eyes and international charm. My heart can't cope with this. His ridiculously huge shoulders are currently framed by the — my — painting. He's too beautiful for my health. I need a distraction. "What were you doing when we came in, anyway?"

"Working."

I cock my brow. "Shirtless?"

"It helps me get into character."

Character?

At my confusion, he softens, reaching for my hand. "Here, let me show you."

I follow him down the hallway, spying the main bedroom ahead, but we stop instead in front of a converted hall closet. "Welcome to my studio."

The walls are covered in black soundproofing foam, with a microphone stand, headphones and a laptop set up inside. There aren't any instruments in here—no guitars (shame) or sheet music. A singer, maybe?

Except that's a script I can see on the screen. So… voiceover? I mean, yeah, with a voice like that, why not? I'd pay for it.

Let's not say that out loud.

"This is a bit of a temporary setup until I can install better equipment, but it works well enough for now. Sorry about before. I was in the middle of recording when I heard the lift." There's pride in his expression. I recognize it from the years I spent watching Ciara talk about the ocean, or Emma talk about governance, or Manny testing out a new cocktail.

It's a whole new side of him. Not the cocky traveler, not the stoic son, but the soft, private part. I can't believe he's just letting me see it.

Lincoln mistakes my awe for confusion. "Ivy, I'd like to introduce you to my alter ego, Mr. Silver."

———

This explains a lot.

As a woman with a healthy libido, I've heard of audio erotica before. I've just never actually listened to any. Five minutes ago, I didn't even know where to find it, but now not only do I have an app to download, but a name to search as soon as I get back to my apartment.

Or would that be creepy? Is it stalking if I've slept with him already and am kinda-sorta fake dating him?

No, wait. He's the one who carried four dozen (I knew it was four!) bouquets into my room this morning while I was sleeping. Listening to him play act a couple of orgasms will be, like, fair restitution.

Or something.

The masquerade makes so much more sense now. I'm almost disappointed I didn't put this together sooner. "And your family doesn't know?"

We're back in his living room, and yes, the sofa is exactly as comfortable as it looks. "Manny knows."

I can't imagine not wanting my family in my business. Even when we don't agree, I don't like keeping them in the dark. "I thought maybe this was why there was so much tension between you and your brother."

He scratches his thumb, looking out the window. "No, that's an issue that goes a lot farther back."

"So what do they think you do?"

"Nothing of value, if you asked them," he says

sadly, still turned away, even though the view is barely more than a rooftop car lot and an empty office complex. If I lean enough to the right, I could probably see the Helix building.

I focus on Lincoln instead.

Mom says I've always been observant. Ciara is the quiet one, her nose in a book, then in a fish tank. One hilarious afternoon, she jumped into the touch pool at the aquarium. Funny for me, at least. Mom was not laughing. She kept asking me what I'd said to my sister to make her do it.

Apparently, jumping into the unknown headfirst was cute when I was onstage as Tree Number One, but not so great when Ciara was trying to hug a cuttlefish.

These days I try to think first, but it's not easy. I'm not a natural planner like Emma. I've seen the lists she makes.

Me? I go with my gut and lead with my mouth. (Okay, that sounded dirtier than I meant it).

I don't always get it right. Like the time I booked a hotel room for Aaron and myself as a surprise romantic staycation, but didn't account for him getting back together with his ex the night before.

That wasn't my favorite birthday.

But my gut is telling me that Lincoln is wrong about this. I've seen how happy Darcy and Astrid are that he's here. How eager they are to get to know him.

I slide my hand into his, tugging until he looks at me. "I think they'd surprise you if you gave them the chance."

He doesn't answer.

Instead, Lincoln curls his palm around mine, and I try to forget that the last time I tried to hold a date's hand, they tore it away from me.

"I'm sorry if the roses make you uncomfortable. I can have them cleared out today."

"What?" I must have misheard him. "No, you will not. They're beautiful and they were a gift. It's rude to take a gift back." I didn't say it to make him smile, but the sight of it is a relief. "Although now that you mention it, I would like to be able to move in my bedroom again. Come on," I say, pulling him by the hand to the elevator. "I have an idea."

CHAPTER 22
SHARING IS CARING

IVY

It takes a few hours to clear them out of my apartment.

We carry four bouquets each, going door to door through the building. Only a handful of people answer when we knock, busy with work or a life, or just not in the mood to talk to us (and honestly, I don't blame them. We probably look like we're trying to sell them a floral subscription).

Any time there's no answer — or in the case of Johanna, who is rushing out the door, and can't talk — we leave the bouquet propped up against their door.

"Shouldn't we leave a note?" Lincoln asks, prompting me to shoot him a teasing glare.

"If Armando hasn't already emailed half the building, I'll faint from shock." His gossip goes harder than TMZ.

Lincoln hasn't said it, but I think he was a little disappointed that I wanted to give them away. His eyes had slipped away from mine when I loaded him up with the first few bouquets. It's not that I'm not grateful, but watching five hundred roses die slowly in my apartment isn't my idea of a good time.

But really, watching as people's eyes light up when we hand them over is amazing.

"Do you think everyone feels like work is a dead end at some point?" We're three-quarters of the way through the building, and my knuckles are getting sore from knocking. "Maybe my midlife crisis is hitting early."

Lincoln taps politely on Mrs. Gilpin's door, then sets the roses down on her welcome mat when she doesn't answer. "I hope for both our sakes that you live long enough that this could barely count as a quarter of your life, but in answer to your question, I suspect a lot of people feel exactly as you do."

I chew on that for a while. Ciara used to joke that words flowed through me as easy as water, but every once in a while, a point needs time to thaw out before I can digest it. If only I could take my time more, maybe I wouldn't get in so many messes. No wonder Mom is worried about me being left to my own devices.

I tuck the two bouquets I'm carrying into my other arm. The cellophane wrapping sticks briefly. All these deliveries are hard work. I slow to a stop in the hallway, resting on the wall. Lincoln mirrors me with a soft smile.

"The first time I got on a stage, the coat they stuck me in was so scratchy I wanted to tear it off for the entire performance. I only had two lines, squashed between storming onstage and slamming a door, but right in the middle, I had to pause, and in those ten seconds, I felt the world stop. Hundreds of eyes glued to me, the burning heat of the spotlight, the lingering smell of fresh paint from the set background."

It was like nothing I'd ever felt before. Tectonic plates shifting beneath my feet, the little click of something unknown slotting into place. "As soon as I was offstage, I was dying to go back on. Even watching the performance from backstage, the frantic energy of what's happening behind the curtain, got me jazzed up."

The way he watches me gives me that same buzz. It's intense. Electric. I want so much more.

"Why didn't you pursue it?"

"Just because I love it doesn't mean I'm good at it," I joke. "Plus, it was kind of drilled into me to get a proper degree. I kept up acting for a while, some improv classes here, a little local theater there, but when things got busy, I moved on." I push off the wall, and Lincoln follows a step behind. The memories of us making a very similar walk not that long ago cause a shiver to roll through me, one I'm glad he can't see from back there.

"Do you miss it?" he asks.

I step up to Dorothy's door and smile at the trans flag she's stuck up before knocking. "Being up there? No, it was terrifying. The good kind of terrifying, but I definitely prefer being in the audience. I do really miss playing dress-up, though, and uh," I flush at the memory, "being someone else for the night."

"You do it well," he says, setting the flowers down.

There's really nothing safe or appropriate about where my thoughts have gone, so I swallow back whatever filthy words my brain wants to blurt out before they have the chance to ruin the moment.

As he stands, the door opens. Dorothy is the same age as my mom, with the same short frame and frantic brown hair too.

"Oh," she says when she spots the roses. Sighs, really, in this soft, surprised way that curls around my heart and squeezes.

"It's a gift," I tell her as she picks them up, and gesture to Lincoln. "From our new landlord."

The smile she directs at him is wide and pure. "I haven't gotten flowers in years. Thank you." It's thick with gratitude, for so much more than the roses in her hands. We've barely talked in the time I've lived here, but I've heard enough in passing to understand. We all have our reasons.

He nods in a stilted movement that is unlike him, and it hits me that he's speechless. It's about time he saw just how much his generosity has meant to us.

What must seem small to him hasn't been small for us, and it's nice to be the one blowing his mind for a change.

Excellent timing, Dot. I could kiss you.

CHAPTER 23
AN ACT OF KINDNESS

LINCOLN

"You're joking. *Blackout* is not your favorite album."

Ivy stops dead in the hallway, her hip cocked to one side. The overhead light highlights the flyaway hairs that have been escaping her bun since she stormed into my apartment. There's a sheen of sweat along the back of her neck and pink dusting the roundness of her cheeks.

She's fucking gorgeous.

"It's surprisingly underrated," I admit. "And some of Britney's best work."

Her eyes widen comically. "Wow. You just said that with your whole chest," she says, but there's so much humor in her eyes I can only laugh.

I've never been a poet, but fuck, I want to try.

The hallways vary from quiet to curious, music or conversations giving small insight into the lives of the people who live here. As we disperse the many flowers throughout the building, I take note of names and faces, of small issues that need addressing — some paint chipping here, a carpet stain there — but mostly, I'm taken with Ivy.

"Am I imagining it, or are you humming 'Diamonds Are Forever'?" I ask when I finally recognize it. This explains why she and Manny get along so well.

She immediately stops, and I wish she wouldn't be so quick to dim her own spark when it's what drew me to her in the first place.

"I might be." She faces me head-on, shoulders back, chin high, her hair tied back. I long to see it flowing as freely as it did that night. Watching her let go was the most wondrous vision. "I have a lot of Bond in my running playlist. It makes me feel like I'm in a movie."

There's a sting to her, like a scorpion. Quick to attack but protective. She's smart too, a little underhanded. A sharp tongue that belies the hint of vulnerability under the surface. It's beautiful.

I drag my gaze along her body, top to toe and back again. "I can see you as an assassin."

Ivy says nothing, but her smile tucks in at the corners as she turns and lays the next bouquet on a welcome mat that says *nice package.*

I don't know how to quantify what we are to each other — strangers, lovers, friends — it feels like a little of all and nothing I've had before. All I know is that I want more of it.

More of her.

When we're down to the final two bouquets, my heart is bursting and my calves burn with the effort of a good workout. I'm shocked when I see it's the afternoon. It's incredibly easy to spend time with her.

"You don't have to do all this, you know." Ivy's voice is careful, and I have to walk ahead of her to see her expression. Her brow is furrowed. "If you think you need to shower someone with gifts to sell them on you, you don't. There's a lot of you to like without it."

It's the nicest thing she could have said to me, but I need her to know that I'm not doing any of this to buy her affections. That was the old Lincoln, the self-indulgent beast of a boy who fooled himself into thinking he was better than his peers because he didn't care about money, all the while throwing lavish parties and lapping up the attention they brought him.

Now I know money isn't worth having if I can't take care of the people I care about, and to be a man worthy of Ivy's attention would be worth more than Deacon's entire fortune.

I set the flowers on the ground before cupping her cheek. "However I can help you, Ivy, I will. No matter who we are to each other, you'll never have anything to worry about. I'll make sure of that. But you don't owe me anything in return."

"Wow," she whispers.

I can't help the way my eyes drop to her mouth. The need to kiss her is all-encompassing, but I don't want her to believe that today was only a ploy to seduce her. If I really want to make this work, and I do, I can't let lust distract me.

"Ah, shit," she says under her breath, her face crumpling. "Did I even thank you for the roses? I didn't, did I?" She shakes her head as she steps out of my reach. "God, I'm such a dick. Thank you. They are really lovely, and I'm a hard person to buy presents for. Ask anyone. I'd rather have no gift at all than one that's had no thought put into it. But these are really nice."

"I'm glad you like them," I say, warmth spreading through me. "And that we've been able to share it with everyone."

"Me too." She places her last bouquet down, and then it's just the two of us. "So, what about you? It's got to be hard to buy something for a man who has access to everything he wants."

Not everything. "I'm happy to receive anything you want to give me." Anything and everything, for the rest of my days.

"Oh really?" she asks, wonderfully incredulous. After growing up surrounded by the collective emotions of a cairn of rocks, I can't get enough of how expressive she is. Up, down, silly, superfluous. I want it all.

Shoving her hands into her pockets, Ivy continues down the hall, completely unaware of how intensely I want to grab her and press her against the faded wall-paper until she's panting my name.

"So your girlfriend comes home all excited and says, 'I got you something you'll love,' only you open it and it's not what you asked for at all. It's…" She stops walking, turns to me. "What's something you hate?"

"People clapping off rhythm."

Her laughter flows as free and wild as a waterfall. "Okay, fair. But come on, gimme something."

I shrug. "Fine, I don't like avocado."

Her jaw drops. "Well, that's that. We have to break up."

I catch her hand and pull her in, drunk off the fumes of her open joy. It's as clear now as it was the night of the masquerade. "Finish your question."

Ivy slips out of my hold and keeps walking, but her smile lingers. "So she comes home, and instead of getting you the speaker system of your dreams…"

It really shouldn't surprise me that she's already guessed what I would ask for.

"She's booked you both a cooking class called 101 Ways to Enjoy Avocado at Home. What do you do?"

We've reached the elevator, and I follow her inside when it arrives, taking the opportunity to openly admire her. "I'd say thank you, because it's the thought that counts."

Ivy scoffs. "Please. If she'd thought at all, she'd have known you would hate that."

Slipping my hands around her hips, I drag her into me. Exactly where she belongs. "Are you angry at my imaginary girlfriend right now?" I ask, close enough I can feel the moment her breath hitches.

"Technically I'm your imaginary girlfriend," she whispers, blinking up at me. "And if I ever buy you a gift you hate, I want you to tell me."

I can't imagine she could do anything I would hate, but I'm willing to dedicate as much time as needed to test the theory. The rest of my life, perhaps? "Would you tell me if the roles were reversed?"

Her bare throat is calling to me, and as I cup her jaw, I know her heart is beating as fast as mine is.

"You haven't given me anything I hated yet." Her eyes catch longingly on my mouth. I'm about to give her exactly what she wants when she swallows and pushes out of my hold, putting a careful distance between us. That's twice, now. "But if you ever even *think* of giving me anything fishing related, your family will need to use it to find your corpse."

"I suppose I'll have to throw out the tackle, then."

"Only if you want to keep yours."

It's wondrous, how quickly she's becoming my favorite person.

CHAPTER 24
THE MAN WITH THE SILVER TONGUE

IVY

It's hardly news to say I fall fast and hard when I like something. Ciara and I have that in common. We don't just taste, we *consume*, sinking our teeth in so deep it becomes a part of us.

So, when Lincoln tells me he records porn ("erotica" Emma reminds me, "and there's a strong story aspect to it. You should listen to a few."), I skip right past "a few" and listen to every single one I can find. Twice.

And while Emma avoids all British voices — "The accent always reminded me too much of Lincoln, funnily enough." Which is immediately interrupted by Charlie's indignant, "Could've just said you didn't want anyone else's voice getting you off these days, jeez" — I have no issues letting his sultry tone and sexy little breaths turn me on.

Because, hey, I'm no saint, no matter how often Mom has asked me to be. And with Lincoln's husky voice captured in surround sound and his permission to "enjoy"?

Yeah, I'm gonna slip on my party shoes and dance straight on down to hell. And it'll be Lincoln's name on my lips as I enter.

I find and replay my favorite clips. Every single one reminds me of him slipping his hand around my throat, his commands working as quickly as his fingers to make me come.

"Don't speak unless you're prepared to lose your voice screaming my name."

Damn, he sounds sexy. It's undeniably him, but also not, sounding deeper, rougher, like rolling storm clouds.

"I'll have you anyway I want you, and you're going to beg me for more."

He's good. Really, really good.

Gotta be the accent. I'm convinced Lincoln could read my phone's terms and conditions agreement, and I'd be on my knees before he reached the second paragraph.

"Look at you, so eager to be filled. To feel my big, fat cock inside you. Is that what you want? No, I need to hear it. You're not going to get anything until you say please. Come on, beg me for my cock."

Jesus. My throat's so dry, Curly McLain's about to roll on into town.

So that's why he was able to make that night as incredible as it was. Why he can play the perfect boyfriend so easily with me.

I just have to stop forgetting it's an act.

CHAPTER 25
LET YOURSELF IN
(NOW STAY)

LINCOLN

I've only ever lived with family before. Never had the occasion to have a partner stay beyond an evening or weekend. When — if — I imagined it, I always expected it to be different from living with Manny or my father — less comfortable in some ways, more in others.

But when I shuffle out of my bedroom to the sun blaring the last of its morning light and find Ivy already settled in on the couch, laptop open on her thighs, a coffee at her lips, completely at ease and looking as though she's never lived anywhere else, well…

I'm happy to discover how wrong I was.

"I see you're letting yourself into my apartment."

She looks up, and her smile rearranges my whole outlook on life. "Is there a problem?"

"Only that I didn't wake up with you beside me," I admit, my voice rough with sleep. I make a mental note to try recording more in the mornings. Perhaps Ivy can be my test audience.

As I lean in to kiss her good morning, the lingering

scent of sweat under soap and the fresh flush of her cheeks tell me she's already run and showered this morning. I'm contemplating abandoning all the day's plans to do nothing but breathe her in when she points to a second mug that is steaming on the coffee table in front of me.

"Tea," she says.

It's dark enough to have been properly steeped, with a dash of milk.

"There was only one button on your kettle machine, so if it's wrong, it's not my fault."

Christ, she's adorable. I'd love nothing more than to distract her with my mouth, but I take the offered tea and groan when, fuck, it's perfect.

She's perfect.

Ivy looks up, waiting for my reaction.

I lower myself onto the seat beside her, draping my free arm around her, pressing us together from shoulder to knee. "It's an interesting way to propose, but I accept."

She lights up at the praise. Yes, I'll take every morning like this.

"What are you working on?" I ask, nodding to her laptop. There's an ungodly number of tabs open, the foremost one a job listing.

She stares down at it, hesitation stitched into every pore. "I decided it was time to get a job."

"You decided, or it's something you're doing to keep your mum happy?"

Her worry lines deepen. "I can't do nothing forever."

Why not? I want to ask. *Move in, let me keep you. I want to.*

"If this is about money—"

"It's not," she says, strongly enough that I believe her. "I miss being productive. Even when I hated working at Helix, at least I felt like I was useful." Her eyes flutter closed as I start to massage the tension from her shoulder. "I just wish going back to work didn't feel so hopeless."

"Ivy, I truly believe you can do anything you put your heart into. There's nothing shameful about a job that pays the bills, but that doesn't mean you have to consign yourself to one reality forever." If anyone knows a thing or two about reinvention, it's me. "Apply for something new. If they don't like your résumé, they won't interview you. If you don't like the interview, don't accept the job. Think of it like the masquerade. You're simply trying it on for size."

She nods with her eyes closed, sighing so sweetly I have to abort whatever plan my cock begins crafting. I give her shoulder one final squeeze before pulling my hand away.

When it becomes clear that Ivy plans to continue her job search from the comfort of my couch, I decide there's no point putting off my own work, either.

There's a flurry of Pulse notifications when I log in. I check the statistics from my last upload, and they've doubled again. It seems "Guarding the Princess" is on track to be the top audio on the platform this month, and I have requests for sequels piling up.

A new prompt catches my eye, tagged under *boyfriend*, which I've been avoiding for a while now.

Truly, the jokes write themselves at this point.

Curious, I open it. It's an anniversary setup; lovers celebrating by trying something new, and while I would normally scroll past, the idea snags my attention.

How would I do it? Ivy and I — if our ruse wasn't fictional — would have a year's worth to catch up on.

I'd start with something grand. If something's worth saying, it's worth saying as loudly as possible. How did Ivy phrase it? *With my whole chest.* Yes, that's how I'd tell her how I felt.

For a while, I sit with my fingers hovering over the keys. It's a wonder Ivy doesn't question it, but she does lean her weight farther into me, humming a tune I'm not familiar with.

I've been purposefully avoiding my own desires when working — it's too easy to blur the professional lines in a job where I'm simulating what I sound like when I come — but if I'm honest, I've been using it as an excuse to avoid it outside of work as well.

But it's not difficult to imagine what I'd want.

Beside me, Ivy is slowly repurposing her résumé into an online application, wearing a stern look, as though she's preparing for battle. Despite her objections, she's forging ahead, unafraid to face the consequences, and I find myself wanting to do the same.

If the wife I imagine as I write so happens to have black hair and a penchant for trouble, then who will know but me?

Once I've opened the floodgates, it's simple, and

two hours later, I have a draft I don't hate and two more started. It's been years since words flowed this easily.

I stand, stretching my back with a groan, and boil the kettle for a second round. Ivy is grumbling as she fills in application after application, swearing every time she has to re-enter "the same goddamn information that's in my résumé. Seriously, it's like they don't want me to apply."

I lean against the kitchen counter and watch her, liking how well she fits. It's an intoxicating future, one I never gave myself permission to imagine before, where I could find someone who accepted what I do, who I am.

Hell, she's met my family, and she's still here. That alone makes her incredible.

I have no interest in a life built around wealth, but a life built around her? That is something I can aspire to.

CHAPTER 26
TELL ME MORE

IVY

Confession? I might be a little addicted to Lincoln's apartment. The shine, the space, the man who fills it.

It's been a month since the redundancy, and one week since I started a temporary archiving assignment that might be more depressing than my old job.

It's all too easy to end the workday and collapse onto his sofa (or into his arms). If he has a problem with me invading his space, then he's a way better actor than I thought, because every time he sees me, his smile melts my heart into a puddle. If it isn't real, I'm going to have to stop dating for the rest of my life because nothing and no one will ever compare to the way he makes me feel.

The job is fine. I hate it, but it's a job, so…

I text Mum every day, and we chat, but we aren't really talking. She'll send me updates on the baby, and I'll reassure her that I'm not living on the streets yet, but that's all. I miss her, but I don't know how to fix this without simply giving up what I want, and I can't do that yet.

I just need a little more time.

At the end of my second week in archival hell, I'm starting to rethink that opinion, but I've had twenty more job rejections today, so bring on week three, I guess.

On the plus side, I've introduced Lincoln to the miracle of *Love Island* (although seriously, how he managed to avoid it is genuinely shocking to me), and it's worth it for his commentary.

After our third episode tonight, our stomachs start rumbling in harmony, and I invade his enormous kitchen rather than head home.

Lincoln leans back against the island, watching me. "Careful, you look too good in here. I may never let you leave."

My heart signs along the dotted line before I stuff it back in its box and get to cooking.

I busy myself with sandwiches. It's not fancy, but it's this or takeout, and I'd like to be the one doing something nice for a change. "Am I allowed to ask about your work?" Said casually, like *hey, no big deal. Whatever.* Not *what you do is really fascinating, and I love hearing you moan, but I'm trying not to be weird about it because even though you've had your dick in me and we're pretend dating, I want us to be friends.*

I'm, like, 60 percent sure Lincoln sees through me.

"Ivy, you may ask me anything you like. What do you want to know?"

All of it. There's not a corner of him I want hidden

from me, no room unentered. Whatever he'll let me see before he closes the door. "Everything."

"It was a surprise to me, honestly. I never had much of an imagination as a kid, unless you count thinking I was untouchable." Carefully, he spreads the butter to each edge, his work far more precise than I was expecting. "Then I went on a date with a woman who had a very successful career doing cam work, and she suggested I could make some money using my voice."

Maybe it's a good thing that his listeners can't see him or the slow sweep of his tongue as it wets his lips. I can see it, and I know what those lips feel like. The path his tongue trailed along my jaw, over my chest, across my…

I clear my throat. "So you started for fun and then couldn't get enough? And you write them yourself?"

"Yes," he says from behind me. "Would you like a demonstration?"

What a ridiculous question. Of course I do. "Maybe later," I say, picking up a butter knife and holding it out to him. He clasps my wrist and plucks it from my grip before bringing my hand to his lips.

A peek over at his knowing grin says he heard what I really wanted to say.

I start slicing tomato. "And that's all it took?" I'm pretty proud of how steady I sound.

"She was very persuasive," he says, low enough my body is reacting. "And flexible."

I flush.

Jesus, I can see my eulogy now. *Here lies Ivy, drowned*

in her arousal. When asked, investigators said she'd carved the term "his fucking voice" into the countertop.

"Ivy?"

I duck my head, moving over to the sink to wash some lettuce. "What else do you want on this? It's not going to be fancy, but I'm making the most of the bare thing you call a pantry. If you want a real meal, you'd have to come to my place." Great, now I'm rambling. Just invite him for a date, why don't I.

A date. With my one-night stand/crush/fake boyfriend… Yeah, that tracks for me.

This is more ridiculous than the lengths the show *Smash* went to convince people Karen could hold a candle to Ivy, as if viewers didn't have ears and a brain.

"I'm quite sure I would follow you off a pier, darling. A home-cooked meal would not be a hardship."

I shake the water off while I compose myself.

Bread buttered, Lincoln walks over and fits himself at my back, even though he has to reach farther to the kettle on the counter. "Tea?" he asks.

A shiver rolls down my spine. It doubles when he brushes my hair off my neck, and I momentarily forget what I'm doing, waiting, breathless, for what's next. But there isn't anything. Just the solid wall of him at my back.

"No, thank you. I don't like tea."

His head hits my shoulder with a soft thump. "You're really testing my resolve here, Ivy. Manny will be very disappointed in you."

I whip around, brandishing the spatula at him,

while he bites back a smile. "A real boyfriend would be nicer to the woman who is about to feed him."

"Tell me more," he whispers, his hands finding their way to my hips, his fingers skimming the waistband of my jeans. Heat races through me, and my eyes flutter closed. "About what your boyfriend can do for you."

A flush races up my neck so fast it breaks the sound barrier.

I step away. This is too close to everything I want to pretend it is. "He'd stop distracting me and get us some plates so we can eat."

Lincoln prefers to eat dinner at his dining table, which is a real adult thing he has in his apartment, but I want to eat on the sofa, so we compromise by eating on his sofa.

I'm trying desperately to keep my senses, but it's so hard. Every day I learn something interesting or sweet or sexy about him and want more. Every time I come here, I'm testing if his fill of me has a limit, waiting and knowing I'll find it one way or another. I always do.

It's all too easy to fit myself into the space beside him, slip into the warmth of his attention, soak in it. Lincoln brushes his pinky finger over mine, hooking them together without a word, and there's a rapture of applause in my chest.

"Ivy," he says, taking my hand in his. "Are you free for dinner next weekend?"

I nod. Is this…? Could he feel something too? Could we be more?

Lincoln's smile tugs on my heart. "Wonderful. I'm

planning a dinner for Reed. Nothing special, just immediate family. I want you with me."

Oh. Of course.

There's not much more my heart can take. I've led it down so many dead ends that I'm not sure I can read the road signs anymore. Maybe I'll never know what it's like to be loved. Maybe one day I'll have given my heart to so many people, there won't be anything left.

Maybe it's already too late.

CHAPTER 27
MY ALTER EGO
LINCOLN

It's going to sound like bullshit, but I mean it when I say it's an honor to play a part in people's pleasure.

For it to be good, you have to get to the heart of what someone needs, and it has to be honest.

It has to be the sort of honesty that most people can't handle. No one realizes how deeply vulnerable they're being when they share their desires. But it speaks to the very heart of us and what we crave. Sometimes these are things we can't name or speak aloud. Safety, power, tenderness.

And I have the power to take those moments and bring them to life.

But not everyone is a fan, and since I revealed my work to her, it's Ivy's opinion I'm most interested in. She's asked a few careful questions, but nothing more. Although, so far, she doesn't seem opposed to the idea.

For a woman so eager to say what she's thinking, it's disorienting when she holds back. But it's all the more meaningful when she finally opens up.

I've spent a long time holding back, so I understand the impulse. But I'm not nearly as brave as Ivy when it comes to letting people in. I'm starting to wonder if it's time.

She pauses the episode we're watching while I collect our empty plates. It's quick work to wash the dishes, and the memory of the hours I worked in a kitchen doing only this makes me smile. After Bruges, Mum cut off my allowance (despite Deacon laughing it off by saying "boys will be boys"), and I had no choice.

If I wanted to survive the last year of Uni, I had to find a room to rent, and more importantly, a job.

Manny and I were not happy roommates at first. He called me a fucking Muppet and found me the shittiest job he could — as the kitchen porter where he worked — and he never let me get away with thinking anything was owed to me. He still says he didn't do shit except dislike me back then, but who could blame him? What had I really earned at that point, except a reputation?

"Lincoln?"

Hanging the plates on the rack, I dry my hands off and turn around to face Ivy. She's got her arms crossed over the back of the couch, her hair twisted into two buns, and curiosity in her eyes.

"Yes?"

"I have a confession." She sets her chin on top of her hands, and I wait. "I listened to a few of your audios. They're really good."

From the way she's avoiding looking at me directly, I suspect *a few* is putting it mildly. I'd wondered when the curiosity would consume her. Now we're getting somewhere.

Throwing the dish towel onto the counter, I cross over to the couch, placing my hands on either side of her elbows to give her my full attention. "Research is important."

Ivy's lips part, and I lean in just enough to hear the soft hitch in her breath.

"I told you — you can ask me anything."

"Um, okay," she says, twisting back around, and good god, I can't decide what's more endearing: how nervous she's suddenly become or the gorgeous pink flush that's staining her cheeks. I'm desperate to kiss her again.

"Your setup is pretty professional. Did the app set you up with all that stuff? I imagine it's not a course they teach at Eton."

Christ, it's hard having any secrets when Ivy is able to magic up the details of my life like her own. It's rather refreshing, if I'm honest. So much of my life has revolved around what isn't said.

I retake my seat beside her, preferring to have this conversation face to face so I can read her reactions. "My earlier attempts were far less impressive, I promise you. But I did my research and spoke about what worked and what didn't with other artists until I had enough practice under my belt to make my own decisions."

"Where do you get your ideas from?"

"Some are my own, others are prompts provided by the platform or on a shared forum."

She sags, demure in a way I've rarely seen her. "Sorry. I guess I was thinking… I don't know. Something sexier, like at the ball." She drops her gaze to her lap, where she's rolling the frayed ends of her distressed jeans between her fingers.

Reaching out, I brush the hair away from her face. I'm rewarded as she blinks back up at me. God, I could let hours disappear without anything but this. Brown eyes, warm like hot chocolate with glimmers of honey throughout.

"I don't know that I can take full credit for that. I was inspired by a beauty with a wicked mind."

Her cheeks darken, although there isn't any other change in her expression. Ivy is a vault. She's expressive in her excitement, and yet everything fragile is kept protected.

"I didn't think I'd like it," she admits. "Most guys aren't great with talking in bed, and the few that tried put me off it until now." She toys with a spare hair tie on her wrist. Two more are already in use where her hair is twisted back. It's so rare to see her let her hair down. "The first time I had sex with a guy, he was running a commentary the whole time. I'm pretty sure he thought he was great at pillow talk, but it was distracting and not even a little bit sexy."

She deserves so much more. The urge to blast away any dissatisfying remnant of her past experience roars in my gut. I'm going to rewrite every fantasy she's ever had until the only way she can come is by hearing my name.

"And that isn't even the worst story I have," she

says, with the tired acceptance of any woman I've ever met. Men should have to pass a test before they're allowed to get their pricks out. But if they did, I could be out of a job. "There was this one guy, an app date. You know how it is. We start kissing on his couch, and then he unzipped, pulled out his dick, and goes, 'Now give it a little kiss.'" Ivy's whole body contorts, as if shaking off the memory. "At first I just stared. All I could think was "you're ruining this blowjob for me."

A laugh rips itself free from my chest, and she ducks her head with a smile. What a fucking treasure she is. I lean closer, missing the bright spark of her eyes. "Please tell me you left him hanging."

"I should have. Nothing ruins a good blowjob more than a man's personality."

And this is where I should cut this line of conversation off, because sitting beside her and not being able to have her is quickly driving me to distraction.

I can't help it. I lift my hand to touch that perfect mouth. Pillowy soft and so eager to please. Whoever the fuck this guy is, he didn't deserve the gift of it.

I stroke the corner of her lips with my thumb. "None of them have known how to handle you, have they?" I bet none of them took the time to appreciate her, too busy taking what they wanted and then fucking off. "Bastards, all of them. Has anyone ever taken the time to truly get to know you?"

"There's not much to know."

Well, that's a fucking joke.

I pull her chin toward me. "I told you, Ivy; we don't lie to each other."

We sit like that for a moment, simply looking at each other. I'm quietly cataloging all the wrongs I'm going to right for her, while she looks like she's trying to decode my programming.

"You're nothing like I expected," she says with something I want badly to believe is awe in her voice. *Please. If there is any chance of redeeming my past mistakes, let it be by meaning something to her.* Ivy finally looks away, smoothing a hand on her knee. "How is it you've never been in love? I mean, I noticed your audios are always two strangers, or a coworker, or a boss. You never play a boyfriend or a husband. Why is that?"

I take a breath. It's a fair question; one I've been asked by Pulse before. When certain tags get popular, they like to encourage everyone to jump in. At the time, I skirted the truth, but I want to give Ivy more than that. "The relationships I've had have been short-lived. When I try to write those scenes, I either feel like a fraud or I put too much of my own heart into them. The result is…" I hesitate.

"Too much of the truth or too much like a lie," she says.

Exactly. Dating was easier when I only cared about impressing a woman long enough to get between her sheets. It's infinitely more complicated now. If it's not my bank account they're chasing, my work disgusts them.

Rarely is it me they see.

Not like Ivy can.

She twists to fully face me, curling her feet under

her, her knees pressing into my thigh. I lay a hand on the closest one, holding her there.

"I know I've only pretended to be your girlfriend, but take it from me; you know what you're doing."

The list of reasons that this can't work is becoming increasingly small. And yet, I can't help but notice how careful she is around me. Close, but never crossing the line. In my mind, the only fictional part of this relationship is our history. But something is holding Ivy back, and I'm determined to find out what it is.

"Is that right?"

She nods, eyes wide, a hint of her steeliness peeking out from under soft cheeks, hinting at the intensity I find compelling. What she's feeling penetrates deeply and rises to the surface in a flash, and I enjoy being swept up in her wave.

"So how does it work? Do you..." she trails off, expecting me to finish the sentence. But it's far more enjoyable to catalog the sweep of her lashes against her cheek as the seconds tick by. "You know," she finishes, waving a hand at my cock in a move that works like a charm to stir it to life.

It takes some serious willpower to keep it at bay.

"Are you sure you want to know? I've heard peeking behind the curtain can kill the magic for some." I can feel the smile as it takes over my face.

Ivy's gaze snaps to mine as her back straightens, her eyes darkening as though I just insulted her. "Well, I'm not some people," she says, and no, she definitely isn't.

I catch her arm where it's been resting on her thigh and stroke the inside of her wrist. It lets me feel the exact moment her pulse spikes. "Do I get turned on? Touch myself while I record? Be clear on what you're asking me."

She blinks, swallows. "Both," she breathes. "Either."

Her heart rabbits under my fingertips. "There have been times it's turned me on, but I won't act on it until after I'm recording. Though now I'm curious," I say, closing the gap between us to drag my lips along her jaw. "What effect did it have on you? Did you listen to them in bed? Were your hands free to wander? Or were you getting off on my voice somewhere else? In public, perhaps? With your headphones on while no one around you knew how wet you were getting?"

Her lips part, her chest rising quicker now. Ivy pulls her wrist free to grip my shirt in her fist. Not pushing me away. Merely holding me in place as we share breath.

"How many orgasms do you think you've given listeners?"

With my free hand, I skim the tips of my fingers down her stomach, lingering at her waistband. Hovering in a promise. Waiting for her to ask. To beg. "You've done the research. Tell me how many you've had, and I'll extrapolate from there."

Her shoulders shake as her skin washes over with goose bumps. Nothing gets me harder than knowing how quickly I can bring her to surrender.

One word from her, and I'll have her on her knees, giving her exactly what I know she's craving.

"Fuck," she gasps, but it comes out as a laugh, cutting through the tension as she lets go of my shirt and reclaims the space I closed, leaning back and catching her breath. I pull my hand back to safer ground. "No wonder you're so popular on there," she says, "I love the way words sound coming from your mouth."

I know she does. It's stitched into every shiver that rumbles through her when I whisper in her ear. The way her body reacts as I lean in. How hungrily she's staring at my cock right now, half hard and wanting along my thigh. "What a coincidence," I reply, knowing she's holding herself back from taking what she wants, but also that I'll wait forever for her. "Because I happen to adore the way you sound coming from my mouth."

The heat that floods her skin is almost as good to watch as it would be to taste.

CHAPTER 28
FATHER DEAREST

LINCOLN

I knew moving would be hard, but it's the little things that keep tripping me up.

I miss the piece of shit apartment Manny and I had. The one that was four blocks from the tube. The fish & chip shop on the corner with proper curry sauce and battered cod roe fatter than my fist.

I miss sitting on Dad's couch, arguing over the football, hearing his Wednesday rants about the price of Hobnobs going up and how all of life's problems could be fixed with an English breakfast or a pint.

I miss being too far away for anyone to have their nose in my business.

It's only been a month since I left, and while a day hasn't gone by that I don't talk to him, it's not the same. Instead of getting to share a pint or a pot of tea while I contort myself in his awful dining chairs, watching him carve new smile lines with each new story from the pub, I'm on the other side of the world, staring at him through a phone.

"I think dinner is a good idea," he says, surer than I am. "I'm proud of you for trying."

Reed doesn't deserve it after the shit he pulled the other day, but I made Dad a promise before I left, and I won't let Reed's bullheadedness deter me.

"Yeah, well. If he could at least show he gives a damn, it would be nice."

"You know how he is." It's a purely Dad answer, straight from the mouth of a man who worked the same job for thirty-eight years of his life. Nothing fancy, but it was "good, steady work." He met Mum when she was in the UK studying at Oxford. Dad said she had no business at a pub in Hackney, but there she was, a beauty beyond compare.

They did well to last as long as they did. Twenty years is a lot, especially when Deacon didn't approve of dad's "simpler leanings." He hated that we lived in the UK for most of the year, only visiting during school hols. That's what ate at them the most, I think. Who they were being asked to be wasn't who they actually were, and it tore them apart.

"You're both too bloody stubborn for your own good," he adds. "Used to be, I couldn't tear you apart. Now it's like pulling teeth." He sighs, and I know he feels partly responsible.

I don't blame Darcy and Reed for choosing Mum, at least not the way Reed blames me for staying with Dad. But I knew she'd be okay without me, and I didn't want Dad to be alone.

Reed and I never quite fit the same after that. A bone knocked out of alignment, rubbing enough to ache and itch. Of course, we never talked about it head-on. Always around it. Always in riddles and rhymes.

"If it all goes tits up, expect a phone call," I joke.

"Ah, yes, well," he says. Dad stammering is a sure sign he's not telling me something. "Maybe text me first. I'm seeing someone, and it'll be awkward if I have to choose between you and them."

"What?" This is news to me. "When did you start seeing someone? And more importantly, why didn't you tell me about it?"

Christ, this must be how everyone else felt about Ivy.

"It's early. I don't want to jinx it."

"Since when did you become superstitious?"

"When it counts, I'll take all the help I can get." And wow. I haven't heard Dad talk about anyone like this before. "Now explain this relationship you accidentally fell into."

Ah, yes. Telling Dad the truth about Ivy wasn't as difficult as I expected, even though he's on strict instruction to keep it to himself.

"Oh, so you don't want to tell me about your girl-friend, but I'm supposed to tell you all about mine?"

"It's that serious, huh?"

I heave a sigh, running a hand through my hair. "It wasn't supposed to be, but…"

The image of him begins to tilt, and he catches his phone before bringing it close to his face. The angle makes him look older than I remember, eyebrows gone almost transparently silver now, a rich network of lines framing his eyes. It's a harsh reminder that time is precious.

He clears his throat. "I've made a lot of mistakes, as you know, and I never thought of myself as someone who should give love advice, but I'll tell you what I'm going to do. I'm going to make sure she wakes up every day knowing how incredible she is, how lucky I am, and do everything I can to make her as happy as she makes me." He really is head-over-heels for this woman. "And flowers don't hurt, either."

Man after my own heart. "I'm two steps ahead of you, there."

"Good. I'm very much hoping to meet this Ivy when I visit," he says, but when I ask him for the details, he starts stammering again. "I don't have the exact dates yet." Which is odd because he's usually so particular about it. It's where Reed gets it from. "But I'll see you when you get back from the reunion."

"Just tell me your flight number, and I'll pick you up at the airport."

His face disappears from the frame. "No need. It's, ah, all sorted. Anyway, have to run, but, ah, we'll talk soon. Love you."

My phone screen taunts me after he hangs up. Just what I needed.

More secrets.

CHAPTER 29
TIME FOR A CHANGE

IVY

I stare up at the ceiling, counting the paint chips, while fireflies swarm worryingly in my belly.

Five weeks since the redundancy (yes, I'm counting). Three whole weeks since I've started working again, fulfilling the role of one point five people for a company that will cut me as soon as they need to maximize their portfolio value.

See, I'm enthusiastic! I don't know what Mom's talking about.

My weekends have become sacred again, a liminal space where I shed the constraints of Office Ivy and take a look at the chaotic jumble that lies beneath. I thought I'd know myself better by now.

Maybe the inescapable horror of answering Slack calls until the day I die has eroded all the interesting parts away.

I kick the sheets off. *No.* I refuse to let this beat me.

There's only one thing left to do.

Emma would tell me to think it through, make a list

of pros and cons, or at least sleep on it first. But I'm sick of feeling lost, of continuing to go through the motions without knowing who I am.

I have an opportunity here. I either take it or I don't. Both are infinitely scary. But there's only one that I really want.

I want to choose myself.

Change has been nipping at my heels, begging for my attention for years now. And I've kept it away through a strict diet of guilt and fear. Of the unknown. Of failing. But change didn't wait for me to be prepared. And it knocked me on my ass, sick of being pushed aside.

So, okay. I'm not ignoring it anymore. Change is here, and I'm ready to admit I need it. This is *my time*. My shot. My chance to shed the past, chalk the ground, step into the new season of my life.

RIP to the old, safe, responsible me.

Now I want to experience. To see for myself what I've only ever read about. There's a yellow (blond?) brick road ahead of me, and I want to follow.

If I only get this one chance, I want to be the kind of person who says yes.

Who can rest at the end of it all, knowing I took that step. Ventured. Explored.

I wish Mom could understand.

She gave up time with us so she could put us through school, commiserate with other moms about the lives they put on pause, the vacations they dreamed of, the dreams they let go of.

All the "somedays" and "nevers."

Well, now is my someday, and I don't want to let it go by.

I'm done letting her worries become my worries. I've spent years doing the sensible thing, and all I'm asking for is this one tiny thing.

I pull the claw clip from my hair, touch the paper-thin ends that fall around my face.

This isn't just for the Ivy staring back at me.

It's for the little girl who picked up a brush and practiced interviews before bed.

Who taught herself dance moves and performed at Christmas like it was a world tour.

Who sat in the dark and wondered if her own life would ever be as magical as the musicals she loved.

I couldn't do much for the little girl I used to be, but I can do this.

As I knew she would, Emma answers before the second ring.

"I'm about to do something wild. Would you come with me?"

"Ivy, you effervescent sunflower. That you could ever think the answer would be a no is an insult."

I laugh. "I'll see you soon."

———

It will go down as the perfect day.

The sunshine, the feeling of being on the cusp of a new era. The riptide of a drastic decision made knowing there's no turning back.

Regret doesn't have a place here. Not anymore.

I've been coming to Jen's salon for years now. It's bold and energizing, with earthy browns and oranges filling the small space. Four chairs face huge wood-framed floor mirrors. There's music playing throughout, which occasionally becomes karaoke when the right song comes on.

Jen greets us with hugs and deposits me in the closest chair, examining the dead ends I've been ignoring. "What are you after today? The usual wash and trim?"

I stare myself down in the mirror, the corner of my lip caught under my teeth, my hair falling straight and strong over my shoulders. A rising tide of adrenaline washes over me.

I want to do this. I need to.

I take a deep breath. "How would you feel about cutting it all off?" I ask.

Her reaction is gleeful, her hands stilling in my hair for only a beat before she's petting, testing, appraising. "Yes," she says, dragging out the word in pure joy. "Are you sure?"

I nod. As sure as Jonathon Groff spitting on the front row. "Positive. And no more straightening." It's time.

She smiles ear to ear as she meets my gaze in the mirror. "Are we embracing the wave, finally?" Her hips wiggle behind me.

If I wasn't already bursting with excitement, I would be now.

It's what I've wanted for years. I've imagined saying yes before, even been tempted once or twice, but I've always backed out at the last minute, hearing my mother's voice in my ear.

But I'm ready, and I'm tired of denying myself.

"Do it. I want to be more Me."

Jen places her hands on my shoulders, her tone warm and reassuring. "Babe, you're about to be the best version of you."

I look over at Emma, whose smile is wide and encouraging. A wave of giddiness hits me, and I know, without a doubt, this is the start of something good.

"What are we waiting for, then?"

It's been so long since I've lingered in the now.

Since I had the luxury to exist longer than the scant hours between Friday afternoon and Monday morning or moved through the world with intention, not running through the weekend because I know the second I look, time will be up, because it's Sunday night and screw doing the dishes because there are only a few more hours before work, and I don't want to waste them doing chores.

There's responsibility in not taking life for granted. The urge to hold these moments in my bare hands and create. Birth something new. Do something exciting.

It's the sort of restlessness I haven't indulged since I was a kid, where whole days could be set aside for a single endeavor. Today's a pool day, tomorrow, we'll race our bikes — a world of minutes ahead of us.

How many have I spent since, staring at a clock? White-knuckling a Bluetooth mouse when the reply came back with my name misspelled? Or pulling Emma away from her desk at lunch because I can't go another second without a real, meaningful conversation. Anything to remember there's more to me, more to life, than a KPI.

"How did your staycation go?" I ask her now, while Jen is busy washing my hair.

Charlie and I agree on many things. Namely that Emma is the fucking best, but also that good vacations don't need a death trap in the sky to get you there (recent experiences excluded).

"It was…" Her pause is so loud I don't have to see her to know she's blushing. "Perfect. The cabin was beautiful. Charlie drove me out to this lookout, and the view… Ivy, I was speechless. Zeus adored having so much space to run around. It was exactly what we needed."

When I'm done, Jen wraps my hair up in the towel and walks me back to the chair.

My damp hair hangs by my face, and I take a slow breath as the *snip-snip-snip* of her scissors cuts the bulk of it away, the cold brush of metal against my jaw sending goose bumps down my neck. I let my eyes fall closed while she works.

"How are you feeling about work?" Emma asks from the seat beside me.

I sigh. "The same. New company, same shit. I just… I know that answering phones and making appointments aren't what I want to be doing, but I still don't know what that is."

"You'll find it. I believe in you," she says, and I know it's the truth.

"Sorry," I say, "I don't want to keep harping on my

stuff all the time."

"Don't be silly. That's what I'm here for. You listened to me when everything with Charlie was going on. And Logan, for that matter."

But it's easier when it's not me. "Just because it makes sense doesn't mean it's easy to accept," I say. "Penelope says I should take stock of everything in my life that I'm grateful for. Focus on that to counterbalance what work can't provide."

As the wet hair falls away, I remember strolling the boulevard with Astrid, fresh spring air in my lungs, waking up a little more with each breath.

"Therapists usually know what they're talking about," Emma says, her tone soft and warm. When we first met, stuck in the same BS workshop for the day, I was fascinated by her — a little distant, a little spiky, downright gorgeous — but in minutes, I realized how much more there was to her. A tongue as sharp as her mind, and underneath it all, a big, squishy heart. "Let me grab my phone," and I hear her rummaging around in her bag. "Okay, let's make a list."

"Don't ever change," I laugh, but I take a deep breath and don't overthink it. "Top of the list is you, obviously, and Fil. Mom and Ciara, definitely." Arguments come and go, but we've stuck together this long. We'll get through this too. "I'm grateful for my body," I add. "This flesh sack puts up with a lot." Including that awful year of college where I subsisted on diet soda and no sleep. "But it's also strong as fuck—"

"And beautiful," Emma adds.

"That goes without saying." I'm determined to love

this body in every way I can, and while I can't complete a pull-up to save my life, my ass is flat-out dangerous, and I love it.

"I'm going to go ahead and add *brave, creative,* and *a wonderful friend,* and don't even think of arguing, because they are facts, not opinions."

Thankfully my eyes are already closed, because it's easier to hold back the tears. Penelope was right. This is exactly what I needed. I might have to time my showers to keep my bills down and track grocery sales to make every cent count, but I am rich with the parts of life that outweigh money.

"Do you think I should learn to crochet?" Maybe learning something new will help. Plus, Bruno in 37F is expecting his first grandchild soon, and baby booties can't be that hard, right?

"I think you can do anything you put your mind to," Emma says, proving she's the human equivalent of a sugar cookie.

My foot taps in rhythm with Jen's cuts. *Snip, snip, snip.*

Nonna used to warn me against impatience. She hated teaching me to make pasta from scratch, because I'd hover over the pot, continuously checking for al dente too soon. "Trust the wait," she'd say.

I still can't. I want to find what I'm searching for, and I want to do it as soon as possible. Why put off happiness? Take it now, because we never know how long we have to enjoy it.

Except rushing the pasta before it was fully cooked

always made it take twice as long, and it never once tasted as good as hers.

I don't plan to keep my eyes closed, but by the time Jen is tapping my shoulder and telling me she's finished, it's as though no time has passed.

My heart stutters when I finally open my eyes, and I blink back hot tears.

"There you are," Jen says, fluffing the ends of my now chin-length waves.

Yes. There I am.

For a second, all I can do is blink at my own reflection. It's been so long since I've seen myself like this — short wild hair, full of volume and life.

Huh. I'd forgotten I looked like this.

Warmth floods my veins. It's like coming home.

My smile arrives on a fresh wave of happiness. I'm shocked I haven't floated away.

This is me. Suddenly the shaky ground I've been teetering on solidifies under me, a brick laid in place, secure. Ready for more.

I can almost see the steel set in my own eyes. This is act one. Now I just have to figure out the rest.

"Oh, Ivy. You're radiant. More so than usual. I can't believe I've never seen you without straight hair before."

Emma gives the kind of compliments that warm like the summer sun, forever soaking themselves into my skin and etching their presence on my heart like a love note on a tree.

Jen's cut is so precise I can't even hide my blush under the sweep of my hair anymore.

I can't even let myself imagine what Lincoln's reaction will be, otherwise I will melt into a puddle so large they could use me to power wash the floor.

"I love it," I manage through a giggle. I can't help it. The happiness is bubbling up in me like a kid blowing into a milkshake. "It's perfect."

"Your boyfriend's going to love it," Jen jokes as I pay, and though I'm smiling, I shake my head.

"No," I say. "This is all for me."

CHAPTER 30
WHO ORDERED THE DISASTER?

IVY

Lincoln is waiting outside my apartment when Emma and I return. He looks incredible (When doesn't he?) in a teal dress shirt that I know without touching will be expensively smooth and my favorite dark jeans, his sleeves rolled up to his elbows and the collar undone enough that his gold chain and a peek of tattoo are visible as we get closer.

I remember how spectacularly rumpled he looked the morning after the masquerade, his shirt half buttoned, jacket slung over his arm. His bedhead alone almost destroyed me enough to drag him back to bed.

As soon as he turns, his lips part. I barely get to ask, "Do you like—" before he has stalked forward and cupped my face in both hands and is kissing me breathless in the hallway.

Fireflies awaken under my skin, humming and buzzing around my heart, lighting up my ribcage. This is not the gentle kiss we shared in front of his family or the deep and deliberate kiss he gave me our first night together.

No, it's so much more. It's hunger and fire and a sweeping wave of ownership that knocks me off my feet until all I can do is hold on and surrender.

"Oh," I breathe as he softly nips on my lower lip. I'm definitely going to need a minute to remember what words are.

Distantly, I hear Emma say, "Lincoln Montgomery Reeves, you better not kiss everyone like that." But Lincoln's palms are still warm on my cheeks, his mouth mere inches from my own.

He stares down, eyes blazing. Oh, wow.

"I take it you like the new look," I finally breath out, my heart pounding in my chest.

"You're ravishing, darling. More so than usual."

I have to close my eyes under the praise, awareness slowly creeping back in. I release his arms, which I've been clinging to, and step back to collect myself, since he doesn't seem all too interested in parting from me. But Emma knows we aren't really dating, so there's no chance to really indulge whatever has come over him.

At least he likes the hair.

"Emma, I hope you've been well."

"I am. Almost as well as you, from the look of it."

I can hear the smile in her voice, but I haven't been able to take my eyes off Lincoln. As if sensing my gaze, he turns back to me.

"Infatuation suits me."

Emma chuckles. "Well, on that note, I'll leave you two to it." She pulls me in for a hug. "You better text me everything," she whispers in my ear. "Have fun at dinner."

———

The restaurant is nice (not that I expected any less), although not quite Lincoln's style. It's all hard, sharp lines and cool, pale tones. There's a low hum of noise, as though sound itself is being carefully traded between guests, no one showing their hand.

Even the exposed kitchen works in almost silence. It's off-putting, but he knows his brother better than I do, so I don't mention it.

Reed and a woman I'm assuming is Felicity, his girlfriend, are already seated when we arrive, and when I know we're in view of them, I pull Lincoln to a stop.

It's indulgent and selfish, but my lips have been burning with the need to touch his since we left, and I'm not going to get many chances to do this, so why not stretch up and kiss him?

Just to touch. To taste. To remember.

He strokes along my jaw, and my heart jumps. "What was that for?"

Lightning skitters along my spine. The way he looks at me is exactly what I've always wished for.

"Just playing my part," I say with a smile, expecting him to joke back, but he doesn't. Instead, he frowns, and I have the all-too-terrible feeling I just said the wrong thing.

"You do know you're in the way, don't you?" Darcy

jokes as she walks by, and I watch as a part of Lincoln's mask slips back into place.

Right. It's not real.

It's not real.

———

Felicity is lovely, with intelligent eyes and a striking gap between her front teeth. Her thick brown hair curls down over a draped blouse in cream that makes her skin glow, and there's the lightest pink dusted over her cheeks. Her smile is soft as I introduce myself. I would love to know how Reed managed to charm her.

Lincoln and I take the seats across from her and Reed, and Darcy plants herself between her brothers, which is clearly on purpose. There's an empty seat beside me, and I wonder where Astrid is. It doesn't seem like her to be late.

"Where's Mum?" Lincoln asks.

Reed unravels his napkin and places it over his lap. "On a last-minute trip to Paris. Something important with an old friend, she said. I've got no more details than that, but you can always check with Darcy if you don't believe me."

Lincoln frowns, ignoring Reed's baited accusation, while I bite my tongue to stop myself from saying anything.

"More important than this?"

The tightening of Reed's jaw is the only indication that he's not as unbothered as he's trying to appear. "Yes, well."

The silence extends, thick and uncomfortable, until the waiter arrives to take our drink order.

I use the distraction to ask Lincoln quietly, "What do you think happened?"

"I'm not sure. It's not like Mum to miss a family dinner, unless she thought being absent would help."

I'm not convinced. To do that, we might actually need a séance. Maybe if we channel the ghosts of people who actually *communicate*, they can finally sort themselves out. There's only so much I can do.

As I'm ordering a glass of chardonnay, the empty chair beside me is filled. Lincoln tenses, and from the overbearing cloud of cologne, I know exactly who has arrived.

"Sorry I'm late, fam." Kyle grins. "Hope I didn't miss anything."

Oh yay, the court asshole approacheth.

I wonder what chemicals I'd need to mix into this wine for it to instantly kill me. If only I hadn't failed chemistry. Maybe I can spend the rest of the meal in Lincoln's lap.

On second thought, if I do that, I'll never leave.

Under the table, Lincoln hooks his foot under my chair and pulls me closer, draping his arm protectively over my shoulders. Close enough.

———

Dinner is more stilted than a *Love is Blind* reunion. I'll never know if there's a different version out there, one where King Kyle isn't getting high off his own self-importance, because biting back every sarcastic response is taking 70 percent of my concentration. The other thirty is busy getting distracted by the soft glide of Lincoln's fingers along my bare shoulder while Felicity tells me about her massage therapy day spa.

"It's not for profit, which was the only way I wanted to do it, and I've partnered with both the training school and the women's shelter to ensure that all of our positions are filled by women who are unfairly looked over for work. Sometimes it's mothers who haven't been in the workforce for a long time, or it's women escaping abusive situations who need a safe and supportive environment. Everything we do is about giving back to the community," she tells me. It's as impressive as it is humbling.

"She's incredible," Reed says, with eyes only for her. I can't disagree.

It's interesting to hear the cross section of accents as we eat. Reed's and Darcy's are subtler, probably on account of them living full time in the states for so long. But next to Kyle and the rest of the Bradbury clan? It's obvious where the differences lie.

Lincoln's voice slips and squeezes between the harsh vowels around me, curling around my shoulders like my favorite sweater.

"So, Ivy." Kyle's arm brushes mine as he faces me, and I plaster on a smile. "What makes you so impressive that you'd inspire the man who never settles down to move across an ocean for you?"

I'm about to tell him to go drown himself in that

ocean when Lincoln's deep, commanding voice does it for me.

"Kyle, if a woman of her caliber had ever deemed you worthy to spend time with, you wouldn't have to ask that question."

"I think it's wonderfully romantic," Felicity adds. She's been giving us heart eyes since we recounted the story of our long-distance courtship (Lincoln literally calls it courting, and I'm blushing too hard to say anything).

Lincoln's eyes are captivating. I can't look away. "I knew the moment I saw her, I needed her in my life."

Felicity sighs.

"You sap," Darcy teases, but she's smiling at us.

"Not sure I believe it," comes from my left, and I turn in time to see Kyle ripping a bread roll apart and throwing a piece into his mouth, smiling as he chews. "A decade of bedding down the hottest chicks I've ever seen, not to mention all those preppy Oxford girls, and not one of them was good enough to stick around for?"

I'm about to stick something in this asshole if he doesn't shut up.

Listening to him talk is worse than getting my period on an overnight Greyhound when I specifically left my tampons behind because packing them "just in case" was overkill.

Cue the instant regret.

"None of them even come close to her," Lincoln says, plucking my deepest desire from my heart as easily as a petal from a rose.

Kyle's staring at Lincoln the same calculating way my old calico Mimi looked at visitors. She'd wait until they'd gotten comfortable, then pounce. And if you didn't pet her just right, she'd scream in your face and dig her nails in before flouncing off. I sit up tall, trying to put as much of a barrier between them as possible, and pull my glass closer.

A little water always worked on Mimi.

Finished with his meal, Kyle throws his napkin down and sprawls back in his chair. He's being the kind of friendly they only are when they're up to something.

What's the word? Smarm. Ugh. He's oozing it. I'm half expecting it to follow him across the floor like a snail trail, sticky and foul. "Look at us, together again. Feels good, doesn't it?"

No one around the table agrees.

It doesn't stop Kyle for a second. "I've been saying it for years. Our parents had the wrong idea, splitting off and doing their own thing. With our powers combined, we could really do something special. Like take the tech company my buddy just started. Ground up, right? And the banks, they're holding out on him, saying he's too green to know what he's doing, and he can't get finance, but—"

"I'd really rather we didn't discuss business tonight," Reed interjects.

"Oh, man. But it's not really business, is it? That's what I'm saying. You three got lucky. Deacon liked you better than the rest of us. With only a small amount of capital, you'd be the first to recognize what a gold mine we have here. And who better to support than family?"

"What kind of tech?" I ask, because I've got an

internal bet going with myself that it's the Silicon Valley equivalent of an MLM.

"Obviously I can't give away anything confidential," he says, and I want to roll my eyes so badly I'm going to strain them. "But it's the next big thing in automatous logistics."

"Oh, I saw something like that on *iCarly*," I lie, purely to annoy the ever-living fuck out of him.

Little of his expression changes; his wide, uncanny smile holds on for dear life as his jaw strains. Oh yeah, he hated that. "Actually," he says in that smarmy way that makes my skin crawl, "it's far more complicated that a kids' show, not that I'd expect you to understand."

He looks proud of himself, as though he's beaten me, and I want to laugh in his face. Oh, please underestimate me. It'll be so much fun.

"Ah," I interrupt, nodding as though I've discovered a key clue. "You were more of a Zack and Cody fan. I get it."

Beside me, Lincoln lets out a soft snort. It's no more than a quick exhale, but it's dripping in humor. Darcy isn't containing a smile, but she is avoiding eye contact, probably so she won't laugh out loud.

Even Reed almost looks amused. Kyle, however, looks like he's regretting my very existence.

"And how do you know it's a good investment?" Reed asks. His expression is calm, but the kind of calm I assume you see before a tiger eats your face off.

"See, that's what's so perfect. I've got an eye for these things. No offense." Kyle may as well wave a red flag at this point, on top of the awful silk button-down he's wearing tonight. "I know you're the big CEO guy here, but I'm telling you, I've got my finger on the pulse, and I know these guys. Honestly, if you want to be really smart, you'd hire me. Bring me onboard. I'll be the best asset you have."

Lincoln tenses every time Kyle's arm brushes mine. It's wildly empowering, having a man like Lincoln — strong, ferocious, Lincoln — ready to protect me. Kyle's inane babble fades into the background while I watch Lincoln's knuckles flex and ripple.

He has great hands.

"I can assure you," Reed says, adjusting his wineglass on the table. His tone borders on bored, but I can see the way his left hand is tightly clenched around his fork. "If I was interested in advice on financial decisions, and I'm not, you'd be the last person I'd think of."

Around us, the other guests continue to eat. Waiters glide seamlessly between tables with polite precision. In the corner, I see a woman cover a laugh with her hand, but I hear nothing above my own thundering pulse.

In the corner of my eye, Kyle nods over a huffed laugh. I don't dare move. Lincoln's hand on my shoulder tightens.

"You say that now," Kyle says, still with a forced cheer. I won't give him credit for much, but it's clear he's shrewd enough to recognize that no one here wants anything to do with him. And still, he keeps trying. "But I'll convince you."

Dinner is cleared from the table, and the distraction allows us all to take a collective breath.

Lincoln slides his hand to the junction of my neck and squeezes, and my breath catches in my throat. "I need to excuse myself for a moment. Will you be all right?" Goose bumps flood my body, tingling along my calves and shoulders and making my nipples hard. I fight the urge to cross my arms over my chest.

"Yes."

He leans in and kisses my cheek before heading toward the bathrooms. I'm still blushing when Kyle runs his fingers down my arm. I flinch away from him, knocking Lincoln's phone to the floor under my chair. Before I can move, Kyle leans down — *too close, too close, too close* — and holds it out to me.

His eyes drop to my blue corset top, and he better pick them up before I pluck them out.

"Your boyfriend," he says, disdain dripping from every word, "dropped this. He should be more careful with his things. You never know when you're going to lose them."

I yank it out of his hands. "He doesn't have anything to worry about there."

"I'm not so sure," he says, making my skin crawl. There's something under his tone I can't quite figure out. But before I do, he's standing and throwing his napkin to the table. "This has been fun, but I'm a busy man with important people to see. Catch you all at the house next month. It's looking like it's going to be the best year yet."

Nobody says goodbye, but it doesn't stop Kyle from walking away. *Good riddance, asshole.*

Remembering Lincoln's phone, I look down.

There's a notification:

Thank you, Mr. Silver, for your ongoing contributions to Pulse^{TM}. As one of our top creators, your monthly earnings have been transferred to your account with a bonus to reflect the excellent boost in plays this month. Keep up the fantastic work!

When Lincoln returns, I stand, ready to get home and as far from Kyle as possible.

CHAPTER 31
TAKE EVERYTHING, GIVE ME FOREVER

LINCOLN

"I need a hug," Ivy says, throwing herself onto the couch before I've even registered the chime of the lift, the words muffled into my shirt because she's already hooked around me like a bloody koala. No idea what I was doing ten seconds ago, because all I can focus on is how incredible she feels in my arms.

It's instinct to hold her back. That'll never be a problem. The issue will be never wanting to let go.

"I take it today didn't go well."

With her face still buried between my neck and shoulder, she shakes her head. Christ, she's adorable.

I'll never be able to give this up.

"Do you want to talk about it?"

I struggle not to laugh when she mutters a petulant "no" in response, then push my phone aside to run a hand along her back.

She sighs, and I feel her fingers curl tighter into my shirt.

My heart skips a beat.

"But you know what really annoys me?" she says. She pushes up off my chest, and then I'm staring up at an Ivy with fire in her eyes. "I knew taking this job would mean no benefits, but I didn't realize it would be so mind-numbing. No phone, no music. They don't even like it when I hum. Do you know what it's like being in here with my thoughts all day?" She taps her temple. "Like a circus, but all the monkeys are played by that one guy from the Airflow commercial."

In my life, I've been lucky enough to travel to over a hundred countries, and nowhere on earth have I met anyone as utterly captivating as Ivy Hawkins.

There won't be any settling after her. If there's any of my heart left to give, I won't be satisfied with anyone else.

"Sounds fascinating." And I mean it. I've never met anyone so endlessly interesting.

"And on top of all that," she says, and I don't think she's even heard me. She's on too much of a roll. "They denied my leave for your family weekend, even though I wouldn't get paid if they let me take it. He said they can't 'spare the bodies' to give me time off. So I told him he's going to have to exhume someone, because I quit."

Ah. Suddenly the clinging makes sense.

She drops her head to my chest. "I should have listened to Mom and gone back to work sooner. Now I have to start all over again."

I attempt to soothe the tension from her shoulders. It keeps surprising me, this blind spot she has for her own brilliance. It makes no sense to me.

She's a prism of attitude and joy, and every time I'm witness to a new side of her — exhausted but obstinately pushing through it to finish her favorite show, freshly showered after a workout and bouncing on the balls of her feet because she's too energized to sit still, anxiously reading yet another job ad while she talks herself out of being qualified for it. The deep breath she needs to take when I compliment her, her eyes falling closed, as though she needs a few seconds to steady herself against it or perhaps tuck it away carefully before it's gone. She should be overrun with praise until it's overflowing. If she'd let me, there'd be no room left for doubt.

"This isn't your fault. Let me help."

Still resting on my chest, she shakes her head. "You've already done so much for me; I can't keep relying on you to swoop in and save me every time."

Well, fuck that. "Yes, you can," I correct her. Ivy says nothing. "And in the interest of not incurring your wrath, I need to let you know that your rent is hereby suspended until further notice."

Her head snaps up, almost clipping me on the chin. "You can't do that."

It's frustrating that she still thinks I wouldn't do anything for her. It's a perception I'll be happy to dispel. "Not the reaction I was hoping for, but all right. I suppose I'm glad Hania gave me her thanks by way of a kiss."

"Lincoln, you can't just — wait. She kissed you?"

It's only a slight exaggeration. More of a peck on the cheek since she was set to sell her beloved piano to cover a recent medical bill, but it's worth the risk to see Ivy's eyes flood with jealousy.

Fuck, I could get drunk on her alone.

"I quickly reminded her that I'm spoken for," I say, sliding my hands along her firm thighs and enjoying the way her gaze drops to my lips. "Now, before you get mad, I should tell you it's a building-wide policy, so that we can replace the lift."

Which currently works perfectly fine, something Ivy knows.

"It doesn't need replacing."

See? No matter. Her eyes flutter when my palms reach the apex of her legs, my thumbs skirting dangerously close to her zipper. "Then we'll fix the fire escapes," I say. We both know I'm lying through my teeth, but it changes nothing. I'm doing this for her, and I won't be taking no for an answer.

"Lincoln," she warns, seeing through the ruse.

I smile widely back at her. "Or we'll build a community garden on the roof and give everyone access. It's up to you." She must know that by now.

"Are you sure?"

About her? Absolutely.

The rent is an easy gesture to make. It'll take a nice chunk out of the funds Deacon used to send me as an attempt to guilt me into leaving London, but I can't think of a more worthy use for it. "Think of it like a belated Christmas gift. The perks of dating a posh git."

Ivy chuckles softly, but her eyes glisten with emotion. "I don't know what a git is, but I'm going to say you don't quality."

I cup her cheek. "Ask my brother. He'd be happy to disagree with you."

Mentioning Reed is a mistake as soon as I say it, Ivy's expression hitting the brakes and slamming right into disappointment. Shit.

"Okay," she says, standing up. "I have to know. Why do you let him believe such horrible things about you?"

Because they're true. Or they were once, and it's easier to let him dismiss a lie than be rejected with the truth.

"Whatever you're thinking is wrong," she says with an uncanny ability to always know what I haven't said. "I know you now, and you're not lazy or selfish, and yet you let him talk about you like you're..." She looks around as though searching for the word. "Like you're Kyle."

Well, now I'm offended.

Ivy stands between my knees, her hands on her hips, resolute in her frustration. "Why do I get the feeling you're using this little arrangement as a buffer and a distraction instead of doing what you moved back here for?" Her brow raises. "What the hell happened between you two?"

I suppose now is as good a time as any to tell her.

I wasn't always a smart man. After the split, Mum tried to make up for the distance by giving me an allowance. Combined with the prestigious university Deacon had arranged my entry to, I was well on my way to being a right bastard.

"I met Kat when I was twenty. Friend of a friend of

a friend, that sort of thing. I was gone on her, but she needed to play it cool, said her dad could never find out. That I needed to pay for all the fancy gifts and dinners she wanted because he checked her spending. Well, I didn't care, did I? Just handed my card over and followed her lead. All the way to Belgium, where her boyfriend found us." I can still remember the ice-cold punch of realization. "Turns out it wasn't her father we were hiding from, but her boyfriend. I thought, *hey, it's shit luck*, but she'll tell him it's over, and that'll be that."

Ivy must already sense where I'm headed as she moves closer, curling her hand around my arm.

I haven't admitted this to anyone other than my brother. "But I was the one with the wool over my eyes. She never saw me as anything other than a bank account."

"What did you do?"

All the wrong things. "Yelled a lot. Her boyfriend started a fight; I finished it. But since his father was a diplomat, I was the only one arrested." The night went from bad to worse as I watched them take my passport. "I called the only person I trusted, and Reed arranged to get me back to London, but only after he'd spent an hour telling me what a bellend I'd become."

After that, I was only granted enough money to get by. "Until you get your head out of your arse and start acting like an adult."

He wasn't wrong, but it hurt to hear, and in that moment, he went from brother to parent. "After that, I ditched the partying, ditched the Eton rejects, and

sorted myself out. Moved in with Manny after I graduated, and the rest carried on from there."

I'm not expecting Ivy to look so hard done by, the
lines of her mouth pinched and cross. "But that's ridiculous. He shouldn't hold one mistake against you for the
rest of your life."

"It was a very expensive mistake."

"And what? Nothing you've done since matters?
Everyone is reckless in their twenties." Christ, her anger
is rewarding.

"Were you?" If so, I want every detail.

"No, but we're not talking about me."

Oh, but I'd like to.

She shifts, glaring at the exit and looking all too
ready to storm off in search of my brother to give him a
piece of her mind. I bite back the smile tugging at my
lips.

"You made a mistake," she huffs, eyes blazing. "A
big one, sure, but no one got hurt, and you learned
from it."

It sends my heart down a familiar detour of gratitude. She's proof I've done one thing right, at least, but I
promised myself a long time ago that I wouldn't turn a
blind eye to my mistakes. "I hurt myself, and things
with Reed have never been the same. If I could take it
back—"

She interrupts me by knocking my foot with hers,
and fuck, I think she might try to fight me. It's the
hottest thing I've ever seen. "Yeah, well, you can't, but
you can stand up for yourself and fix things."

That's it. I give in to the urge and pull her back into

my lap, stopping short of showing her exactly how much I want to devour her but giving in to the need to hold her. Much better. "You're incredibly sexy. Do you know that?"

She fights it for a moment but can't stop the smile tugging at her lips. "You've mentioned it."

"And wise," I add, kissing her cheek.

She lets out a soft snort that ghosts my lips. "I actually embarrassed myself a lot in senior year."

"I can't imagine it."

"Then you're not thinking hard enough," she laughs, playfully pushing me away and, even more regrettably, sliding off my lap. I make do with throwing one arm around her shoulders while she reaches forward for the remote.

It turns out I've been living for the moment for far too long, because I'm unprepared for how viscerally I can imagine a future with her, one where she inhabits as much of this apartment as she does my mind. All of it.

I need her humming when she's deep in thought, keeping me company while I work. I need her filling my kitchen with her cooking the same way she fills my life with a spark I haven't felt for years. I need her phenomenal body within reach every day and night if I have any hope of satisfying my craving for her.

"Thank you for the rent," she finally says. "I know you're not obligated to help me, considering this relationship isn't real."

But she's wrong. Nothing has ever been more real than this.

"If you don't like it, you're welcome to break up with me," I challenge.

She says nothing, looking only at her hands.

My hand is laid against the back of the couch, and as I wait for her answer, I curl my palm around the back of her neck, tracing the tan lines where her sports bra stops, stroking the warm skin until it elicits a shiver. My mouth waters with the need to taste the salt of her skin. "Well?"

She opens her eyes, her voice breathless, unable to hide the effect I'm having on her. "Maybe tomorrow. I'm too busy today."

CHAPTER 32
FEELINGS? NO THANK YOU, I'M FULL

IVY

I met Villainina in the hallway between our apartments. She crashed through her door, opposite mine, late for her performance at the city's first and best (and second seediest) drag bar. I'm honestly trash for sequins, but it was the way she took one look at me and said "love the shoes; we can work on the rest" that made me obsessed.

I laughed and shouted "your lace is showing" at her back (it wasn't) and she flipped me off with a smile.

Filipe knocked on my door the next night, sans the Villainina look but with all of the attitude, and we've been sparring buddies since — literally and figuratively — Fil's trained in capoeira, but we stick to boxing drills to burn off the booze and bitchiness.

"Just tell him you want to date for real," Fil says, throwing his pads to the floor and wiping the sweat off his forehead with his forearm.

"Oh my god," I say dramatically, peeling off the Velcro and unwinding my wraps. "Why didn't I think of that? I should just be honest. Because a man has never lied about his feelings."

Filipe laughs, grabbing two water bottles from his fridge. "Trust me, I heard it as soon as it came out of my mouth." He tosses me a bottle, then downs half of his own in one long gulp. "It's really not a choice, is it?"

I shake my head as I swallow, relishing the icy relief. "Remember Rhys?" I ask, throwing myself down on Fil's settee. "Emails me in the middle of the night — emails, like it's the late nineteen hundreds — about how I'm the first person he's been able to open up to, how we have something special. Then he goes and blocks my number before I've even woken up."

I sigh.

"Men," we groan in unison.

"So you're just not going to say anything? That sounds healthy," Fil says, gulping down the last of his water and tossing the empty bottle toward the trash. "What if he's waiting for you? Rejection has got to be better than not knowing."

It knocks at the little door in my mind where I've been stuffing all my hopes that perhaps this could be exactly as good as it's been. That I'm not imagining anything at all. But then, that's what I thought with all the others. "My big mouth is what got us into this situation in the first place. I'm not going to make everything ten times worse by admitting I'm falling for him too."

Fil isn't moved by my logic. "So instead, you're going to keep up the charade, and hurt yourself over and over again until you can't take it anymore. What a great plan."

"Wow, just punch me straight in the face next time," I groan.

Of course I'd date Lincoln. I'm hopeless, I'm not deranged. He's intriguing, confident, self-possessed. Kind of adorable, when he's with his sister or Manny, and then, holy shit, is he a demon in the sack. A fucking natural disaster in the way he can fuck me up and mesmerize me.

"I want to. It's just..." I'm scared. "Everything with him is so big and intense, and it's great. But I've been swept up in it before, getting my hopes up based on nothing, only to find out I'm stranded out on emotion island by myself."

I like Lincoln with a fierceness that is embarrassing. He's confident and fun, and every time I look at his hands, I get overwhelmed with the urge to have them tearing off my clothes or dragging me in for a world-bending kiss.

But that's not what I'm afraid of. The scary, heart-racing, can't-breathe problem is that I've started lying in bed imagining our future together.

Fil takes the seat next to me, dabbing at the sweat on his neck with a towel.

"I'm screwed, aren't I?" I ask him.

"You'll survive," Fil says, but I don't think I will.

CHAPTER 33
GROWING FOND OF YOU

IVY

Whoever said change is as good as a vacation never had to answer the question "What can you bring to this role?" three thousand times. I swear, the whole process would be a lot easier if I could answer honestly. *Can operate computer. Will trade labor for money.*

Like, come on, what am I supposed to say? That life before this job opportunity was meaningless and now, wonderfully, I've found my true heart's purpose?

I just want to buy eggs.

It probably should be concerning that when I hear a key in my front door, I don't immediately call the authorities. Instead, I call out "over here" and smile as Lincoln approaches.

It doesn't seem right that someone whose upper body should have its own judicial system can fit through a human-sized door or sit anywhere smaller than a throne.

We've taken to spending time together every day, and every unannounced visit warms my heart a little more. I thought it was just me he liked helping, but it's not, is it? It's everyone. Like he can't help himself. Like he needs it, using his charm to discover exactly what people need and then being the guy who gifts it to them.

Mom would be absolutely horrified to know a man is helping himself into my apartment, but I find it soothing. No matter what I might need him for, I know Lincoln wouldn't hesitate to get to me.

It's a level of devotion I've never had before, and I'm struggling to not get too used to it.

"A little late for spring cleaning, isn't it? Or is this a new design trend I'm not aware of?"

I look up from where I'm swimming under a pool of clothes. "I felt like a change."

More like I felt like shedding the rest of my cocoon.

I've spent years keeping the odd parts of myself stuffed into a back room, mementos of youth packed away with a school uniform and an affinity for happy squeals. God, there was a time I used to literally jump for joy.

It's the dress I bought on a whim and have never had a reason to wear. The patent pink stilettos from three fashion cycles ago that I'm too terrified to wear out because someone will clock that I'm not "with the times" but I can't bring myself to throw away because I've never worn them. It's the costume jewelry I bought for myself with my first paycheck that now sits, tangled and buried at the bottom of a shoebox.

Breadcrumbs of a person I want to be but have never dared.

"Evidently. Can I help? I have some experience rescuing maidens."

There's no fighting the blush that floods my cheeks, but I aim a tiny glare at him anyway. Lincoln grins back.

"These pants or this skirt?" I hold up the items for his scrutiny. I can't explain it, but I woke up this morning, took one look at my wardrobe, and didn't want to see anything in there that wasn't me anymore.

I don't care whether it's a Canadian tuxedo or a plaid maxi castoff from a Stevie Nicks impersonator. If it's got flair, I want it. I'll wear it. Fil's philosophy is that clothes transform, and I've seen Villainina come to life in drag. My wardrobe needs to express who I am. Who I want to be.

Bright or seductive or ethereal. Cozy or focused or ready for anything. Maybe that's why deciding is so difficult. I want too much. I want it all.

Loud florals; mismatched sets; soft, off-the-shoulder sweaters in deep, ominous colors. Shoes I can dance in, just in case the situation arises. Finishing touches on finishing touches.

But none of that fit with serious Ivy. Button-down shirts and business pants and action items never left any room for whimsy.

Somewhere along the line, I started to resent that.

"Actually," I say, throwing both onto the scrap pile, "never mind."

Usually, after the big hair change, the lead's life gets better. Me? I'm still confused. I'm just hotter now.

"Glad I could be of assistance," Lincoln jokes, crouching down to pluck a yellow summer dress from the pile. It's soft and floaty, with ties on the shoulders, and never fails to make me feel amazing. "Funny, I have this exact same one in blue."

"Give me that," I laugh, taking it from him and placing it firmly in *Keep*. "You're supposed to help me work out what to get rid of."

His smile curls just so, and my body shivers. "In that case, you can start with everything you're wearing right now."

Christ. There's nothing I want more.

Apart from the roguish smile, he's wearing olive dress pants and a white collared shirt with flowers embroidered along the buttons. It makes his skin glow golden.

"Maybe another time."

I get stuck rediscovering a pair of flared shorts that I mourned the loss of last year, and it's not until I'm midway through my mental rendition of "Together Again" and Lincoln is handing me a glass of water that I realize he's been here for over an hour, sitting comfortably on my sofa and watching with a smile.

Somewhere in our fake relationship, we've become real friends, and I'm praying that after our inevitable (and personally devastating) breakup, I might be lucky enough to keep this.

It takes me another hour to sort everything, and when I finally look up, it's Lincoln's turn to be lost in work. He must have run upstairs to grab his laptop, because he's now hunched intently over his keyboard, reading.

He claims to not be an actor (he'll accept performer,

though, which is conveniently also a train of thought that I have to cancel before I remember the way his fingers felt inside—Nope) but he is voracious about writing.

Sometimes he'll ask for my opinion on a script and then launch into a deep dive on John Truby's *The Anatomy of Story*. It's fascinating to listen to him connect threads of technique with various philosophical teachings on passion.

It's clear his work means something to him. Yes, it's salacious, but he cares about it beyond that. Enough to take his time, to write scenes he's proud of, to breathe life into them. He talks about pacing and motivation, what exercises help him with modulation and breath control, the singing classes he's taken to improve his range and pitch. I think I could spend a lifetime listening to him talk and never get bored.

I could spend a second listening to his recordings.

I've developed an unfortunate addiction to the sound of his sighs. Memories rise to the surface every time, imprints of his rock steady chest enveloping my back, the pressure of his palm on my throat, long fingers commanding me to bare the most delicate parts of myself to him. It makes me want to give him everything, to loosen my grip on my shields and let him in. The very thought of it is terrifying. And still, I want it.

There's nothing more attractive than a touch of softness, no matter where I find it. Sometimes it's in the eyes, glowing with kindness as we trade bios during happy hour, a hint of deeper meaning behind the surface-level backstory we're sharing. Sometimes, it's in the thighs, thicker than my hands can hold and a pleasure to kneel between no matter the owner. In that moment, I hold greatness under my palms and wield ecstasy with my lips in a feedback loop that keeps on giving.

My personal favorite, though, is finding softness where I least expect it. God, this probably says so much about me — and is likely the entire reason I keep falling for all the wrong people — but that moment when a broody man gently holds my hand or a jiu-jitsu queen brushes the hair out of my face?

I'm a goner.

Now that I know what to look for, I see Lincoln's softness clear as day. It exists where his heart is, on his sleeve, as long as you know to look there.

There's pride in the work he does, the creativity it takes. A hunger I've had the pleasure of being the focus of before.

Components, parts, that I'm adding up to a whole.

With every day, he becomes more interesting, more arresting, more wonderful. It's awful (entirely because it's not anywhere close to being awful at all).

If Reed really, truly believes Lincoln to be unambitious, or lazy, he doesn't know his brother at all.

CHAPTER 34
KISSES, GIFTS, GESTURES

LINCOLN

The Playhouse Theatre is an intimate space in midtown, a relic of an older time but still standing strong. It's gotten a facelift in the last few years, and they've done a commendable job keeping to the original aesthetic. Of course, it's not the building that has captured my attention.

While Ivy takes in the view, I only have eyes for her. Wonder and hope brighten her eyes like stars, like those I remember reflected in them the night of the masquerade, standing with her heart beating under my fingertips and my own reaching out for her in a way I didn't understand until now.

Christ, if she doesn't stop looking so gorgeous, I'll have to throw myself into oncoming traffic, or better yet, propose.

Ivy turns to me, her mouth open. "When you said you had a surprise for me, I wasn't expecting this."

"Do you like it? I've never bought a theatre before."

"What? Lincoln, no you can't buy me a theatre. What the hell would I do with it?"

"Whatever you like."

She stares up at me, lip caught between her teeth, her eyes intense with an emotion I can't quite read.

It's possible I just fucked up.

Then Ivy is stretching up, pulling me down with one hand clenched in my shirt and kissing me once, hard.

It's everything I've been holding back from taking, but it's barely a bruise before she's pulling back.

Worse than missing the chance to return it, is the sight of regret pinching the spot between her eyes.

"Wait, sorry. I shouldn't have done that. Can we just cut that and pretend it never happened?"

I doubt I'll ever forget a single moment with her for the rest of my life, but I nod anyway and watch the relief sap the tension from her body.

"Great," she says, taking a step back. I already miss having her in my arms. "God, you can't be real. I keep thinking I'm going to wake up from this dream, but you're still here." She's staring up at the freshly painted awnings. There's no doubt the building is a beauty, but there's nothing else I'd rather be looking at but her.

"How did you even arrange this?" she asks. "They don't do venue tours after two."

The backstage door swings open, and Francis looks gleeful. "Yes, but Don Juan here has friends in high places," he says in his clipped British tone.

Ivy's jaw drops open. "You're Francis Byrne. I absolutely adored you in *The Sacred Link.*"

Francis's eyes sparkle, and I know immediately Ivy has him under her spell. *Join the club.*

CHAPTER 35
DRAMA, DARLING

IVY

Francis Byrne is standing in front of me. The Francis Byrne. He's so close I could touch him.

His hand covers his heart. "I was phenomenal in that, wasn't I? One of my best, even if I was robbed of the Olivier by that bastard Alfonso. But we shouldn't linger on old wounds."

Behind me, Lincoln stifles a laugh, which makes me think this is a scab Francis has been picking at for a while.

Holy shit, Lincoln knows Francis Byrne. I can't believe he didn't tell me.

I wish Astrid were here.

"And who is this ravishing creature?" Francis leans back dramatically and gives me a once over. He's as tall as Lincoln, but lean, his hair shock white, his face wrinkled with age and experience, with deep-set eyes that skewer you in place.

He's a bastion of the stage and he's standing four feet away from me.

Lincoln's hand curls around my waist. "The someone special I told you about."

He mentioned me? To *Francis Byrne*? Is this what an out-of-body experience feels like?

I hold out my hand, half expecting to wake up the moment we touch. "I'm Ivy."

"A pleasure, Ivy." Francis takes my hand and gives it an air kiss. It's so charmingly dramatic I'm ten seconds away from linking our arms together so we can skip down the aisle.

I can't believe Lincoln did this for me.

Francis walks back into the theater and beckons us to follow. "Come, let me give you the grand tour."

I've lost count of the shows I've seen at the Play-house. Getting a tour has been on my bucket list since my first, but it's sat at the back of the list for years, waiting for a rainy day.

Here Lincoln is, making it pour.

Stepping inside is like stepping back in time, like stepping into a dream. The red-cushioned seats, the gilded archways, the buffed and polished and re-scuffed stage.

With rehearsals underway, the stage crew is hard at work around us, taking directions given to them via managers' headsets. Francis introduces his costar, Julian, who is currently sprawled back on a leather sofa at center stage, talking over the script with someone who is nodding a lot and unable to get a word in.

The air smells of set paint and a little like wet socks, and I'm so happy I could cry.

Lincoln waves me on before we go backstage, and I

follow Francis alone into the belly of the beast. When we reach the largest of the dressing rooms, he lingers at the door, watching as I venture into the auspicious space and letting me stare giddily at everything. "Lincoln says you're a performer yourself. Why aren't you up here?"

I laugh. "Because I was terrible at it." There's a signed photo of Audra McDonald on the wall. I want to sneak it out so badly. "I do miss dressing up, though."

"You don't need to be onstage for that."

True.

Makeup litters the counter, and I suddenly see the joyful chaos around me in a new light. Huh. I guess you can take the girl out of the theater, but...

I turn to Francis, who is eyeing me with curiosity. He's been acting for twice my lifetime. There's probably not a role around that he hasn't played, but the man in front of me doesn't seem confused about who he is when he's offstage.

It must be nice.

"Is it difficult?" I ask. "Being someone new all the time? Do you ever feel like you've lost yourself?"

To his credit, Francis smiles, warm and knowing. Actor to actor. "Constantly. We all play roles in life. Some we choose, others we don't. The trick is always knowing who you're performing for and how to return to what is true."

I think of Lincoln, of Astrid, my mom. All the times I've swallowed down how I'm feeling. All the times I've thought of my future and felt trapped.

A compassionate lie, a camouflaged truth, a polite smile. Smiling when I want to scream. Or cry.

I've caught myself at my most tender, searching for words, attempting to capture them in voice notes I never send. Ramblings I express, then delete before another person might know them.

"You know, for the longest time, I thought maybe I liked pretending to be other people because they were more interesting than I was." I pick up a lavish green velvet cloak and drape it over my shoulders, swaying it back and forth. It's divine. I need five. Immediately. "Now I think maybe I gravitated toward interesting people because I recognized myself in them."

I turn to the mirror.

"No one ever told me I might be lost as an adult. What was the point of all those conversations with career counselors?" I was supposed to have this worked out a decade ago.

What happens if I never find myself? Am I doomed to wander, never satisfied? It's not fair to tie myself to another person if I don't have solid footing first. I'll always have one foot lifted, anxious to plant myself. And without roots, how can anything grow?

Francis takes a long breath. I shouldn't be boring him with this. The guy's a renowned thespian. But he doesn't look put out. No, he's looking at me the way Nonna used to. The way Astrid did as we shopped. I'm starting to feel like a group project.

"Can I give you a little advice?"

I nod. "Please."

"Don't wait for it. Find what makes you happy and

grab on with both hands. Don't wait and pine for it later."

I almost want to laugh. Patience isn't really my style. I used to pace in the wings before my cue, lightning zipping through my veins like the Flash, pinballing around my ribs. I miss the adrenaline rush of performing. The split second before I step out from behind the black curtain, where time comes to a standstill.

One last deep breath before launching myself onstage.

"What if I don't know what makes me happy?"

"You'll never know the answer to *what if,* so you must be happy with what is. And if you aren't, then you work to change that."

Shit. Crying in front of Sir Francis was not on my to-do list, but cross it off. He reaches past me and hands me an honest to god handkerchief. It's embroidered with his initials. "You're already on your way. Crying in the dressing room is a rite of passage in this theater."

At the end of the tour, Francis sits on the edge of the stage, and I take a seat beside Lincoln in the front row. His arm goes around my shoulders as soon as I've sat down. "How was it?" he asks.

"Incredible," I say honestly, feeling another piece of my puzzle click into place. I don't know how I'm ever going to thank him.

"Now, Lincoln," Francis says, "if you are at all the gentleman you profess to be, you need to make sure this wonderful woman is in that seat on opening night."

"You know I will," Lincoln says.

"You don't have to do that," I say. "This is more than enough." I can't believe I'm turning down front-row tickets, but Lincoln has already done so much for me when all I've done is make him lie to his family and pretend to be my boyfriend.

"Ridiculous," Francis responds. "Let the man spoil you, dear."

"Oh, we're not..." I trail off. "He's just trying to make me feel better since I was fired," I explain. "I mean, you saw me before. I'm still trying to figure out what I'm going to do, and Lincoln has been very nice about it."

About a lot of things.

Francis narrows his eyes, a smile playing on his lips. He doesn't look away from me, even as he asks, "Are you often in the habit of pulling favors for complete strangers, Lincoln?"

"No, only the people I care about."

Francis smiles wider, and I feel my face heat. "Fascinating." He then jumps up and claps so loudly I feel the air shake. "You must stay and watch us rehearse," he says before loudly whispering, "Julian needs the extra help."

"More like you want to preen," Julian calls out, picking lint off his cape as he stands. "And I'm not overselling the confession."

"You bloody well are," Francis retorts.

Julian rolls his eyes. "Ivy, be a dear and tell Francis he's an aging husk and his best days are behind him."

I laugh, and Francis turns back to wink at me before

he straightens his cuffs and takes ownership of the room.

Damn. He doesn't just command the stage, he rules it. There's no taking my eyes off him, eager not to miss out on a single reaction.

"I felt a similar awe watching you work the room that night," Lincoln says softly. I flush. I still remember the weight of his eyes following me as intimately as my shadow.

I also remember how powerful it was to free myself. The fun of letting my imagination run wild. Like I was sifting through a box of childhood mementos and remembering who I used to be.

How did Lincoln know I needed that, even before he knew anything else about me?

"The first show I ever saw was in this theater," I tell him, swallowing past the lump in my throat. I was in middle school. I can't even remember which class it was for, only that it was this musical I hadn't heard of.

I didn't know then that my heart would immediately be yanked from its moors, pumped with the voices of the chorus, and then — just for good measure — gloriously pulverized with "On My Own."

"Mum took me to my first play," he says, a soft smile on his face. "I was fourteen and bored off my arse, but Mum loved it, and it was nice to see her happy."

My heart aches. Family means so much to him, but everyone is so busy keeping the peace, they don't see how much it's keeping them apart. If there was ever a time for Lincoln to catch my foot-in-mouth disease, now would be it. Maybe then they'd all stop quietly pining for the past.

"Astrid would love this." Maybe I shouldn't meddle, but I can't stand aside and not try. Not after all the advice they've given me. Besides, when Lincoln decides he doesn't need me for practice anymore, I want to know that they're okay.

Family is too important.

"She thanked me, you know, for finally convincing you to move back. I hated that she didn't know how much she means to you."

It's hard, sometimes, to read anything in his expression, but when he speaks, his tone is somber. "I'm sorry for making you lie to her."

Making me? "I'm the one who started this, and if you ever want to end it—"

"I don't," he says immediately. Something raw and selfish inside me roars. I don't want to either. "But," he adds, and my stomach sinks into my sneakers. "I won't make you continue if you're uncomfortable."

"The reunion's a week away," I say, because as much as I know I should, I can't bring myself to end this yet. I just want a little more of it first.

"I don't care about that. Ivy, I only want you to be happy."

Crack. That'll be the thin ice my heart is currently skating on.

I swallow. "I am happy," I half-lie. He doesn't look convinced.

"Just so you know," I say, picking up our linked hands as a distraction. "Today has been amazing, but just holding hands is good too. Sometimes all you need is knowing that there's someone there for you."

Lincoln reaches up with his free hand, brushing my cheek as he attempts to tame my hair behind my ear. It's fighting him, popping out again. I can't bring myself to stop him, too enamored with the pinch of determination creasing his brow. On his third try, I have to bite the inside of my cheek to keep from laughing.

With a sigh that makes me smile, he relents. "I've never really been known for my subtlety. It's something I'm working on."

"Please don't," I say suddenly. He's too close to miss the heat I can feel warming my cheeks. "I mean, unless you want to. But I like it. Subtlety is overrated."

"Good, because I don't want to stop spoiling you."

He will, someday.

CHAPTER 36
THE WORST PERSON (IT'S PROBABLY ME)

LINCOLN

When Manny and I coexist on the same soil, we only ever need to phone when there's a problem.

Which is why dread blooms, quick and bloody as a black eye, in my gut as soon as his name flashes up on my screen.

"Problem?" I ask, clinging to unlikely hope.

"I'd say a big fucking problem, yeah."

There's weight in the silence between every word, a language I recognize as the warning it is. "I'm on my way. Whatever it is, keep it there."

"Mate, if I could get it to leave, we wouldn't be talking."

Oh, hell.

As soon as I see Kyle, I know it's going to get worse before it gets better. Much, much worse.

"Ah, the lord of the manor has arrived," he says, a grin splitting his face open in a way my fist is jealous of.

He's never been here. It's a shock to see him in all his polo-shaped glory, dirtying up a space reserved for all the best parts of my life. I want to drag him out of here by the collar of that ridiculous shirt.

There's a glint in his eye that says he really wants me to ask what he thinks of the place, pretty painted insults sitting ripe on his tongue, ready for flinging.

As if I'd give him the satisfaction.

"What do you want?"

"Hey," he says, faking offense. "Is that how you greet your favorite cousin? No hello? How are you? I mean, this place isn't much to look at," he sneers, "but you don't have to be ashamed. We're family."

Manny steps out from behind the bar, and it's a good thing he isn't set to open for another hour. "I swear to god, if you don't shut your mouth right now—"

"It's all right. I'll take care of this." I hold a hand up to Manny, who shakes his head at me and grumbles.

"Smart man," Kyle says, making my skin crawl. "Now, how about we head upstairs so we can talk? I've got something that might interest you."

I fucking doubt that.

"Spill it or fuck off, Kyle. I don't have time."

As kids, we never managed to be in the same circles. I'm not sure if that was Mum's doing or pure luck, but I've always been grateful. Every second spent in Kyle's presence has been a test of patience and a lesson in fuckery.

All three of us had our own way of dealing with him. Reed ignored him (typical, that). Darcy spoke back, wielding words like weapons until Kyle was riled up.

I dared him to try me. He never did.

Until now.

I'm expecting him to deflate, huff and puff until the house wins and he slinks off back to whatever J Crew–infested nightmare he came from. But he smiles like he's holding a royal flush and pulls his phone out of his pocket.

As soon as the audio starts, I know it's too late.

"Fuck, man," Manny says as makes a grab for his phone.

"Nuh-uh-uh," Kyle says, pulling it out of reach.

I cross my arms over my chest, glad when Kyle's smile falters as he takes in the muscles I've developed over the last decade. *Yeah, knobhead, and I know how to use them.* "All right, I get it. Stop the fucking recording."

"Oh," he says. "Do you want to talk to me now?"

Kyle is the world's biggest tosser. I don't know how he found out, but he clearly thinks he has leverage now. "What the fuck do you want?"

"Well, at first, I was going to just ask for an investment. But then I realized that's too small. What happens when we need to raise more capital? No. What I want is an in at the company. Something high up. VP sounds good."

He's doing all this for a job? "Good luck with that."

"You're going to make it happen."

Like hell I will.

"Or," he says, dangling the phone from his creepy fingers. "I introduce Reed to your alter ego. Now, I don't know about you, but I don't think he's going to be too impressed with your filthy little side hustle. What's it costing him, huh? To keep you afloat while you piss away the family money?"

At least Kyle is stupid enough to show his hand.

He continues. "And that's before anyone from the press finds out. How are the shareholders going to feel when they discover their CEO's brother is getting paid to get his rocks off online?"

I don't fuck with shame, not about this. I enjoy what I do, but I also know that this is the exact reaction I've been trying to avoid.

Reed doesn't want to talk at the best of times, and Mum is always looking at me like I'm lost to her. The last thing I want to do is make that worse.

So I bluff.

"I don't give a shit. Tell whoever you want."

But it doesn't work. "You'd really do that to your own brother? You already made a bad enough impression when you got arrested."

I fucking hate that he knows about that, but he is right. As much as I hate to admit it, and I never would to this tit, I've been keeping it from Reed because I know he'll see it as one more mark against my name.

But it's going to be impossible to convince him to hire Kyle. "Who says he'll even go for it?"

"That's not my problem, is it? That's for you to figure out."

Man, he's a prick. "All right." I shrug. "Let's say I entertain this bullshit plan of yours. What happens if he says no? You don't gain anything by telling him about me."

"That's where you're wrong. I don't get the job, sure,

but I still win. Do you know how fucking annoying you all are? Think you're so much better than the rest of us, cause Grandaddy Deacon loved you more. But you aren't better, and I'm looking forward to seeing you knocked down off that fucking pedestal."

Fucking hell. "And if I tell him first? Ruin your little game?"

"You won't." I hate how confident he is, smiling as he chews. I want to see him choke on that gum. "Otherwise, he'd already know. But sure, call him right now. Let's see what he thinks." I know punching him in the face won't help the situation, but it sure would make me feel a hell of a lot better.

No. I need to buy myself some time, work out how to fix this before it blows up in my face. "Get the fuck out."

It's a blessing that he listens. Manny turns to me as soon as Kyle's gone. "Bloody hell. What are you going to do?"

The last thing I want to. "I'm going to speak with my brother."

CHAPTER 37
THE INTERVIEW

IVY

When Darcy invites me, and only me, to a "little chat" in her office, I know the jig is up. There's no other explanation.

As soon as I open the door to Darcy's office, I'm in love. Based on her whole "eclectic houndstooth" vibe, I knew I wasn't about to walk into a showroom of *Forbes*'s Top Ten Beige variants. But wow, you could have given me twenty guesses and I never would have picked the mustard wallpaper meets earthy opulence that's here.

"Holy shit, can I live here?" I blurt out as she waves me in, my brain three seconds behind me as I finally see she's on a call. "Sorry," I mouth with a wince.

"Yes," she smiles, gesturing to the chairs in front of her desk. They're velvety brown and oversized and may actually swallow me whole. "Fantastic news. I'll mark it on the calendar and send through an invite shortly."

When she hangs up, her smile has shifted into something softer, broader, more real. "Come in, take a seat."

The suede chair is even softer than I imagined, welcoming me like a family member as I sit down. "Bossiness runs in the family, I see."

Darcy casts me a shrewd look. "It does. You'll want to get used to that."

I cross my legs, glad I chose today to wear the boots Astrid bought me. They'll be confident enough for the both of us. "I can handle myself."

And like saying the magic word, she relaxes, looking as gleeful as when she snuck onto the plane to surprise us. "I had that impression, yes."

Though it's lighter than her brother's, her accent is still there, rounding out her vowels in a striking way. I wonder if it's unshakable or if she's holding on to it for sentimentality.

"You're good for my brother," she says, apropos of nothing. Sentimentality it is, then.

"I'm glad," I say, my breath caught in my chest. "He deserves someone who's good to him."

"I agree." She leans forward, primly tucking her hair behind one ear. "Ivy, how much do you know about what we do here?"

The title block on Darcy's desk says Head of Marketing and Communications. After the masquerade, I was more curious than ever about Lincoln's family, but knowing that they run a successful paintbrush manufacturing company — with deep ties to the community and a strong enough partnership with multiple art colleges that they've even personally funded fully paid scholarships — doesn't tell me anything about what Darcy's job is.

"A little," I bluff.

She clasps her hands together on the desk, her fingers stacked with gold rings, and draws out the silence that follows, trapping me under her gaze. It's far too reminiscent of her brothers'. Did they all stand in front of the mirror and practice? It's uncanny. And unnerving.

My high school drama exam consisted solely of a five-minute monologue that had to be performed in front of the class. We weren't allowed costumes or props, only use of the stage. But improvising in front of two dozen sets of eyes was less intimidating than this.

Eventually, Darcy tilts her head. "Do you have any sales experience?"

Wait. Huh? I'm so lost.

My face must be doing the talking for me, because she adds, "I can see you have a strong background in customer engagement, which is useful." She flips over the printout in her hands, and I lean closer.

"Is that my résumé?"

She nods, still reading. "Would you say you pick up new systems quickly?" Dropping the paper to face me head-on, she clasps her hands over her desk again.

"Sorry, is this an interview?"

Darcy looks up, bright blue hitting me like a spot-light. "Yes."

What?

"But... why?"

To my surprise, she laughs, as though I've told a

great joke. "Did you know that the night of the masquerade, the auction made more than it has in three years?"

I have no idea where this is going or why it involves me, but I can't pull that thread without unraveling the whole ball of wax, so I shake my head and hope it'll make sense soon.

"Obviously, I wasn't there, but Mum mentioned quite a few people who paid double or even triple for some pieces. When I followed up, I heard some very interesting stories."

I knew that melted owl was going to come back to haunt me.

"That's great news, but I don't see what it has to do with me."

Darcy stares me down for a moment, then, abruptly, she stands and walks around her desk. She moves quickly. It's the same kinetic energy Lincoln gets when he's talking about his work. "I'll be straight with you, Ivy. I need a communications lead, and I'd like you to apply for it," she says, a lot closer now that she's sitting in the chair beside me. My nerves coalesce like stone, heavy with meaning.

"Me? But I've never done anything in communications."

There's a glint in Darcy's eyes. "I beg to differ. The auction proves that. Although, if you accept, I would prefer you use your powers for good. But I can't deny it was an effective approach. And, somewhat unsurprisingly, we have a soft spot here for creativity." She straightens the cuffs of her checkered blouse. "Look, this role requires someone who can think on their feet. The rest we can teach you."

"That's, I, what?" Mark the calendar. I'm officially speechless.

Weeks of applying for jobs, and this is the first time I've felt a pop and zing of excitement brewing under my skin. Usually, there's a load-bearing depression accompanying the click on Send Application. I never considered an option where I would actually look forward to work.

"Take some time to think about it. I know it's a jump from your current role, but I spoke with Emma—"

My heart pounds. Does that mean she knows about the redundancy? No, Emma would have told me. "You did?"

"She had a lot of great things to say about you. As does most of my family." Darcy leans over to her desk, reaching for an envelope before passing it to me. "I've had HR put together an offer. I believe you'll find it quite competitive."

Blinking, I take the envelope from her. This is... I don't even know what this is. "How long do I have to think about it?" I ask, because the last time I acted without thinking, I ended up with a fake boyfriend.

Except, that's also the same reason I'm sitting here, so maybe I should stop being so hard on myself.

"Let me know by the end of next week."

I don't think it's going to take me that long to decide, and from the sparkle in Darcy's grin, she already knows it.

CHAPTER 38
MY BROTHER, MY JUDGE

Reed's office is awash in navy. Even the ceiling didn't survive whatever decorating phase Darcy went through. It's nice. Elegant. Strong. Handsome.

A good representation of my brother.

He fits here, sitting tall behind his desk, concern etched deep in the lines of his face, as though this very room is the source of his issues.

Or maybe it's me.

Wind the clock back, and it's like looking at a ten-year-old Reed, drowning in one of Deacon's blazers, barking orders.

"Of course you're here without any warning," he says as I drop into the chair across from his desk. It's deep and comfortable, which absolutely means it's my sister's handiwork. "If you're here to see Darcy, she's in the middle of something important."

"I came to see you, actually."

His surprise is evident in the lift of one straight eyebrow, but he says nothing. Instead, his shoulders relax and he pushes back from his desk to walk to a side table which — of course — has a teapot and several company-branded mugs.

Reed turns his head in question, and I nod. It strikes me that he doesn't have an assistant, and he's made no move to close the door to his office, despite the free-flowing chatter that makes its way in from the team working outside.

It's deliberate, in the way I know Reed to be, that he's available to them. That he's a leader, but he's also a part of the team.

He passes me a mug and returns to his desk, holding his own. We've never been this polite. If one of us brings up the weather, I'm leaving.

"What the hell is that?" I ask, grimacing at the speckled brown puck Reed is holding up to his mouth.

He lowers it, glowering. "It's blueberry and chia. Not all food is dripping in preservatives. Some of it is actually good for you."

The only thing that husk of concrete is good for is as a coaster. I reach over and bat it out of his hands, watching as the damn thing drops to the floor with a deep boom. Jesus.

"That was a perfectly good biscuit, you brute."

I roll my eyes. "Looks more like cat litter to me."

Reed scoffs, picking up his tea and crossing his legs. "Why are you here, Lincoln? Apart from messing up my carpet."

It takes a second to remember that I'm not here to argue with him.

"What's that?" he asks as I pull the slim packet out of my pocket.

"A peace offering," I say, waving it at him.

"Give me that," Reed hisses as he snatches the packet out of my hands. He's quick to open it, stuffing a biscuit in his mouth before I can blink.

"Oh god, that's good," he groans, taking two more before throwing the pack back at me. I catch it midair.

I didn't notice earlier, but there's some gray coming through at his temples, showing easily through his darker hair and matching the slate waistcoat he's sporting nicely.

I still remember the boy who let Darcy paint his nails while telling her how to maximize her customer base. Can still picture the lanky kid who confided his first crush to me, who helped me study, who couldn't bluff his way through a card game if his life depended on it.

Christ, when did we all get so bloody old?

"Where the bloody hell did you get proper ginger-snaps?" he asks.

"Care package from dad. He's seeing someone and refuses to tell me anything. Thinks he can buy me off with sweets."

"Which he can," Reed replies through his chewing.

"Of course he fucking can, but I'm not going to tell him that, am I? I'm holding out for Quality Street." I sink back into the leather as easily as our glide into gentle ribbing.

If only every aspect of our relationship were so simple.

"Too right." Reed fights a smile, but the laugh lines around his mouth give him away, and when he gives into it, the damn thing takes over his face.

It's disorienting enough to hurt.

I swallow it down. "Anyway, I thought you didn't eat sugar anymore."

"I do when it's this fucking good," he says, dipping his last bite into my tea, letting it soak but pulling it right before it crumbles. So much like Dad, it's uncanny. If I close my eyes, I could be back in Dad's flat, last night's match on the telly.

Reed swearing can only mean the stress has reached a critical level. I've got the strangest feeling I just helped the man fall off some kind of wagon.

"How's business?"

Reed is looking at me like I've told him I cheer for Liverpool. Is wanting to know how he is such a ridiculous idea?

Then he heaves a sigh as heavy as I've heard from him and sags back into his chair. "Frustrating, if I'm honest. Our biggest competitor is pushing for a merger that would result in layoffs for 80 percent of our staff and minimum wage for the remaining 20 percent."

"I hope you told him to stick it."

"And then some," he says. Good. "Little pissant is trying to price us out of the market now with mass-produced plastic." Reed loosens his tie, scoffs. "If I had any sense, I'd have passed on the job and gone off to become a swimsuit model like you did."

I put down my tea to smile mockingly. "No chance. You're too pale."

He surprises me by throwing his head back in a laugh, and the noise outside the room stops in response. I wonder how many of them were expecting us to brawl instead.

"Fuck you. I don't know how you lucked out of it; the last time Felicity and I went on holiday, I got burnt in a downpour."

I laugh, imagining him soaked down to his knobby knees, red as a slapped arse.

"A lot of people are lucky you made this choice, then." It's a concession I wouldn't have made a few months ago. But now that I've seen some of his work firsthand, the picture I had of him as lord and tyrant of Deacon's soulless empire is shifting into something surprisingly meaningful. Maybe it's time to reframe who I thought he was. "You're good at this. Much better than he was."

He nods his thanks, and we silently agree to let the moment pass. It isn't until I've reached the end of my cuppa that he asks, "How was the theater?"

Jesus. I put the empty mug on his desk. "How did you even know about that?"

He raises his brows as if to ask if I'm serious, and yes, I am. It's hard to believe now, but there was a time not that long ago where I actually had a private life.

"It's impossible to have a secret in this family," he says with a shrug, and boy, do I wish that was true.

"You'd be surprised."

He sets his mug aside, and I would put money that his foot is jumping under the desk. It's his go-to when he's tense. "So, you and Ivy really are serious, then?"

His tone is even, but I haven't forgotten how quickly he questioned her motives. It sets my shoulders back. "What about it?"

He holds his hands up, understanding he's crossed a line. "Didn't mean anything by it. I'm just asking. You look happy."

It's easy to be, with her. "I am."

"That's good. I'm glad," he says, even going so far as to look genuine about it, and honestly? I want to believe him.

He was meant to be my wingman, my best man. A friend, at least. Not the stranger we've become to each other.

Grabbing a couple tissues from a box on his desk, Reed bends over to collect what's left of the cardboard I saved him from ingesting.

"Do you remember summer in London?" I ask.

Reed sits up, tossing the remains into a bin by his feet. His hair is flopping forward and his tie is askew. "What, those two days in June each year? Yeah, I remember it."

I snort a laugh. "A bit of sun hits, and it's like anything is possible. No problem is too great, and you want to soak up as much as you can."

He looks over, expectant. Pushes his hair back into place.

"She makes me feel like that," I say, the truth of it undeniable. There are so few between me and him, obscured beneath our pride. But Ivy deserves nothing less.

Reed's gaze jumps to a silver frame on his desk,

where I bloody well hope Felicity's photo is. "I know exactly what you mean." It's a small bridge, but one I'll cling to.

I came here to talk to him, to call Kyle's bluff and get ahead of this mess before it starts, but everything's wrong. It's Reed. It's this office. I keep expecting him to strike me down with his "you're a disappointment" head tilt. It's like every trip to the principal's office.

That he's been, dare I say it, pleasant, is only reminding me of what I have to lose.

I say I don't care about Reed's opinion, but I do.

I've always cared. Otherwise I would have told him. I would have thrown it in his face as proof that I had disappointed him as deeply as he had me. It wasn't until Kyle made Reed knowing a reality that I understood how, underneath it all, I still want my brother's approval. Still want to make him proud.

Up until now, he's thought me lazy. But what will he make of this? Will I be irredeemable to him after this? The final bridge to burn?

"Hey," I say, leaning forward to rest my elbows on my knees. "Fancy a cheeky pint?"

He doesn't reply at first, but he does look at the door. Could he be considering it? "The last time I said yes to that, I ended up serenading a lamppost at two in the morning."

I chuckle. "Yeah, it was a pretty good night, that."

The smile fades away. "What's this about, then?"

The scrutiny sets me back in my chair. Always calculating, my brother. "Why does it have to be about anything?"

There's the head tilt. Christ.

"Fine. What do you know about Kyle these days?"

The principal's office feeling is back as Reed stares warily. "I didn't realize you two were close."

"We aren't." I'd rather cut off my own cock. "He's a little shit. I want nothing to do with him, and you know it."

"Do I? You seemed awfully cozy the other night. Two years of not seeing you for so much as a birthday, and last week, you plan a dinner and invite him? If you aren't friends, what is it?"

There was a time I wouldn't have hesitated to tell Reed everything. Having him on my side, us against the world? We were invincible. But this is bigger than him and me. It's Mum and Darce and every bloody person working here.

I can't blow up their livelihoods. Even in the off-chance Reed doesn't blow his top, what's stopping Kyle from leaking it publicly? The business might be smaller than it was back in Deacon's day, but those colleges might pull the scholarships once it's known the owner's brother fakes orgasms for a living.

Well. Mostly fakes.

"He hasn't pressured you into investing in that ridiculous venture, has he? If you're in too deep, I'll call my lawyer."

Does he really think I'd give that sanctimonious wanker a single cent? "I wouldn't trust him with a bog roll."

"Then what?"

I run my hand over my jaw, looking past him. "He

came to see me today." There are more framed photos hanging over Reed's shoulder. The one that has my attention is three decades old, taken at Dad's old place. It was one of the few Christmases we spent in London before Deacon guilted Mum about keeping us away. All five of us are huddled around a tiny tree, in pajamas and robes, smiles wide with hot chocolate mustaches.

I'd forgotten about it until now. I never knew Reed had this photo. Probably would have if I ever came into the office.

I look away. "He's still on about that job."

"Why would he come to you about that?" Reed's eyebrows raise with a sudden clarity. "Ah, I see. He talks to you. You come here bearing gifts. And I'm supposed to… what? Hire him as sales VP?"

I'm trying not to get pissed, but it's always been an impossible feat whenever Reed starts a lecture. He takes my silence as confirmation.

"Let me guess, if I don't agree now, he'll try again at the house this weekend?" He shakes his head, disappointment seeping from every pore. "Is this why you said you don't need money? He's roped you into some sort of scheme, and this is the next step?"

"No." I drop the word like a boulder, and Reed sits back and turns his head. Now he can't even look at me. Fuck Kyle.

I hate what I'm about to ask. Hate that it's going to confirm Reed's worst suspicions of me. But this place means everything to him and Darcy, and I won't be the reason it fails.

Staring down at my knees, I bid a silent farewell to

any good blood between us. "If you know he won't give up, why not just make him a nonoperational title and shut him up?"

Reed's voice is as cold as the night I stopped talking to him. "Because he's a pest, and once he knows he can get what he wants, he won't stop. I can't believe you're even entertaining this. But then, you don't have anything to lose, do you? It's so much easier to sit there and ask me to take the risk. How about you leave the critical thinking to me and you worry about yourself?"

Of course he can't imagine thinking is my strong suit. Only the great Reed Reeves is capable of that.

I push out of the chair, but even though I'm the only one standing, Reed's looking at me like he's standing on the high ground. "This is your fault, by the way. If you hadn't cut them out of the estate—"

"You don't have the faintest clue what you're talking about."

Oh really? "But then you have practice at cutting people off."

He rolls his jaw slowly, taking his time. It's his trick. Give himself enough time to gather his thoughts, restock his arsenal. While I'm busy shooting from the hip, Reed's collecting reinforcements. It's another reason he was the only choice to take over from Deacon.

"One day you'll appreciate the decisions I made for this family," he says, and it's clear this conversation has hit its inevitable dead end. "Perhaps then you'll start taking your life seriously and see I'm trying to help you."

No, he's only determined to get me to act according to his rules. Reed's tenants for right and wrong.

"Just because you wanted to become Deacon's clone doesn't mean I want to." If he doesn't want to hear what I have to say, then I'll deal with Kyle myself. "Call me when you get your head out of your arse."

It's only when several people jump out of their seats that I regret slamming his door behind me.

CHAPTER 39
DEFEAT DOESN'T SUIT YOU, DEAR

IVY

The peak of summer brings back a much-missed warmth. Unfortunately, my allergies hitched a ride as well. Still, I brave the pollen strongholds to soak in every ounce of Vitamin D I can.

Sometimes my lungs can't fully expand until I've walked outside. Other days I don't feel quite myself until I'm looping a reformer strap on my wrist, Emma's glowing smile reflected back at me on my left. Other times it's not until I'm sitting next to Lincoln on his sofa, listening to him practice a script.

I'm still searching. Maybe what I'm looking for isn't tangible.

Except then I find Lincoln, and it's as if everything I could ever want to see or touch has been distilled into a single point. A nexus of want. Mind, body, soul. Longing in unison.

As soon as the elevator doors open, I'm on him, taking the laptop out of his hands and climbing onto the couch to straddle his lap. "I have news."

Since leaving Darcy's office, coming here is all I've thought about. Of course, traffic was bumper to bumper all the way down 17th Street, so what should have been a fifteen-minute bus ride turned into an hour. It did give me time to text Emma and Fil, though.

Emma said to sleep on it (called it), then added that Charlie said to go with my gut. Fil's message included at least three GIFs and most said the same thing.

I agree with all of them. Which is why I need Lincoln to be the tiebreaker. I also want to know what he thinks, what he'd do in my situation.

Lincoln drops his hands to my hips. "Hello, darling."

I'm all ready to launch into Darcy's offer, but something is wrong. He's too quiet, too stiff.

"What is it?" I ask.

His gaze is lowered, stuck somewhere around my collarbone, while his hands — his freaking *hands* — knead and massage my thighs. I'm trying to keep it together because this seems important, even if my blood is racing right now.

"Nothing I can't handle."

I'm sure. I cover his hands with mine, stilling them. "Tell me." *Let me be here for you.*

He fights it, his jaw rolling under calm eyes. He's so damn effusive.

"Kyle knows about Pulse."

Dread lands heavy in my gut. Oh, shit. Of all the people to find out, I can only imagine that asshole's reaction. Even if he didn't immediately go for an insult (and I'll run naked down Main Street if he didn't), he definitely followed it up with something disgusting.

He's so fucking predictable.

Lincoln's lips pull taut. "The one time the prick decides to rub his two fucking brain cells together, and it had to be now."

"Fuck, Lincoln. I'm so sorry." But it's a good point. How did he find out? I can't imagine Kyle downloading any app made by women, for women.

If I dial 666, will the devil appear? I think it's time he created a new hell, and I have the perfect guinea pig.

"Now, darling, I know you aren't going to say something ridiculous like this was your fault." Lincoln tucks a strand of hair behind my ear, brushing his fingers along my jaw. He knows how much I love that, but I won't let him distract me.

Because I'm suddenly remembering the dinner. Fuck. *The dinner.* The notification. I press my head into my hands. "It is my fault, and that's twice now my mouth has gotten you into big trouble." It's a wonder he hasn't broken up with me yet.

"How do you figure that?"

"Reed's dinner. I knocked your cell off the table, and Kyle picked it up. There was a message from Pulse on your phone, addressed to Mr. Silver. I didn't even think."

He curls his hand around my chin, lifting until I'm hit with the full force of his gaze. Every time I think I'm prepared for it, I find myself falling all over again.

"Ivy, you did nothing wrong."

Tingles spread down my spine. "What's his game, anyway? Why bring it up?"

It's a ridiculous question. I know it before I've asked. Lincoln said it at the masquerade — the only reason Kyle does anything is because he wants something.

Lincoln drags a hand through his hair, but it's already a lost cause, spilling out of place. "My sodding turd of a cousin wants me to convince Reed to hire him."

"As what? The village idiot?"

Finally, a laugh breaks free, the first sign of the sun under his stormy expression. "Quite. No, he wants a title role or he'll send the audio to my brother. Not that it'll get him what he wants. Reed would rather lick the seat of a toilet than hire him. Or me."

Fuck Kyle. It's Lincoln's business to tell his family about his life in his own way, on his terms. I won't let that asshat ruin it for him.

"So there's no stopping him?" I refuse to believe that, but if it is true, then… "Okay, worst-case scenario, he shows Reed. What does it even matter if you record erotica anyway?"

I'm not naive, but this is his family we're talking about. Love is more important than some outdated — and, frankly, misguided — perception of sex work.

It hurts to see how resigned he is to accepting their judgment. It's so far from the charismatic, confident man he is. "Even if he doesn't, and it's a very distant if, I'm imagining the highly cautious businesses my brother's company relies on will care a great deal."

Fuck. He's right. "We have to get ahead of it. Then he won't have any leverage. Just tell Reed what's going on, and we can—"

"No," he says, and the word drops between us like a stone. "My brother has made it perfectly clear he isn't interested in what I have to say, especially where Kyle is concerned. Even if he did listen long enough for me to tell him about the blackmail, I'm not interested in the sermon he'll deliver once he discovers I fake orgasms for a living."

I can't believe what I'm hearing. He's never spoken about his work this way before. It's as if his mouth is moving, but someone else's words are coming out. "Don't say it like that. It's more than that, and you know it."

"Reed won't see it that way."

Defeat doesn't suit him. I'm used to all the easy charm of a man who has never worried about money in his life, stitched and woven around an iron-clad determination, and a body that will finish the job if his words aren't enough.

Not this.

"Who cares? You're just going to roll over and play dead instead of being an adult and facing this? What about Darcy?"

He shakes his head, dashing my hopes. His hands have stopped moving now, every part of him tenses under me. "I adore my sister, but she's the worst liar on the planet. If we tell her, I'll barely have the sentence out before the whole family knows."

It's hard to leave his lap, but I need to think. Slowly,

I push away from him, and the fact that Lincoln doesn't even try to stop me makes everything worse.

My painting is still hanging on the wall behind him. I stare at those little paint dots and pray for inspiration. "Okay, then. We handle it ourselves. This has got to have something to do with how weird Kyle's been, right? All the sucking up?"

He nods, smoothing his hands down his jeans, shoulders slumped. "I had the same thought."

I gasp. "Oh my god," I say, grabbing Lincoln's bicep. "Oh my god." Of course. Why the hell didn't I put this together before? "The day we flew out to the factory. Reed was all tense and broody and dragged you back for a family meeting."

"I remember."

"You said it was a security thing, right?"

He hums in agreement.

Come on, he's a smart guy. Why isn't he getting this yet? "Bit of a coincidence, isn't it?" I ask, and I see the penny drop.

A smile finally cuts through his broody fog. "You think Kyle — a man who probably pays someone to wipe his own arse for him — tried to hack into the trust?"

"Wait, hack?" He's right. Kyle's password is probably something like 69God. He couldn't hack into a pencil case.

"The accounts are protected, thankfully. But Reed was alerted when someone attempted to access them, and when that didn't work, tried to brute-force their way into it."

Jesus, it sounds like something out of a bad movie. "Can't they tell who it was?"

Lincoln carefully avoids my gaze, playing with the pull tie on the side of my shirt, rubbing the cotton between his fingers. "Not that he told me, but we're not exactly swapping recipes with each other right now, so that could either mean nothing, or they don't have enough to point at anyone."

I trust Lincoln's instincts, but my gut is telling me it's Kyle, and it knows how to clock douchebags.

"So, it could have been Kyle." His silence is enough to tell me he doesn't believe it yet. That's fine. I can work on that. "I'm not saying he did it himself. You said he pays other people to do the dirty work. What I want to know is why."

"That's easy," Lincoln says. "Money."

I groan. The guy needs a new move. "God, that's so boring."

My Lincoln reappears when he laughs and pulls me back into his lap, strong hands bracketing my hips. "I'll tell him you're disappointed."

There's a conversation I'd pay to see. Fuck, I knew Kyle was a dick, but this is low even for him. "I want to dig into this douchebag. No one treats you like this and gets away with it."

I don't know if there's a word for the man who is my fake boyfriend/friend/landlord who once bent me over and railed me to the best orgasm of my life, but the one thing I know is that I'm fucked.

The worst part? It's not even the sex. Don't get me wrong, the sex was phenomenal. A multitalented, multidimensional kind of amazing. I can't tell whether it's better or worse to look at his hands and remember them gripping my throat and filling me up until I was begging for his cock.

The issue is the way he uses those same hands to reassure me. Brushing the sensitive part of my neck with his thumb, laying his palm on my thigh under the table, holding my hand as we talk.

There's fondness in his eyes now, sparkling like glitter in sunlight. Like he thinks it's sweet that I care. Like he isn't used to anyone who isn't family giving a shit. It breaks my heart. "You don't need to involve yourself for me. This is a family problem. I'll handle it."

It shouldn't hurt as much as it does, but what else did I expect? He's right. It's not my family, not even close. I'm only the make-believe girlfriend, the rehearsal for the real thing. Nothing more.

I scramble off his lap. It's ungraceful and obvious, and I couldn't care less right now because he's looking at me with those sweet silver eyes, and if I don't get out of here, I might actually start believing my own lies.

"Right, of course. Family. I'll, uh, get out of your hair, then."

"Ivy?"

I don't look back as I call for the elevator and leave. Now I remember why I didn't want to let myself fall for the fantasy. Because when reality hits, it hits hard.

CHAPTER 40
AH

LINCOLN

As soon as Ivy stands, I know I've fucked up. Shit. I'm cursing myself as the lift closes behind her, a game plan forming in my mind as I wait for it to return. I won't lose her, not to my fumbling and not to Kyle's bloody machinations.

"Ivy," I say, knocking gently at her door. My instincts are going haywire, halfway to dialing a jeweler as part of a grand apology, even as I know it's not the right choice this time. This needs tact. Honesty. Everything I'm unpracticed in.

The relief when she opens the door almost sends me to my knees, right here in the hallway. I grip the doorframe, steeling myself. "Tell me what's wrong."

That she doesn't immediately launch into what's bothering her is the biggest sign that this goes deeper than my tosspot of a cousin. I've learned enough now to know that Ivy only hides behind silence when the truth is too big to bear.

When there's a real possibility of being hurt.

"Come here," I say, pulling her into a hug. I have to fix this. There's pain in her eyes, and there shouldn't be. Not now, not ever. Knowing I'm the cause of it, even a little, pains me.

She presses herself into me, slipping her hands under my shirt as she hugs back, the touch of her skin on mine a vice I might never shake. All I can do is press my lips to her temple, breathe in the glory of her soft, clean scent, and try to memorize how good she feels in my arms.

Muffled shouting and a car horn seep out from Fil's apartment, whatever film he's watching playing at full volume. Wafting down the hall is the smell of someone's dinner, rich and spicy. Somewhere out there, Kyle holds the fragile tether of my reputation in his slimy hands.

But the only person worth thinking about right now is quietly clinging to me, and I don't know why.

"Sorry that I keep messing with your life like this," she mumbles against my chest. Christ, how did I ever think my heart was prepared for her?

She's killing me.

"Don't you dare apologize. It's been a long time since someone cared about me who wasn't already family." Perhaps never. "I'm grateful."

She slips out of my hands, and I miss her immediately. "Just make sure you remember that for your next girlfriend," she says, as if there could ever be a next after her.

I open my mouth to say this when it hits me. Ah. How ridiculous I've been to miss it until now.

Ivy believes this to only be a game. Another role she's been thrust into. And games are fun, but they're short-lived.

If she doesn't trust this to last, I'll take great pleasure in proving her wrong. Because when you manage to catch starlight in your hands, you don't let it go.

"You didn't need to rush over." She walks inside, and I take the open door as an invitation to follow. Inside is the chaos I've come to love with her. "Dealing with Kyle is more important."

Is she joking? "There's nothing more important to me than you. I'm simply used to taking on issues alone. I didn't consider you'd want to help."

"Are you kidding me? We're friends, and that means your battles are my battles. So sit your perfect ass down and let's see what we can find."

I won't push. Now isn't the time. In my experience, words wouldn't be enough anyhow. What Ivy needs is proof. To see that I'll keep to my word. That I won't walk away at the nearest opportunity.

I can do that for her. I have no plans to go anywhere, and I'll wait as long as it takes to convince her.

One day, I'm going to need her to marry me.

She looks toward the kitchen and hums. "Want me to run upstairs and get your kettle first?"

I don't dare tear my eyes from hers, hoping she can hear the honesty in my next words. "I have everything I need right here."

She ducks my gaze to throw herself down on her tiny couch, pulling her laptop onto her crossed legs.

Two strides put me right there next to her, where I always hope to be, with no distance between us.

What Kyle seems to misunderstand about life is that money can't touch what is really important, because this right here — Ivy, hair loose, curls wild, like a dream come to life — is worth more than any wealth in the world.

CHAPTER 41
ARE YOU READY FOR THIS?

IVY

The day we leave for the Bradbury reunion, I swear there is birdsong outside my window. It follows me on my morning run. Maybe in another universe, it's the sign that this weekend is only meant for good things.

A universe where local wildlife dance if I whistle the right tune.

But this is real life.

I bet Snow White never had to clean bird poop out of her hair.

———

My black suitcase fits neatly next to Lincoln's leather bag in his trunk (once he cleared up the confusion that was "pop it in the boot." I'm definitely going to have to start carrying around a little notebook of British translations).

The estate is two hours away, but I still overpacked (yes, even tampons), which Emma promises me is better for weekends like this. My wardrobe is prepared for anything.

Me? Ask me again later.

Lincoln closes the "boot" with a soft thud. "All right. You have everything you need, and now…" He slips a hand around my stomach, his mouth dipped down to my ear. "So do I."

I smile as I slip out of his grip and into the passenger seat. Lincoln offered to let me drive my faded yellow Subaru, but the temptation to slip into the passenger seat of his McLaren was too great.

The dark red leather is soft and smooth, and one quick turn might send me sliding into the footwell.

Lincoln starts the car, curling his hand around my thigh and pulling my body closer to him. "I'm going to preemptively apologize for this weekend. The extended family can be a lot. If at any point you wish to leave, I will drop everything and take you home."

Something lurches in my chest at the thought of being alone in our building without him. Slowly but surely, home has expanded to mean more than the four walls of my apartment, growing to include his as well, or perhaps just any place where he is.

"I won't leave you," I say, because the rest feels too big to say out loud. Besides, if we're going to face the wolves, I can't stomach the thought of not trying to protect him from it.

I'm the one who got us into this mess.

"I don't know what I've done to deserve you."

I stare down at his long fingers, too close and too far from where I want them to be.

"I'm keeping a list," I say.

He squeezes my thigh, and my whole body responds in kind, like an echo. "Are you now?"

No, but if I was, there wouldn't be enough paper in the world to contain all the things I like about him.

"All right," I say once we've reached the highway out of town. I turn as much as I can in the passenger seat, slipping off my shoes and tucking my feet under me to get comfortable. "Quiz me."

I spent all night memorizing the Bradbury family tree so that I wouldn't embarrass myself this weekend. Top of the heap is Joe, Deacon's twin brother, and an ex-agriculture pilot. His lifetime partner Art is, hilariously, a tenured art history professor at the college whose students donated their work for the masquerade auction. (It really is a small world, after all.)

Then there's Betty, Deacon's widow. "She's lovely, although you won't see much of her," Lincoln adds, after I tick her off my mental list. "She's always been a quiet one. Spends most of her time in her reading room."

Deacon's kids come next. Five in total. Richard is the eldest, the owner of the estate and, deeply unfortunately, Kyle's dad. He and his wife Helen must have known they'd spawned a demon, because they never had another kid.

Lincoln's laugh fills the car when I voice this. "Have I mentioned how much I adore your imagination?"

It takes two miles before my face cools down.

Next in line is Judy, a retired family lawyer, and maybe the one I'm the most scared of. Attorneys (with the exception of Astrid, who is completely lovely) can hardly be good if they aren't able to sniff out the truth. I'm convinced that with one look at me, Judy will know about the time I snuck quiz notes into my pen in fifth grade.

If anyone's going to discover the truth about Lincoln and me, it'll be her. The best plan is for me to stay as far away from her as possible.

"No one's expecting you to be an expert." Lincoln laughs when I shush him.

"What if I call her Julie by mistake?"

"She'll probably try to cleave your eye out with her nails," Lincoln says, his words dripping with sarcasm.

Oh, God. She will, won't she?

"Not helping," I say before I send up a silent prayer.

After Judy (*Judy, Judy, Judy*) is Dale, who looks boring in every way I could name. Apart from being one of twelve Dale Bradburys in the state, his online presence was exactly what you'd expect for a sixty-something white guy who grew up with money — board member at a one-word corporation, who posts opinion pieces on LinkedIn denouncing the "woke agenda."

As soon as I saw that he'd titled himself an "international thought leader" I closed the tab and had to rewatch an hour of *The Walking Dead* to shake off the urge to call this weekend off (the good seasons; I'm not a masochist).

Second youngest is Sally, who spends more time talking about her husband than her kids, if her Instagram is anything to go by. To be fair, in his heyday, he was a pretty decent wide receiver.

"And last, your mom," I say. "Who I might like more than you."

Lincoln spares a quick smile in my direction before facing the road. "Not too much more, I hope." His hands look massive on the wheel, ten and two like my instructor taught. Why is responsible driving so hot?

I pull my feet up onto the seat, wiggling my toes in my socks with a sigh. The last thing I want is to mess this up more than I already have. "I promise to be on my best behavior this weekend."

"Who says I want that?" He reaches across the console, and I watch, enraptured and tingling, as he threads his fingers with mine, bringing my hand up to his lips for a kiss without taking his eyes off the road. My heart practices somersaults in my chest.

"No matter how this weekend goes, I'm glad you're here. I'd rather an awful weekend with you than a thousand good nights with anyone else."

Somewhere out there is an Ivy who gets to have this. I'm sure of it. An Ivy who isn't questioning everything he says, each touch, every look, until it's impossible to know what's real.

All I can really trust is my own heart. I always knew my biggest adventure would be falling in love. It's a journey I've taken over and over and over again.

Except I did it alone.

This isn't love for Lincoln, but he's still given me the adventure I wanted. I'll always be grateful for that.

I want to take the job with Darcy. It's new and interesting, and I really think I could do it. What did Charlie say? That shit is transferable.

When Lincoln and I break up, I know Darcy won't rescind the offer. She strikes me as better than that. But I would still see her every day, still get to know her and be reminded of the life I borrowed for a short while.

Just as I will every time I go downstairs to see Manny.

Even if I never spoke to Lincoln again — and honestly, the chances of that are slim to none, he'd make sure of it — there would still be the memory of him, smudges left on the lens everywhere I look.

No. I know myself.

I'll read too much into it. Every glance, every smile. Each brush of our hands. They'll be caught and replayed until I hardly remember what is real or imagined anymore.

If I have any chance of getting over him, I'll have to move. Say goodbye to everything that leads back to him. At least until I can patch my heart up enough to survive hearing his name.

Once this weekend is over, so are we, and I'll need to find the courage to walk away.

CHAPTER 42
RICH PEOPLE LOVE AMBIENCE

IVY

The Bradbury grounds and estate emerge with the saturation turned all the way up. Even with sunglasses on, I shield my eyes, the sun so bright it's burned the blue out of the sky.

I've seen enough *Real Housewives* to know that the bigger the house, the bigger the ego. Deacon's ego must have contributed to global warming with how big it is.

You could land a small plane in the driveway. There's a botanical garden filled with carved statues and a fountain that probably charges for entry. And I can't believe I'm about to walk into it wearing flared blue jeans and scuffed sneakers.

There's a tennis court, a stable (empty, to my bitter disappointment), and an excess of gold *on the outside.* It's monstrous and epically gaudy.

I'm in heaven.

Despite my excitement, I can't imagine what it must have been like for Lincoln and his siblings being stuck here every summer. The nearest neighbor is miles away. Whole school populations couldn't fill this place.

I feel lonely just looking at it.

"The upkeep on this place must be wild," I say as Lincoln parks out front. If he tells me I need to start bowing and memorizing thirty types of forks, I won't be held responsible for my actions.

For the past fifteen minutes, he's been the kind of quiet I'm starting to hate on him. The one that says he's stuffing himself into the shape of someone he isn't. On second thought, coming here might have been a terrible idea.

I take a collective breath and follow him out of the car.

"You came!" Darcy calls out, stepping gracefully out of the entrance and making her way over to us.

The extent of my fashion knowledge starts and ends with the floral-patterned leggings I used to wear as a freewheeling toddler — which I kinda miss, if I'm honest — but her flowing brown skirt and off-the-shoulder top suit the aesthetic. Her hair falls perfectly straight, shining a glimmering, soft gold in the after-noon sun.

I ready myself for a weekend of being under-dressed.

"I wouldn't miss it," I say.

"You won't be saying that by morning," she promises. But it doesn't matter, because what I told Lincoln is the truth. I'm here for him, and I'm not going anywhere until this weekend is over.

As Lincoln collects our bags, two older figures step

out of the house, their expressions blank enough that it's either arrogance or cosmetic.

Considering these are Kyle's parents we're talking about, I feel good saying it's the first.

"Lincoln," Richard says, the word a greeting and a warning. He doesn't bother looking at me.

Gotta say, having met their demon of a son, I was expecting worse. More... pizzazz. There's a patch of hair the size of a quarter left at the tip of his widow's peak, and it must be clinging for dear life because it's all that's left on the wasteland that is his scalp.

Beside him, Helen applies a smile, as though she just now remembered it's a thing humans do. Her dark hair is trimmed into a bob so thick it reminds me of the hedges that line the top of the driveway. They're both dressed in head-to-toe summer beige, and honestly, I could kick myself for even being surprised. All that's missing is a small dog and a Stetson.

We all turn at the arrival of several cars.

Kyle arrives first, in a car that looks like a piece of coal mated with a spaceship. It's big and loud, and I can see the ozone layer deteriorating before my eyes as he skids to a stop.

He bypasses us with a snide grin, shaking his own father's hand before going for a hug with Helen. The only person who gets a real reaction from her is, of course, her son. I did not need the evidence to tell me that Kyle has a mommy complex, but ew, there it is. In all its lip kissing glory.

Several doors slam, and Sally waves a hand in passing that is either her saying hello or telling us to fuck off, and actually, from the way she pushes past her husband, her nose pointed in the air, I'm guessing it's both. Neither her husband nor her sons say a word to us as they head inside.

"I'm starting to think I should be offended," I whisper.

Darcy leans in. "It's just the breeding, love. Lots of sketchy cousins. Don't take it personally."

I snort loudly. I can think of one in particular.

The last arrival is the dreaded Judy.

As she steps out of a silver sports car in a loose linen shirt and capris, her straw-colored hair falls around her face and shoulders as though she demanded it stay in line or else. The thump of her car door (a surprisingly humble white Honda) echoes as she faces off against Richard. And if I see one tumbleweed, I'm getting straight back in the car.

"Hayden is visiting his father. You get me instead."

Her eyes slowly take us all in, pausing long enough on me that I feel my stomach bottom out. I'm sure if I looked down, I'd find it shriveled between my beat-up sneakers. Her expression is inscrutable.

"I feel like she's looking into my soul, discovering I failed at cursive, and will never forgive me," I whisper in Darcy's direction.

I can hear the smile in Lincoln's voice when he leans in to reply. "Aunt J's okay if she likes you."

"Oh, great," I whisper. How the hell am I going to make that happen?

We're informed (only because Judy actually asks)

that Betty is napping and Joe is walking in the gardens with Art. Judy excuses herself in that direction without another word.

Okay, then.

Looking so bored I'm half worried he's having a stroke, Richard finally spares a look in my direction, taking in my outfit before saying, "Please remember to dress appropriately this weekend. You may lounge in whatever you like at home, but consider the impression you're giving while you're here."

He sighs heavily and heads back inside without another word.

"Don't take it personally," Darcy says when it's just the three of us again. "He's like that with everyone."

It is personal. But the joke's on him, because I just pulled a fresh batch of grudges out of the oven, and I'm feeling generous.

Lincoln's choice to stay with his father for so long makes so much more sense now. Like a flashing billboard warning that I really shouldn't have waved off as many times as I did.

"Is it too late to turn around?" I ask.

"Never," he answers, but I know as long as he's here, so am I.

"Don't you dare leave me here alone," Darcy says, grabbing my hand and striding confidently toward the house. "You're the only reason I've been looking forward to this weekend."

• • •

Our room isn't a room. I mean, technically it's a room, with four walls, a coffered ceiling, marble floors, and a connected bathroom (not to mention the giant four-poster bed that I definitely can't look directly at without thinking about the last time Lincoln and I slept next to each other).

But it's so far from any other room I've been in. For one, it's the size of my entire apartment. There's a working fireplace with a gray chaise facing it, matching gray curtains over floor-to-ceiling windows that look out over the empty stable, and a huge white rug that must be a bitch to clean.

Glossy white side tables and a dresser sit at odds with the historical foundations, a stark reminder that money doesn't equal taste.

I miss the warmth and color of Lincoln's apartment. I miss squeezing onto my ratty sofa watching *Too Hot To Handle* while he works — until he gets so invested he puts his laptop away, and I finally get to curl up under his arm.

I'll miss it all more when it's gone.

Darcy perches on the end of the bed I'm avoiding, rolling her eyes when Lincoln shoos her off it again. "They had you in the terrace room right next to Kyle, so I moved you here. If you need me, I'm right across the hall." She strides over, giving me another hug before disappearing through the door.

The only other mansion I've set foot in was Emma's parents' old place next door, which is a ridiculous term to use for a building located miles away. "You really must have hated it here to walk all the way to the Conways."

Lincoln's standing at the dresser, unpacking. "I think you answered your own question. Although technically I only went to keep an eye on Darcy." He sets a pair of dress shoes on the floor. "We were given free rein while we were here, but it was lonely. Our friends were an ocean and a time zone away, so we spent a lot of time escaping when we could or haunting this place when we couldn't."

"I can't imagine being here as a kid." There are marks carved into the edge of the mantel; the kind I remember doodling in the corners of textbooks in school. I trail my fingers over the grooves. "This place is more mausoleum than home."

"That was Deacon for you. More myth than man," he says, hanging up his dinner jacket. It's all very civilized for a guy who works topless most of the time. "He didn't really know how to talk to children, so he wouldn't. Mum was always his favorite, but he never approved of Dad, and he never hid how happy he was when they split. I expected him to leave everything to her, to be honest."

I can't imagine anything Astrid would hate more. "Do you think Reed asked for it? To keep it from going to anyone else?" I can only imagine the damage if it had gone to Richard instead. Reed can be a stick-in-the-mud, but it doesn't feel like a stretch for him to swoop in and rescue the company away from greedier hands.

Lincoln only sighs. "I'm not sure what to think, but I can tell you it's caused nothing but problems."

Once I finally give in, I can't stop staring at the bed. It looks sturdy, like it could handle itself if, say, two people were to really go at it. Not that I'm imaging such a thing. Or wanting to test it out.

I'm definitely not picturing Lincoln hovering over me in a white mask, wearing nothing but a smile.

"Darling?"

I snap myself out of it, dropping onto the chaise so I can't see the bed anymore. "I've been thinking," I say, and he stops unpacking to face me, crossing his ankles and leaning casually against the dresser. I don't know when it happened, but the top two buttons of his shirt have come undone. My heart skips a beat.

"Maybe if we got some dirt on Kyle, we could counteract his blackmail. A guy like that definitely has skeletons in his closet. If we can get something big enough, we can turn the tables on him."

He considers it while I make eye contact with the snake on his collarbone. "I'm not convinced it would matter. Kyle's fuck-ups are a badly kept secret. He won't care if anyone knows about his skeletons. But he knows I do."

"This is bullshit," I say, slipping out of my sneakers and socks. I need to change before dinner, even if I'd rather see if I can make Richard's veins pop by showing up in jeans.

"You won't find an argument here," Lincoln says, and when I look up, he's pulled his shirt out of his pants, revealing more of his toned body with each button he pops open. The sight of it is wreaking havoc on my nervous system. "I should pay him off. I don't know what amount will satisfy him, but it's an option."

It's enough to get me off my ass and in Lincoln's business, pressing my finger to his chest (and if I happen to notice how hot and firm it is while I'm there, it's just a bonus). "You can't pay him off. Then he'll win. And even if you don't care about that — which you should — he'll never stop. As soon as he knows he can get money out of you, he'll keep coming back for more. The only way to beat him is to either destroy the leverage he has over you by telling Reed about the job yourself or find something Kyle wants more than the money."

He smooths his hands down my arms. "Then I suppose we're shit out of luck, because there is nothing Kyle cares about more than that, and Reed will never go for it. I've already tried."

It's enough to make a girl scream. "So you're just going to give up?" I don't know who I'm angrier at right now, Lincoln for rolling over, or Kyle for generally being the worst. Scratch that, it's more like The Worst (™).

"I'm not giving up," he says with the edge I've been waiting for, the one I remember from that night. Finally.

"I could key his car. It won't change anything, but it'll make me feel better."

My pulse skips when his eyes drop to my lips. Then again when he licks his own. There's no way I'm sleeping tonight. "That's not very sporting of you."

I step away, fishing a dress out of my bag for tonight

and willing the heat out of my cheeks. "I think we passed sporting a few miles back. Somewhere around blackmail boulevard?"

"Fair point, darling." He catches my wrist before I can slip into the bathroom and kisses my cheek. "Let's call that plan B."

CHAPTER 43
LET'S GET THROUGH TONIGHT

IVY

This is so not my scene. I'd rather be debating with Manny over which *Dexter* villain is superior (we're at a stalemate because while Manny is right, Trinity is brutal, I fully believe that if Brian were still alive, he and Dex would be a fatalistic duo).

Going out usually means bars where I can lick barbecue sauce off my fingers and sing along when I've had one too many drinks, not six courses and strained conversation. The only plus is that my assigned seat (seriously, I can't make this shit up) is between my two favorite people.

Dinner is every bit as awkward as I expected, and Kyle is relentlessly smug, although he does shut up several times in deference to his father.

Interesting. I wonder if we can use that.

I do get to finally complete my set of Bradbury siblings when Dale arrives. He's late, a fact Richard doesn't let pass unnoticed, and from his scathing commentary, must be typical.

Dale reminds me of every owner of a regional car dealership that does its own ads. Thinning hair to match his brother's, an air of arrogance, a little round everywhere. He looks like the kind of guy who wears socks under sandals.

He, too, slips into younger brother mode tonight, his posture sagging every time Richard talks over him. Dale's wife keeps herself as invisible as Helen does, and I keep coming back to the same question — why would anyone willingly come back here?

Meanwhile, Betty is exactly as Lincoln described, a shock of white hair pinned back with a bright blue clasp. She's shorter than me, four-foot-nine at best, and barely says a word when we're introduced. But she's the first person to smile at me, so I already like her.

Not so welcoming is Joe, who scowls his way through every bite. He might be the only person who wants out of here more than I do. With hair as silver as Lincoln's eyes, the only time his mask cracks is when Art, in a blaring yellow-patterned shirt, whispers something in his ear. I can't be sure in the candlelight, but I could swear Joe smiles. I'd sell my grandmother to know what they're gossiping about.

It's a relief to see Astrid again. I don't know what she did in Paris, but she's practically glowing. "How was your trip?" I ask, desperate for details and a distraction.

"Wonderful. It went better than I could have hoped," she says, and is being cryptic a rule in this family or what?

It must have been good, because I can't get any other details from her throughout the main course.

Apart from Kyle's insidious grin disgusting me from the other end of the table, it's a pretty dull event. Richard is sullen, like he resents us all for being here, even though he's the one who invited us, and everyone eats quickly, like we all silently agreed to get the first night over as quickly as possible.

In fact, I'm so eager to get away that it isn't until Lincoln unlocks our door (with an antique key, no less; Jesus fuck, rich people are dramatic), that I remember one glaring problem.

One huge, pillow-topped, Egyptian-sheeted, canopied, bed-sized problem.

"You should take the bed tonight," I blurt, already rolling my suitcase over to the chaise. "I can suffer on the space couch." My back will file several complaints, but better me than Lincoln. If I see him hanging off this thing, I'll laugh myself into an early grave.

"No." He throws his duffel onto the seat and steps in front of me, guiding me by the shoulders back to the bed. "I'm definitely not letting you sleep on that thing. I'll be fine."

The words jump so quickly to my tongue it's as if they were waiting in the wings for this very moment. "We could share."

Lincoln's gaze meets mine. His hair is cavalier, windswept. Gorgeous.

I've never used the word debonair to describe anyone in my life, but now I take a mental picture of

Lincoln in his black shirt and strong jaw, and I frame it under the word within my memory.

"It's a very tempting offer," he eventually says.

I couldn't agree more.

"Extremely tempting," I say, my breath hitching when his eyes dart down to my lips. In fact, I think I stop breathing entirely while I wait for him to kiss me, but when he leans in, it's only to kiss my cheek instead.

The disappointment hits hard and fast, and I shuffle into the bathroom before he can see it on my face.

Fil was right. I can't keep this up.

When I finally emerge in my tank top and shorts, Lincoln has changed into the white shirt/gray sweats combo I'm used to.

I roll over as far to my side as I can, putting my back to him. But Lincoln isn't as cautious. As soon as he's under the covers, he grabs my waist and hauls me halfway across the bed so I'm tucked in tight against his chest.

"That's better," he says, his voice a low rumble in my ear. He smells of the mint toothpaste I stole off him (I forgot mine, okay? I was very busy panicking this morning).

Grabbing his hand, I pull him tighter around me. If this weekend is all I get, I'm damn well going to enjoy it.

The seconds tick by. Lincoln is hot at my back while the cold night air chills my exposed shoulders. Usually, I like leaving a window open at night, hearing the sounds of cars and people passing by. Sometimes Armando has a party, and I get lulled to sleep with impromptu karaoke.

It's void of sound here. No music, no laughter, no life at all.

Only Lincoln's steady breathing and the erratic beat of my heart while I listen to him.

Maybe that's why I quietly admit, "You know, Ivy is actually my middle name. My first name is Gianna, after my mom, but Ivy always felt right. Like I could be my own person." Whoever that is.

His lips brush my ear as he speaks. "It suits you, as all things do."

The dark hides my smile. Such a smooth talker.

"Okay, I spilled," I say, nudging him. "Your turn."

He hums, a rumble I feel down to my toes. "Is that so?"

"No secrets, remember?" I whisper, feeling like the liar I am.

He says nothing for a while, and I sink into the feel of his fingers quietly mapping out my body in the dark, never straying into dangerous territory, simply memorizing me with his hands.

My first music teacher was a bit of a prodigy on the piano, could play with his eyes closed and always looked as though the music played him, rather than the other way around. As though it was a frequency he was especially attuned to, and his hands were his way of letting it flow through him.

Lincoln touches me the way Mr. Spencer played.

Passionate. Adoring.

Eventually, long enough that I've almost forgotten what I asked, he admits softly, "I don't have a middle name."

I turn over to face him, and while I can't make out his expression, I swear I can see him smiling. "Tell me everything."

He grazes my nose with his. "It started while Darcy and Emma were kids. Some wanker made Emma cry over her name, and I joked that mine was worse. Guessing it would make her smile, and after a while, she completely forgot why she was upset. I kept meaning to tell her the truth, but she enjoys the game, and it's never bothered me."

Jesus. Even as a kid, he was putting others first. Knowing what they needed and helping them.

"Are you cold?" he asks when I shiver against him.

In fact, I am, but I like it. In truth, I love summer exactly because the temperature drops so suddenly here at night. As though the world's temperature gauge is a little buggy, blinking out only in this spot at this precise time, year in, year out, but working enough that no one's bothered to fix it. The chill is a relief.

"Yes, but you'll think it's silly," I say.

"There isn't a single thing about you that I don't want to know, and not any of it could ever be considered silly."

It's times like these where words fail me.

I stare up into the darkness, basking in the anchor of him as the night settles across my neck and shoulders. "When we were kids, our apartment caught heat like an iron stove, and the only way to clear it out at night was to keep the windows open. Ciara and I would lie on the floor under the window and count down the sunset, waiting for the first gust of cold air to come through." I close my eyes and sink back into Lincoln a little more.

"It always felt like magic. Like every scrape Mom kissed better, or the swell of the orchestra when love conquers evil. We'd lie there so long I could hear my teeth chattering. It was like finding a portal between worlds — hot and cold, day and night. It's the first time I ever thought maybe being different was a good thing. That someday there might be a person out there who would enjoy my oddness too."

"There is," he says with so much certainty that my heart threatens to stop, fumbling and skittering over its next few beats.

Sometimes when Emma is sweet, or Ciara sends me a video of my nephew Remi, I'll fill up on so much love it overflows, and for a moment, I can't move, preoccupied with remembering how to breathe, holding myself together while my chest aches.

Lincoln makes me feel that way.

I hug him tighter, closing my eyes while he continues to stroke my back, sending shivers down my spine. I wonder if this is what Other Ivy is doing, off in the alternate universe where our relationship is real and not a performance for his family.

Does she get this every night? I could handle that.

"Good night, darling," he says softly, and it's so perfect I could cry.

It's bad this time, the sheer, unadulterated wanting of him. Every once in a while, it'll hit, and I need to steady myself, the room tilting like standing too fast, the swoop of my heart in my chest the only indication that it's not the world that he's irrevocably moved, but the very core of me.

If only I'd said no to the masquerade. I wouldn't know the feel of his hand in mine or how it sounds when he whispers my name in my ear to get my attention, as if it's ever strayed far from him.

I wouldn't know how deeply I could love, and how painful it is to not be loved back.

Two more days. That's all I need to survive.

CHAPTER 44
THE BALL'S IN YOUR COURT

LINCOLN

If I thought waking up to her in my apartment was pleasant, waking up to Ivy curled around me is electrifying. This is what I missed out on after the masquerade.

This is what I've been searching for.

She's always beautiful, but the mornings provide an extra glow, illuminating her from the inside out. "Did you sleep well?" I brush the hair off her cheek, watching her eyes flutter closed before she blinks back at me.

"Mmm," she hums with a smile. "I'm angry at how nice this bed is. Do you think there's a way to sneak it back with us? I could get used to waking up like this."

So could I, and it has nothing to do with the mattress. She comes willingly when I press my fingers into the hot give of her skin and hook her thigh over mine. "I'd recommend holding off judgment. You haven't tried my bed yet."

Ivy licks her lips. "That's true, but if it turns out your bed is better, how am I supposed to go back to sleeping in mine?"

"You don't," I say, my voice low and rough with sleep. Leaning down, I kiss along her jaw. "If you think I'm going to spend another night sleeping without you, I'm not doing my job right."

She exhales a sigh, melting against me. There's nothing I want more than to peel off her clothes and take my time in devouring her, but I need to know where she stands first. Still, I can't help but test the boundaries a fraction, crushing her to me, letting her feel how hard I am, tasting the sleep lingering on her skin.

I can feel the fight in her. I'd rather she threw caution out the window, but that's a decision Ivy needs to make on her own. Whatever it takes to convince her that I want this, I'll do it. The rest is up to her.

When she pushes back, I let her roll away, but I don't hide how much I want her.

Soon, I'll ask her to clarify what this is, leaving no doubt in her mind that I want all of her, in every way. I'm in this 100 percent, and I want nothing less in return.

By the time we slink down to breakfast, the room is nearly empty.

"About time you two joined us," Richard says from the head of the table. He stands and throws his napkin down. "Perhaps tomorrow you can respect everyone enough to be on time." Silence follows him as he walks out.

Arsehole.

Reed, Felicity, and Darcy are huddled together at one end, and Ivy and I make our way to them. Before I can sit, Reed has kicked my chair out, shifting it out of my hands the way he used to when we were kids.

"What the ever-loving hell was that for?" I ask.

The chair scrapes against the floor as I pull it back and sit down, filling our plates with food while Ivy pours me a tea.

"No thanks to you, I've ruined my diet," Reed pouts. Felicity leans forward to loudly whisper, "He's been stress baking gingersnaps."

While Darce smirks into her tea, Ivy openly laughs at Reed's misfortune while her hands are cupped around a mug of coffee that's more milk than caffeine.

"You're welcome," I joke. "Eat enough of them, and it might finally dislodge the stick that's up your arse."

Reed sips his tea with one hand while flipping me off with the other, and it takes me back twenty years in a blink. Christ, was he a pissy teenager.

Maybe this weekend won't be all bad.

"So how do you all spend the day?" Ivy asks, stuffing a croissant with berries before taking a bite. "Is there a game hall I haven't seen yet, or are we to line up single file so Richard can judge us formally?"

Reed rests his elbows on the table, a bad habit he's never grown out of. He's dressed casually, in a blue T-shirt and mismatched navy shorts. There's a fucking fedora on the table by his arm, and it's killing me not to take the piss out of him for it. "I overheard Kyle mention he wants to detox in the sauna, so that counts out anything involving the pool," he says, and I agree. "If you're a hand at tennis, Ivy, I was going to head to the court."

Ivy shifts eagerly in her chair. "I haven't played since middle school, but I've already missed my morning run, so I'd love to join you."

I try not to be jealous, but I'm not that much of a saint.

"Doubles?" Reed asks, turning to me with enough of a smirk that he knows exactly what I'm thinking.

"Count me out," Darcy says, pushing her empty cup away from her. "You're both too competitive. But I will referee. I don't trust either of you to not cheat." She ignores our mutual sounds of protest. "And I, for one, do not want to scare Ivy off so soon."

From the look on Ivy's face, I rather think it would have the opposite effect, but it makes me happy to hear Darcy so openly welcome her.

"Felicity?" Ivy asks. "Want to be my partner?"

"Tennis partner," I correct, not caring how nonsensical it sounds. There's no one in this room who would need the clarification, but it makes Ivy's cheeks flush any time I assert my claim on her, so I'll keep doing it.

Reed rolls his eyes while Darcy laughs at me, and for the first time in possibly my whole life, I'm glad to be here.

Proof positive that Ivy makes everything better.

"Sorry, but I don't play," Felicity says. "Haven't since I tore my rotator cuff in college."

"Not to worry," Reed says, standing. "We can rotate game play. Lincoln will likely need to rest his aching feet after one game."

"Speak for yourself, old man. It's not a competition," I say. "But if it was, you would lose."

Darcy brushes invisible crumbles off her skirt as she stands. "I hope you know what you signed up for, Ivy. A lifetime of this."

I curl my hand around Ivy's, knowing a single lifetime with her won't be enough, but I'll take it anyway.

What's the harm in a friendly match?

Darcy would argue — and does — that there should be a ban on my family in particular being allowed to host games of any sort. We've never been polite enough to each other to manage losing very well.

Or winning, for that matter.

Reed — always the organizer — has everything set up for us. The first issue comes when we're deciding who will play first. "Take a seat," he says. "First round is on me."

I should perhaps analyze why Ivy's calculating smile turns me on quite this much, but I'm also worried Reed won't go easy on her — I haven't forgotten how quickly he blamed her when there was little reason — so I step in. "No. You're against me. Ivy will play the winner."

He tips his head in silent agreement, but Ivy isn't as easy to convince, taking the racket from my hands and pointing it at the loungers, where Darcy and Felicity are spectating. "You, sit." She swings the racket to Reed. "You, serve."

"Yes, ma'am," he says, doing as instructed.

It's been years since I've seen Reed play, and while he's a little rusty, he's precise enough with every hit that I suspect he's taking it easy on her. Against anyone else, he'd win easily.

But Ivy is a rocket on the court, moving faster than Reed's expecting (faster than I'm expecting, honestly), sprinting like a squirrel to parry every backhand with one of her own.

Right around the time she's leading three-one, the moment is interrupted by the walking shitstain that is my cousin. "Does everyone get a round with Ivy?" Kyle leers as he strides over. "Count me in next."

I stalk toward him, my fists clenched, but Reed is over like a shot, his racket held to my chest, like that's going to hold me back. "If you're in such a hurry to lose," Reed says, "then we play doubles. Ivy and me versus you and Lincoln."

Kyle beams a winner's smile at me as he jogs backward to the baseline, and it prickles under my skin. *You haven't won anything yet, dickhead.*

As Reed and Kyle stare each other down from opposite ends of the court, I pull Ivy aside.

"Don't worry. I'll go easy on you," Ivy says, bouncing on the balls of her feet. She's practically giddy. But we both know that's not why I came over.

"Are you sure?"

Her whole face softens with fond concern, then the spark is back. She playfully pats my hip with her racket.

"Please. Ruin a millionaire's day? Sounds like a wish come true," she says, winking at me before turning to call out to Kyle. "Are we doing this or what?"

I'd rather invite Boris Johnson over for a sex party than be stuck within fifty meters of Kyle on any given day, and right now, I'm as close to bludgeoning him with this racket as I've ever been.

Instead, I play to lose. It goes against all my instincts when playing against my brother, but it's worth it to watch Kyle huff and puff his way around backcourt. I'm betting on him hemorrhaging before the sixth game.

As a bonus, I have plenty of time to admire Ivy's excellent form. As well as her tennis skills.

Reed manages an impressive dropshot to make it forty-love in our third game — take a wild guess who is losing — and while Kyle is losing his shit, I get the pleasure of seeing Ivy teach my brother an exploding fist bump. It heals something deep in my bones I hadn't realized was broken.

"What the fuck?" Kyle screams at me. "Do you want to get your balls back from your girlfriend or are you going to keep being useless?"

It's the wrong thing to say. Ivy's expression is set to kill, and on her next serve, she shoots an ace that has Kyle twisting to reach it.

He doesn't make it.

I wince as his foot twists under him, and the next thing I know, he's on his back, clutching at his leg and swearing up a storm. Fuck.

Felicity is on her feet before I can get to him, running into the house for ice, while Reed pulls his phone out, no doubt calling for a doctor. Kyle's on the floor, screaming bloody murder, but I barely hear a word.

No. My focus is Ivy, who's gone white.

CHAPTER 45
JOIN THE CLUB

IVY

Kyle gets helped back to the house by Dale's son (whose name I can't remember; I've been calling Fido because he's Kyle's little lap dog), overplaying his injury the entire way. He'll probably have a lawsuit drawn up before I even make it back inside.

I'm supposed to be here helping Lincoln, and instead, I'm pretty sure I just made shit a whole lot worse.

Beside me, he clearly has no such worries. "Serves him right," he says, placing his hands on my shoulders and checking me over, even though I'm fine. "Are you okay?"

I nod, the adrenaline still pulsating in my veins. It's not helping that he looks genuinely worried about me, making my weak heart beat double-time.

"Good," he says, pulling me into his chest. "Fucking Kyle."

"No, thank you," I whisper, wrapping my arms around him and breathing in his sun-kissed heat.

"That was an impressive move." Reed appears in my periphery. "Is everything all right?"

"Yes," I answer, stepping back from Lincoln. "Though I think for everyone's safety, I'm going to quit while I'm ahead."

Reed offers me a kind smile. It's the same one I've gotten from every one of the Reeveses, and I find I like this side of him. Better than the overbearing and judgy brother act. Maybe there is hope for them to work things out, after all.

"How about you?" he asks Lincoln. "Keen for another round? Best of three?"

Lincoln looks to me, a clear question in his eyes. I lean up on my tiptoes to kiss him on the cheek. "Keep playing. I'm going to grab a drink of water and hopefully not send anyone to the ICU on the way."

He tilts my head up and kisses me gently, the graze of his lips against mine sending a thrill through my entire body. "Be good," he says softly. "I'll come find you soon."

———

With nothing but my own curiosity to guide me, I do what any nosy person would do in my position. I wander.

There are tapestries on the walls (multiples, what a life) and — no lie — pillars holding up the ceiling in at least two of the sitting rooms. I mean, they're probably just decorative, but if the designer's goal was to intimidate the fuck out of every person who walks in, they've hit it out of the park.

I swear, if I find a library with a ladder in it, I'm going pre-makeover Eliza Doolittle on that thing.

The ceilings are about twelve feet high, held aloft by cracked plaster walls and damaged joists. My footsteps echo down the long hallway. I've never felt smaller.

Deacon's affinity for opulence is everywhere, although I'm not sure he'd care for the state of things. Dust clings to the draperies. Gold accents have darkened and dulled. And there's a cold, empty shadow hovering like a ghost in every room.

All this money, gone to waste. They could donate this building for community events or bulldoze it and use the land for low-income housing. Or anything. That's the point. There are a million possibilities open with this much money, and the Bradburys have done none of them.

It stings to walk the halls, knowing that a single room is filled with shit that could have covered my college tuition.

The way everyone (including Emma) talks about Deacon, he was a dick of the highest order. But I have to give him the teensiest bit of credit — all the gilding and theatrics make for one hell of a home. Every time I step around a corner, I'm expecting to find his ghost, judging my outfit and complaining that I'm being too loud. It doesn't take someone with my sister's intellect to work out why Astrid and her kids distanced themselves from the rest of the family. It also really makes me want to meet Lincoln's dad someday. I have a strong feeling I'd like him a lot.

Out of nowhere, a hand grabs my arm, pulling me into a room that's either a large cupboard or a small den.

"Oh, good. Just the person I was looking for," Judy says. Oh no.

A wall of shelves dominates the room, littered with boxes with their contents spilling out. There's a heavy wooden table pushed to one side, the pieces of a large puzzle spread out on it, and in the corner closest to the windows is Art, in a bright paisley shirt, stuffed into a worn-out armchair that must be as old as he is.

I think I just found their secret hideout.

"I've been hoping to talk to you," Judy says, pulling out the seat beside her at the table. Scattered on its surface are a sea of blue and white pieces surrounding a half-finished recreation of a cloudy sky over water. She probably looked for the most difficult one in the store.

I sit beside her and attempt a friendly smile, but really, my heart is thumping in my chest. Every time she sets her steely eyes on me, I feel like fish food.

"How are you liking it here so far?" she asks. It feels like a test.

"It's lovely," I lie.

Judy snorts a low laugh and turns around. "Did you hear that, Art? It's been lovely."

"About as lovely as a root canal," he deadpans while trying to hide a smile.

"Okay," I say, taking a gamble. "Maybe lovely is the wrong word. It's been…"

Judy surprises me by suggesting, "Bleak?" and Art adds, "Vexing?"

Huh. I may have completely misjudged them. They are hiding away here among a life's worth of odd purchases. Maybe they find this weekend as difficult as Lincoln does. It's a good cubby too. I'm pretty sure that's a piano hiding underneath a stack of newspapers.

How would Lincoln phrase it? "An adjustment."

In a move that surprises me so much I have to hold on to the table so I don't fall out of my chair, Judy laughs. It's a short bark that becomes a sigh when she casts a look over at Art.

"This is the last year, Art. I swear it. I'm sick of dragging myself here for their elevator pitch guilt trip. It's not my problem that they want to live in this hellhole. If they're struggling for money so badly, just sell the damn place."

Art hums. He's hunched over a small red box that's spilling wires out of its insides, and I can't tell whether he's trying to fix it or destroy it. "They wouldn't be in this mess if they stopped cleaning up that boy's messes."

Art, you beautiful man, now you have my attention. "What kind of messes?" I ask. This could be what I need to help Lincoln.

Judy smirks as she scours the table for a puzzle piece, her nails short but perfectly manicured. "Enough to get cut off finally."

Of course. That's why he's so hell-bent on getting Reed's investment.

Art's hands are paused mid-task as he stares at Judy

with the same gleeful interest that's bubbling in me. So much for my spy mission. I think I just hit the jackpot without even trying. "They finally grew a pair, huh? About time."

He picks up a screwdriver and starts twisting something I can't see. "Bribed that boy's entire way through schooling, and they expected him to turn out any differently? Deacon would be rolling in his grave if he knew about the ten million Kyle sank last year. And then," he says, waving the tool in the air, "they have the gall to accuse us of hiding some secret wealth from them and still expect us to play nice this weekend. Joe is livid."

Wow, so Dick's a dick. Color me shocked.

"Like father, like son," Judy says shrewdly. "Dad never listened when I told him Richie learned it from him. Even after he discovered his money had bought them a collegiate wing in exchange for the president ignoring Kyle's three sexual assault charges, he still refused to accept his part in it."

Art locks eyes with her, a small smile playing on his lips. "Careful, we're not supposed to know about that."

Jesus. I need to find Lincoln.

Judy sets the last piece of the lighthouse in place and lets out a soft laugh. "Just like how I'm pretending not to notice that the Louis Kalff lamp is missing from behind you?"

"I have no idea what you're talking about," he says proudly, and it's so obviously a lie I can't help but smile.

Art taps on the side of the box with his fist, but there's nothing but a blank screen. Judy clicks another piece into place. "Art, give it up. You've been trying to fix that old thing for twelve years. Put it out of its misery and put the radio on before I start hearing voices."

He does, and the soft strum of folk music springs forth from a portable radio I hadn't noticed. Art sinks back into the armchair and picks up a pad and pencil.

Judy looks up from her puzzle. "Has Kyle asked you for a loan yet?"

"Yesterday, in fact," Art replies, sounding as done with Kyle's BS as I am. We should start a club. Come to think of it, I might have just been pulled into my first meeting. "Joe's starting to waver, but I reminded him of exactly how much we've given that boy and the precise amount of zero he's repaid." There is black coating Art's fingertips and the edge of his palm. "I overheard him angling Dale for a job."

Judy's hand stills, a piece of cloud hanging in the air before she pushes it into place with a soft click. The calculating pinch between her eyes is back. "That's interesting. He came at me with the same request, albeit clumsily aimed at getting Hayden to add him as coproducer."

This grabs Art's attention, his head popping up in a shot, eyebrows raised in disbelief. "For the *Timeline* reboot?"

Judy nods.

"He asked Reed for a job too," I add, sensing chum in the water. Screw talking to Richard. It's clear his whole agenda is covering for his kid, but the rest of the family? The wheels are already turning. Maybe it's time to give them a little nudge. And, hey, my mouth got me into this mess; I might as well let it have some fun.

"Really?"

With fresh gossip on offer, Judy and Art turn to me. I keep my expression clear, even though I'm buzzing inside. "Yeah. Right after he pitched everyone on investing in his buddy's start-up. Reed shut both down."

"I wouldn't expect anything less, considering the verbal lashing Reed gave all of them at the will reading. Kyle must be getting desperate," Art says, immediately making him my new favorite person.

"Serves him right after those embezzlement rumors surfaced." Judy stretches her neck out. She's in a more casual outfit than I expected — a shift dress that seems at odds with all her right angles. There's pale pink on her nails and a hint of lip gloss on her thin lips. But she makes it work.

Art brushes excess charcoal off his pad, humming along to the radio. Papa passed when I was still a baby, but Nonna told Ciara and me stories; how he loved to ballroom dance, and would sit outside for hours, listening to birds sing. Wherever he is now, I like to imagine him in a garden, striped shirt and sun hat, a smile on his face.

Art reminds me of him, which I know is ridiculous and not even possible, but he hasn't stopped smiling since Judy hauled me in here. How does a man so full of life voluntarily stifle himself in this stuffy house every year?

I have to know.

"Art, why do you come here if you hate it so much?"

"Oh, it's not all bad," he says. "I never laugh half as hard as the drive home, when Joe is reading everyone for filth."

"Joe's funny?" I ask. I honestly can't picture it.

"Oh, yes," he says gleefully. "You wouldn't have recognized him fifty years ago. He was a rogue of the highest order."

"Like Lincoln," I say without thinking.

"Indeed," he replies, his eyes shining with mirth. It doesn't seem like it should work, Art's jubilance and Joe's intensity, but maybe there's balance in it. Maybe that's what real love is, falling for every version of your partner as you grow and change together, over and over again.

I wonder who Lincoln will be in fifty years. I want to meet him. To see if his eyes still sparkle with mischief. If he still takes an hour to wake up in the mornings. If he'll still look at me as though I'm the only one he ever wants to see.

"What are you sketching?" I ask, walking over to him.

He hands the pad to me, and just as I suspected, it's full of Joe. "He was my first model," he says. "Stumbled into my studio like a newborn foal one day, and I was smitten." As I flip through the pages, there are studies on hands, smiles, wrinkles, but even in these disparate parts, there is love in every line. "I never thought he'd be interested in me," Art says. "With his button-ups and vests, who his family was, it meant hiding a lot. We were "roommates" for a very long time."

"They're beautiful." I hand back the pad.

Art clasps his hand around mine briefly. "There will always be someone to disagree with who you are or how you live, but I can no longer allow the world to tell me who I am is wrong. The older you get, the more you recognize that no amount of 'comfort' is worth denying humanity. Let the bigots be uncomfortable."

"Bold words in this house," I chance, and Art smiles. "Here I was hoping I could spice things up by mentioning my torrid bisexuality at dinner tonight."

"Please do. Joe will love it," he chuckles. "I always knew Lincoln would find a good one." His scrutiny is gentler than Judy's, but no less intimidating.

All of a sudden, I don't want to lie anymore. Not about Lincoln. The way I feel about him is too big, too real.

"He's the good one, really." And fuck it, why shouldn't his family know? "He worked in a kitchen for years after what happened in Brussels, never spending a cent Deacon sent him, and he only ever uses it to help others. He made it affordable to live in my building again, and he wouldn't admit it, but I know he's been babysitting for Sheryl's two boys when she gets called into work." In fact, everyone who lives there has a story about how he's helped them, in big and small ways. Turning an empty space in the basement into a free gym, upgrading the laundry, installing shelves in Armando's kitchen. (Which I'm 90 percent sure was so Armando could stare at his thighs in jeans for an hour, and honestly, I can't blame him.) "I didn't know him when he was a kid, but I know the man he's become, and I'm proud to have him in my life."

Art and Judy share a look before he places his sketch pad down. I look over to find Judy has abandoned her puzzle.

"This weekend just got a lot more interesting," Art says, mischief shimmering in his eyes. "How about I break out the secret bottle of red we keep here, and you can tell us some more stories?"

I cross my arms over my chest. "On one condition: you tell me everything you know about Kyle and why he would try to steal from the trust."

Art's jaw drops into a laugh. "Ivy, welcome to the family."

CHAPTER 46
MATTERS OF THE
HEART

IVY

When we hit the end of the bottle, I excuse myself. My eyes are already stinging as I find the fastest way outside, avoiding any chance of bumping into Kyle by taking the front doors, and walk over to the pergola I spotted yesterday when we arrived.

I need fresh air. I need to pull myself together.

Outside, the kiss of the sun helps. Leaning against a pillar, I close my eyes, drinking in its fierce heat, taking long, slow breaths to dislodge the ache in my chest.

I can't stop thinking about Mom.

It's so obvious Lincoln has family who cares about him. Maybe not all of them, but enough. And he doesn't see it. He hears their care only as criticism, not concern.

Suddenly, I'm hearing Mom's fears for the first time. How many times have I leaped and left her to stand on the sidelines to watch and hope her words would be enough to keep me safe?

I'm so grateful for her, but I can't remember if I've ever told her that.

When she picks up, I skip right past pleasantries with "I love you" and follow it immediately with "I'm sorry that you have to worry about me so much."

"Don't be silly," she replies, and the sound of a TV gets quieter until I hear the click of a door closing. "I will always worry about you and your sister. But I know I don't always trust you to make your own decisions."

"No, you don't. I have good instincts, Mom, and I'm ready to try things my way for a little while. I want you to be okay with that, but I won't change my mind if you aren't."

"I know." The fondness in her voice brings tears to my eyes. "Just promise me you'll keep me in the loop. I don't handle surprises well."

That's an understatement. "I promise. I couldn't keep a secret from you if I tried." And I've tried. "In fact, you should probably sit down, because there are a few things I need to tell you. Starting with my landlord…"

Sometimes I wonder if my heart works correctly.

Lincoln wants the whole nine yards with someone, and I can't even decide which ice cream flavor is my favorite. I shouldn't even be eating ice cream because I'm almost certain I'm lactose intolerant.

Pain lances through my heart, sharp and deep, because I'm stealing something from Lincoln, even if he's offering it up freely and plentifully.

It hurt waking up next to him, my nose buried in his

neck, the faint rumblings of his hummed exhales against my lips.

It hurt when he woke up and smiled at me, fuzzy with sleep and so sweet I wanted to rip my heart out of my chest, so I didn't have to feel it anymore.

He might want me now, but how long will that last? Maybe he just misses the sex. I know I do. (Every hopeful corner of my heart is screaming that he doesn't. That he wants more. But it's still in time-out from the last person it pulled this shit with, so she can scream into the void while I keep us both protected).

Living the fantasy is easy. The reality is so much scarier.

We need to talk about it, but every time I try, it hurts enough that I can't get the words out.

I'm just asking for one love story before I go. Just one. That's not too much to ask for, is it? One person out of eight billion?

It can't be normal to want this much. Some days it feels endless and beyond reach. So much so that I'm scared I'll never be able to fill the well inside me. That even if I'm lucky enough to meet someone, I'll ruin it simply by wanting.

What if I find love and it's not enough?

What if I'm not enough?

LOVE, the kind that eclipses lowercase and blares with the wattage of a Broadway marquee, dogs my steps like Eurydice. Longing threatens to choke me with every breath. But I'm terrified if I ever attempt to search for it, I'll turn and find out the truth — it's not there and never will be.

So, I don't look, and I keep on pretending.

But sometimes… Sometimes I can almost believe it, especially when Lincoln looks at me.

Maybe that's why faking it with Lincoln isn't easy anymore. Everything he does fills the gap, but I have to keep reminding myself it's not real.

When it isn't a show for his family, it's a study for his work or practice for his dream girl.

And I agreed to it. Hell, I started it. It wasn't Lincoln's foot getting lodged in my mouth at the ball, getting into this mess. It wasn't Lincoln who said too much at the restaurant and led Kyle to blackmailing him.

This is my own fault.

Just like in school. Just like every other time I've slipped on my own imagination and fallen head-over-heels into a fantasy.

Limerence is a hell of a drug.

Which is why I need to put an end to this. As soon as the weekend is over, I'm going to bow out. Curtain call, no reprises, no encores. Done.

I want the steel in his voice when he fights for me, the gentleness in his eyes when he's reassuring me, the strength of his desire when he's kissing me.

I want his slow wake-ups and sly grins and undivided attention.

I want the overboard gifts and poetic seductions and the grip of his hand in mine.

I want, I want, I want.

It's all I've known since we met, an endless sea of

want that might drown me if he wasn't keeping me afloat.

Wanting has always been easier than having.

Wanting requires nothing but an object of desire. It's fulfilling, an act of giving over to myself, of finding every gap in my heart and pouring myself into it until the emptiness is less noticeable.

Having risks everything.

It takes holding out all the soft, fragile parts and saying "This is me" and "I'm yours," knowing how easily they can be broken.

It's so much easier to pretend, because the alternative? The idea that this is real? It's terrifying.

And I've never wanted anything more.

CHAPTER 47
THE NIGHT IS YOUNG AND ROMANTIC

IVY

By the time I get off the phone with Mom, it's a rush to get ready before dinner. But I still manage to squeeze every juicy secret I've learned from Judy and Art into a half an hour ramble. Maybe it's the thrill of finally being a step ahead, but I don't hesitate to slip into the yellow dress, wearing my family pendants on a fine gold chain, and hope it's not obvious to Lincoln when my heart skips a beat as he takes one look and calls me "absolutely gorgeous."

He hadn't been able to get a word in while I'd dissected all the Kyle information I'd gathered, nodding and humming in the way he does when he's in deep thought. But it was impossible to miss the clench of his jaw or the steel in his eyes. The moment we left our room, he fit his hand in mine, and he hasn't let go since.

Dinner is no less awkward the second go around, but at least now when I catch Judy's eyes on me, I'm not worried she's going to skewer me with her salad fork.

She's still quietly terrifying, her fine hair slicked

behind her ears and falling in harsh lines to her shoulders. But now that I can look at her without fear of turning into a pillar of salt, I can see that she and Astrid have the same nose.

Tonight is scallop ceviche followed by poached seabass. It's delicious, but I'm sure it would taste even better if the soundtrack for tonight wasn't the dull scrape of knives and forks under a hum of barely contained distaste from our host. Richard once again manages to dominate the conversation (I use that term extremely loosely).

The best part of the meal is that Kyle is holed up, nursing his injury in his room.

When we finally get to escape after dinner, Lincoln surprises me by pulling me to the right, in the direction of the gardens rather than the left of our bedroom. "Come, it's a beautiful night."

He should know by now that I'll follow him anywhere.

Palatial is the only word that comes to mind as we cross through a thick wall of hedges into the gardens. They are a panorama of green, even in the moonlight. Lush on the outside but overgrown the farther in we walk. Like all things Bradbury, it's about looking like you care, but not actually doing it.

I'm half expecting to be announced as we enter the inner grounds where the fountain lies, as though there are people hiding in the bushes waiting to say, "Mr. Lincoln Reeves and guest," or perhaps one day — my poor, romantic heart supplies — "Mr. and Mrs. Lincoln Reeves."

I've never been decided on marriage.

That's what I tell people.

The reality is I did picture it once, a long, long time ago. Ciara and I loved to play dress-up, and when I discovered Mom's veil packed away in the attic, I did what most kids do. I slipped it on and stared at my reflection and told myself that one day, a prince would come whisk me away.

I was six.

Twenty years later, and I guess I'm still that little girl, only now my prince is a six-foot-four tattooed millionaire who fills my room with roses and has an accent that makes my knees weak.

Hidden behind the tall hedge that separates us from the house, we walk toward the fountain at the center of the gardens, where cold, uncomfortable stone benches stand watch. The steady trickle of water is hypnotic. Everything else is a world away. We are completely alone.

The sun disappeared beyond the horizon a few hours ago, and any lingering warmth has abruptly retreated now, the night air whipping through my body like a cold front.

"Here," Lincoln says. "I'll keep you warm."

I slip easily into his arms, where heat is rolling off him in waves. Clasping my hand, Lincoln begins to sway us in a silent dance.

It's so beautiful, so perfect, and all I want to do is cry.

He can't know it, but he's given me a gift. A lifetime

of memories to treasure, moments to live and relive, over and over again.

I sigh and press myself closer still, though I'll never be close enough.

"I've always hated coming here," he says. "Misery everywhere, breeding resentment." We continue to sway. "I thought it was impossible to make good memories here, but you've proved me wrong," he says softly, and the gentle stroke of his fingers along my spine is so deeply good that tears begin to prickle at my eyes. I bury my face in his shirt and nod, not trusting my voice. "Never thought I'd get this, either."

Lincoln's grip tightens around my hand, mirroring my heart, which clenches tight enough I can almost hear it cracking. How could I ever explain to him how long I've wanted to hear those words? It would be so easy to dive in, to go all-in and forget how much of this has been for show.

"It's not like you to be so quiet," he says. "What are you thinking about?"

"You," I admit. "Us."

Even in the darkness, his smile is devastating to my senses. "You have good instincts, darling. You should trust them."

Trust… how perfect that we've come full circle.

He asked me once if I trusted him, and I do. In some ways, more than myself. But do I trust real life not to tear us apart? Do I trust we can make it work when he hasn't been in a long-term relationship? When I haven't?

What if he's only fulfilling my needs? Or am I just a

prototype for his fantasies? A dress rehearsal before the real thing?

The questions pile up like dirty dishes in my mind, and I know I can't put off the answers any longer.

"Unless you regret tying yourself to me?" he asks with enough concern that I know I can't do this anymore.

"No," I insist in a rush. "Not at all. That's not…" I shake my head.

Words, words, words. Constantly getting me in trouble. Always getting in my way when they'll cause the most damage.

Never there when I need them.

It's been happening since school. If I went a week without a teacher telling me to be quiet, they worried there was something wrong. I've long accepted that my inability to shut my mouth at the right time would get me in trouble, and I've simply learned how to navigate my way out of it. But it's when the words dry up, when my emotions grow so large even language isn't enough to capture it, that I know I'm in too deep.

"Because I'm glad for it," Lincoln says, dipping his chin as if to kiss me.

I might stop breathing in the second I wait for something to happen, but I've gone so still I ruin it, and Lincoln pulls back before our lips can meet.

He takes a seat on a nearby bench, pulling me in with both hands. "Something's wrong," he says, eyes shining up at me.

"How could anything be wrong in this perfect place?"

But as always, he sees beneath the facade, straight to the heart of me. I let my breath go. "Tell me something true," I plead, threading my hand into his beautiful hair, needing an anchor.

"Kyle is a wanker."

I can't help a small laugh. "I already knew that. Tell me something else. Something I don't know."

He draws his hands up my thighs and hips, the heat of his palms easy to feel through the thin material of my dress. "If you let me, I'm going to make every moment of your future as wonderful as you are."

It's the kind of thing I wouldn't blink twice at if he'd said it around his family. But there's no one here but us. No one to play the part for.

"I wish this was real," I whisper into the dark.

There's day-old stubble on his cheek. It scratches my palm a little as he leans into my touch, his eyes never leaving mine. The sincerity there is almost too much to take. "It is for me. Tell me what I need to do to make it real for you too."

It's a good thing he's holding me up, because I'm not sure I can feel my legs anymore.

"Is this not real?" he asks, pulling my hand up to kiss. "Is this?" He kisses the corner of my mouth. "What you feel is real."

You think I don't know that? What I'm feeling is the problem.

I don't want to be everyone's taste. I'm acquired. I want to linger.

I want to be the bar by which all other performances are measured and compared.

The legacy.

I drop my forehead against his shoulder. It's broad, and I remember the way they flexed under my palms that night. Physically, I'm strong. But no deadlift in the world can protect my heart in this moment.

"Lincoln, I…" My breath escapes, shaky. "I don't think I can do this anymore." It's too hard.

His chest rises and falls in a controlled inhale. "And what's that?"

"Pretend," I whisper against his shirt. Maybe it's ridiculous to be having this conversation with my head buried in his chest, but if I look up, I'll lose my nerve. "I know I said it didn't mean anything, but I was wrong. I can't pretend anymore because I've really fallen in love with you."

Lincoln takes my chin in his grip, tilting my head back until we lock eyes. The anger and fear I've been expecting isn't there, only warmth. Fondness. Love.

"I know, darling."

CHAPTER 48
I LOVE YOU (BELIEVE ME)

LINCOLN

Now I know why there's always been an ache in my chest, a hunger never satisfied. A part of myself held just out of reach.

My devotion has been with her, waiting to find its way back to me.

"You know?" Ivy asks, blinking up at me with fear in her eyes. It'll be the last time she ever doubts my devotion. I'll make sure of that.

"I told you — you don't need to hide anything from me."

I'll be glad to be rid of the pretense. I can't look at her and not feel my heart swell with love. There's no hiding from how much I want to keep her. I want her to know that every word I've ever said has been real.

"Darling," I say, hating the fall of her shoulders, the hurt that creases her brow. It's killing me. "Come here." Gently, I pull her into my arms, just to hold her.

"My heart is yours," I say, hoping to coax it back as I

ghost my knuckles along her jaw. She's the sun, moon, and stars, and I'm merely a lonely astronaut, caught in orbit around her. "Wholeheartedly and without reservation. It's been devoted to you since we met, and I don't care how that sounds. Take it. Take anything you want. I'll give it freely. Nothing could possibly compare now that I've fallen for you. A hundred — no, a million — sunsets, wouldn't suffice."

The moonlight shimmers off her skin, cool where she should always be warm. For years, I've attempted to fulfill the fantasies of strangers, but right now, I'd settle for being hers. She's everything all at once, a little at a time. The meaning of life condensed and distilled. It's never too much, could never be such a thing.

"I'm not going anywhere," I tell her, meaning every word. "You're not going anywhere. I just found you. I'm never letting you out of my sight. I'm only sorry that being with me means choosing all of this," I wave toward the house, "as well."

"I happen to like some of this," she says.

"Then I don't see a problem, because I've fallen in love with you, and though I'd prefer not to, I'm not going to give you up without a fight."

Ivy blinks. "You're in love with me?"

"Desperately."

She's a powerhouse. An ever-burning star, rocketing through the night sky. And even when she's passed, the memory of her light stays with you, lighting the wick of hope within you.

"But I'm messy," she says, and it wouldn't be Ivy if she wasn't attempting to talk her way out of even this.

"You're relaxed."

She huffs, disbelieving. "I'm emotional."

I slide my hands to her back, guiding her more firmly between my legs until I can rest my chin on her stomach. Starlight surrounds her. "Your passion is one of the things I love best about you."

"And I wake up early." I start nodding, undeterred. "And I'll talk your ear off, and I'll hum all the time—"

I pull her into a kiss, licking into her sweet mouth until I feel her melting against me.

"I'll still love you," I say, the words captured in the small gap between us. "I love every version of you that exists and every version I've yet to meet. And even if you don't believe me, it's okay." I reach for her, sliding my hands up her neck, cupping her jaw. "Because I'll get to prove it to you." Her lips are soft as I kiss them. "Over and over again. Every minute of every day." More kisses, each gentler than the last. "And I'll keep on loving you, through every fight, every broken sleep—"

"Every awful weekend?" she suggests, gripping my forearms, a tear breaking free from her lashes. I kiss this too.

"May we have many," I joke in a whisper, my chest lifting when she finally smiles.

"You're too much." Ivy clings to my shirt, pulling.

"I'll try to stop," I say between kisses.

"Don't," she breathes. "Never stop."

There's nothing left to do except kiss her, slowly, deliberately, knowing now we have time, so much time, forever — because I won't allow anything less. "Your very existence commands my attention. Being in love with you comes naturally. There is no choice. I could stop it no easier than I could my heart from beating."

CHAPTER 49
YOU, ME, US

IVY

The sound of a car starting as we exit the garden almost knocks me off my feet. I'd be on my ass if Lincoln didn't catch me.

"Is that Astrid?" I squint through the dark, but all I can make out is a tan coat. It's almost midnight. "Where is she going?"

"I'm sure I don't know," he says, but his concern saturates every word. When I check, his expression is pinched, stress hardening the corners of his eyes, mouth.

"Hey," I say, squeezing his hand. "I'm sure it's nothing." There's an ache in my chest, to dig in, distract, offer solace with hands and lips and teeth. But the line between real and role is already too blurred, and I'm too tired to fake a smile if he refuses. "Maybe she has a secret lover," I joke.

"Excuse me?"

"I asked her about Paris, and she answered like

she'd snuck out her window to make out with someone."

"I do not want the details."

"Party pooper," I say as we watch Astrid quietly ease her car down the driveway.

"When it's your mum, we'll see how you like it." Okay, fine, he has a point.

"Still, I'm kind of proud of her. Sneaking out to see her secret boyfriend? It's so sexy."

Lincoln growls, and before I can react, he picks me up over his shoulder and walks through the side entrance and up the stairs.

I bounce as he drops me onto the bed, momentarily blinded by my blood singing in my veins. I'm going to need him to do that again. A hundred times. Then follow me onto it and cage me in and ravage me. I'm disappointed when he doesn't, merely standing at the end of the bed while he slips his jacket off and folds it. Fuck if that isn't doing it for me, though.

"Never use the words sexy to describe my mum."

"Oh, she's too old to be sexy?"

"No one's too old to be anything, especially that. But that doesn't stop her from being my mum."

"Well, I think she's incredibly sexy. It must be where you get it from." Finally he climbs onto the bed, covering my mouth with his hand while I giggle underneath.

"Now where were we?" he asks, kissing me.

The first time we slept together, it was fire and heat, and I wanted it faster, my blood racing in my veins.

Now time slows, and I want to stop it, take our time, soak in every touch until I know the shape of it as well as my own face. I can't let him go long enough to make it easy, but he doesn't seem to care. We kiss, long, sweeping arcs of tongue, remembering and relearning all at the same time.

I think I'm babbling. Can hear hushed promises between breaths, between kisses, the words pouring out of me as neatly as water.

"Oh god," I say, pulling at his shirt, tugging up, up, up, until it's off and I finally get my hands on his skin. "We could have been doing this for weeks." I'm scrambling to get my hands, my mouth, on those tattoos.

"Slow down," he says. But he's just as eager, pulling my dress up over my head. "We have all night."

It's not enough time. A lifetime wouldn't be enough.

"Hey," Lincoln says. With his hand in my hair, he tips my head back and holds me there, his eyes dark. Everything in me calms. "I love you. Everything I am is yours."

Oh god, this is it. It's real.

Words escape for the second time tonight, but it's okay, because he knows. Just like he's always known. What I need. Who I am.

I can't get enough of him, barely leaving enough space for either of us to undress, but he manages it. So capable. Fuck, I love him.

"Fuck me," I gasp, and Lincoln responds by wrapping his thick arms around my back and lifting me into his arms, our mouths never separating as he settles me in his lap. I can feel how hard he is, and I moan into his mouth at the thought of him inside me again, finally, after all this time.

When he starts to pull away, I stop him. I don't want anything between us. Not anymore.

"I've got the all-clear if you want to go without," I tell him.

Lincoln digs his fingers into my ass with a low growl. "Fuck, of course I want you. Are you sure?"

I nod, frantic.

"All right," he says, kissing me and adjusting his grip to tease my clit with his fingertips. "Nothing to report for me either," he adds, softly stroking me.

My thighs are wet already, and I rub against his cock, making sure he knows how sure I am. I want this. I need him.

"Fuck, darling. Don't worry. I've got you."

He lifts me up with one hand, using the other to position himself. We fumble it the first time, but I don't care, because he's here, and he loves me, and I get to touch his laughter with my tongue and drink in his groan when he finally slides inside me, raw.

Yes.

Lincoln runs his hands up my back, tangles them in my hair, and I let my head fall back. He takes the opportunity to run his teeth down the sensitive part of my neck before soothing it with his tongue.

All while being buried deep.

I swear I can feel his heartbeat through his cock. Or maybe that's mine. He attacks me with a kiss when I squeeze around him, my silent plea for him to move, to fuck me like he promised.

"I love you," he breathes into my mouth, rising to his knees and slamming his hand against the wall behind me.

Then he moves.

God. Fuck. How did I ever exist without him? Without this?

He fucks me with the same single-minded determination he uses for everything, filling me in long, deep thrusts, his fingers leaving bruises on my hip. His words stamping their place on every corner of my heart.

"I want every part of you, all of it. I love your messes. Christ, you don't know what it does to me to wake up and see you in my apartment. You don't even have to be there, just leave something behind—"

I tangle my hands in his perfect hair, gripping it between my fingers, kissing everywhere I can reach, rolling my clit against him.

"Whoever and wherever you want to be, I want you. I've looked my whole life for you. I'm not letting go now."

When I come, it rolls over me in a wave so overwhelming I bury my face in Lincoln's shoulder, my cry muffled against his skin. Sweat sticks my hair to my forehead, and he pushes it back as he picks up his pace, and god, his thighs must be burning, but he doesn't stop until he's groaning into a kiss, and I feel the hot pulse of his dick as he comes inside me.

Exhausted, we slump into the bed in a conjoined heap, neither of us seeming to want to let go yet. If it didn't mean staying in this cold monument, I'd stay like this for a week.

Lincoln dots a series of gentle kisses over my face, his palms searing as they cup my cheeks. I'm too busy floating to do much more than lie there and sink into them.

Because this isn't any other Ivy, and it isn't Lincoln playing a game. It's him and me and us, and the ice my heart has been treading over has completely and utterly melted, slipping into the warm bath of his affection.

It's incredible.

No holding back, not anymore.

No, I'm going to give everything over, because he wants it, but more than that, he can handle it. Gently. With care. With love. And he does.

"Love you," I whisper when he disappears and returns with a washcloth, cleaning me up with a tenderness that threatens to spill my heart out onto the sheets.

I should probably do something back, not just lie here and soak in the pleasure, but it's hard enough to think. Besides, he doesn't look like he's complaining. He likes me this way — compliant, supplicant. Loves it.

So do I.

Strange to think all I needed to do was give myself permission for this. A lifetime of worrying about chasing passion, and why?

Maybe the rest was fleeting, but Lincoln isn't. Could never be. He's immovable.

Persistent.

When he says he's going to prove his love, over and over, I know he means it. And even though he doesn't need to prove it beyond this, because I believed him before he ever said the words, felt it in every kiss since the beginning, before I would ever let myself accept it, I know he won't stop. I won't stop.

CHAPTER 50

DON'T WORRY, BE HAPPY

LINCOLN

I'm expecting to wake up to Ivy wrapped around me again, only this time I won't need to hold myself back from kissing my way down her body until I can feast on her.

There's no better way to wake up, in my opinion.

But she's not touching me at all when I finally blink my eyes open. She's lying on her side out of my reach, which is a crime I immediately seek to rectify.

The sheet is pulled up over her head, and when I slip it off only to get blinded by the light of her phone screen, I realize why.

Ivy rolls over, looking sheepish. "I didn't want to startle you."

"Yes, this is far more reassuring." When I pluck the phone from her fingers, leaving it out of her reach, Ivy playfully kicks out, but only ends up tangling our legs together.

"Come here, beautiful." I take advantage of the position and wrap my arms around her until there's no space left between us.

She tastes as divine now as she did last night, maybe more so, because she doesn't hold back as I kiss her. No more pulling away. God, I'm so fucking done with that, and, it seems, so is Ivy. She's clinging to me like she wants to crawl under my skin and live there.

Fuck knows I'd rather attend one of Manny's poetry jams than deal with government tape. I don't need a piece of paper to confirm how committed I am. To myself or anyone else. As long as I can spend the rest of my life with her.

That said, I do like the idea of wearing a ring, of a little piece of her I could have with me. Could just get the damn thing tattooed on, since she's already imprinted on every corner of my heart.

Speaking of permanent markings, I finally get to indulge myself, nipping and licking my way down her torso. "Tell me about the tattoos."

"You first," she breathes, arching into me, then whining when I rise up on my elbows and wait her out. "Fine."

"Good girl," I whisper into her skin.

Ivy starts with the turtle doves. "This was a gift to myself for my twenty-first birthday, because it's nice, believing love is close by. No matter how many times it feels like I've given a piece of my heart away and not gotten it back, this part will always stay with me."

It's heartbreaking that she could ever be treated like that. Whatever she's missing, I'll patch with my own.

"Now this one," I say, licking over the cursive *Wait for me* that lies at the base of her ribs.

"It's a quote from *Hadestown*," she says, gasping when I suck her nipple into my mouth. It's indescribable to have someone as strong-willed as Ivy following my command. "I'm thinking of getting roses added to it."

I crawl back up to taste the smile from her lips.

"I've always wanted a paw or a cat somewhere, in honor of my old calico, Mimi. This one here," she points to the tattoo of a set of lips, in bright pink, purple, and blue on her left thigh, "is an homage to *Rocky Horror*, but bi, because why not?"

I follow her with my mouth. "Indeed."

Ivy squirms under my tongue. "Don't make fun of me. I saw that *He-Man* sword on your calf."

I fit myself between her legs, licking up the seam of her pussy. "I wouldn't dream of it, darling."

Breakfast can wait.

———

I slip out of our bedroom on strict instructions to only return with food and an exorbitant amount of coffee. It's a command easily followed, since I have no better plans today than to count every way I can please her.

However, my good mood sours when Kyle corners me in the hallway.

He's been on my ass since we arrived, like a fungal infection I can't shake. Every time I want to get Reed alone, something I expect Kyle should want, there he is, slithering his way in, needing to make sure I hold up my side of the deal. He's not wrong to do so. I'd rather attend a gun rally than do him a favor, but what choice do I have?

"I really thought you'd try harder than this," he says. "But I guess you really are as useless as everyone's always said."

"Big words coming from such a small man. I've heard a few things about you this weekend. Mum and Daddy finally cut you off, I see."

But the reaction I'm hoping for never comes, and dread returns as Kyle just laughs. "That's how you want to play it? Fine. Go fuck yourself. I'll get what I deserve either way."

"Finally, something we can agree on."

He sneers. "Don't say I didn't warn you."

There's no chance Reed is going to give Kyle a job. He hates him more than I do, which means there's only one way this ends, and that's with him finding out about Pulse.

I should be the one to tell him. Rip the Band-Aid off and face it. But his opinion of me is already on shaky ground, and I'm not exactly in a rush to ruin it for good.

Kyle's never followed through on anything in his life. Maybe all of this is a fool's game, a bluff played by a desperate man. What does he stand to gain by exposing me? Nothing.

It's in his best interest to keep it and try again.

Later, when shit hits the fan, I'll look back on this decision and laugh.

CHAPTER 51
MUM'S THE WORD (DON'T HATE ME)

LINCOLN

Why am I fighting this? Reed has made no secret of how little he respects me, and that's without knowing the truth.

I've been maintaining a lie for so long, I managed to convince myself that, eventually, he'd see me as I hope to be, not as the foolish kid he's set on remembering me as.

Perhaps it's worth calling Kyle's bluff and seeing how this plays out. Rip off the Band-Aid. Call the game.

Leave the past where it belongs.

I take petty pleasure in loading up on food for Ivy — berries, croissants, a generous serving of yogurt (with a sneaky side of marmalade, because I will convince her it's delicious if it kills me). Richard says nothing, but his breathing has a distinctly loud disdain embedded in it.

When I reach the stairs back to the bedrooms, I find Darcy attempting in vain to get information out of Mum about her trip. I'm more interested in what the hell she was doing sneaking out last night, but if Ivy is right, I don't need the visual. Or the confirmation.

Before I can pass, Mum's arm shoots out. "Lincoln, do you have a moment?"

My hands are full, so I simply raise them in explanation, only to find them abruptly empty when Darcy steals the dishes off me. "I'll take these to Ivy," she says innocently. They've definitely been talking about me, then. "I even promise to let her put pants on first."

I follow Mum to one of the draftier sitting rooms, where Richard has knocked down Deacon's mahogany bookshelves and replaced them with a fake stone wall and a flatscreen television. It physically hurts to look at, and a small part of me weeps at what might have become of the first edition Alexandre Dumas collection I'd always hoped to inherit.

"How are you?" Mum asks, sitting uncomfortably straight on a leather bench seat that looks as though it was carved in stone. As I sit beside her, I realize it feels that way as well.

"Fine," I say, condensing down a thousand feelings into as quick an answer as I can hope to achieve. Where would I even start? The fact that I'm deeply in love with the most amazing woman? That Kyle is currently attempting to blackmail his way into Reed's pocket? That I still miss London and Dad, but also, inexplicably, her, even though she's right here, because I haven't the first clue how to talk to her?

Surely "fine" covers all that.

"How was Paris?" I ask in return.

"My trip was," she smiles, "enlightening." There are

twin pink spots on her cheeks. I know without a doubt Ivy guessed correctly, and I definitely do not want any more details than that.

But I am absolutely certain I need to be there when Reed gets a clue. He'll probably short out.

In the years since the divorce, we've never spoken about it — who stayed, who left, who got hurt. Not one word, because why would we ever talk about the wound when we can pick at it, never let it heal?

Ivy is right. I have been distracting myself. "Do you blame me for choosing Dad?"

Mum doesn't look mad, or even disappointed. No, she smiles. It's small, and yes, sad, but still genuine, and it cracks open something in my chest that I'm not prepared for.

"I was hurt in the beginning," she says, looking down at her lap, where she's habitually rubbing her thumb and forefinger together. She catches herself, stops, flattens her hands over her skirt. There are more wrinkles than I remember. "Can I be honest? I think we're both old enough for it now."

I nod and prepare myself.

"It made it harder, that your father and I separated amicably. If I hated him, I could have blamed him for taking you away from me. But I didn't. And if I couldn't blame him, and I couldn't blame you, all that left was the hurt and a distance between us I've been attempting to bridge ever since."

A few years ago, I would have argued this point. What good were her intentions if they never reached me? We should have had this conversation years ago.

But I'm as much to blame as anyone. "I know I haven't made it easy for you."

She offers me an understanding smile. "No, but I'm proud of you for that. And I'm proud of you for the choice you made. I know how much it meant to your father, and despite my hurt, I've always been glad knowing that you were together, looking after each other."

"Keeping an eye on each other, you mean." I rub at my jaw, the scratch of new growth telling me it's not just a haircut I'm overdue for. Though I suspect Ivy will have some opinions on both, if last night (and this morning) is any indication.

Mum raises her hand to my cheek, a move she used to employ when I'd messed up. I suppose she felt it softened the blow of her disappointment. But this time, it comes with undisguised humor. It reminds me so much of Darcy, I almost want to laugh. "Lincoln, I mean this with love, but you are, and have always been, your father's son. I knew the moment he held you that I was in trouble."

Perhaps trouble is all I've ever been. "It would have been easier if I was more sensible, like Reed."

She *tsks*. "Reed is too sensible for his own good. He could learn a thing or two from you, frankly. We all can. Darling, you're exactly who you're meant to be. Yourself. We've all made missteps, and the best of us learn from them. You need to give yourself more credit. So does your brother."

It's more than I ever expected to hear, and for a moment, all I can do is stare at the awful painted foam stuck on the wall while my heart does something complicated in my chest.

She stares at me the way only a mother can, with absolute authority. "I don't see why you're so intent on misreading how much we care about you. But that hasn't stopped us yet, and love, nothing will."

Perhaps. If I am guilty of getting it wrong, of only seeing what I was set on believing and nothing else, we've lost a lot of time.

To her credit, Mum quickly hides her surprise when I hug her, pressing a gentle squeeze to my shoulders before pulling back. As a kindness, I won't bring up the tears in her eyes. "Thank you," I say. "I needed to hear that."

CHAPTER 52
CAT'S OUT
LINCOLN

Kyle hobbles into the dining room at dinner, exaggerating his injury like he's playing the World Cup. No one's seen him since breakfast, and I'd hoped Ivy and I could get through our last night without his smug face ruining it.

The meal is an exercise in patience. It's hard to believe that I once thought Deacon's parties were excruciating, an excuse for him to puff himself up and lord over us all for three days straight. They're a walk in the park compared to this.

Richard seems intent on making us dread every second we're here, like some ridiculous comeuppance for being denied his "rightful inheritance." As if we aren't all sitting in the multimillion-dollar estate he was left.

Joe looks like he's regretting being alive for any of it. If I thought Art could lie convincingly, Joe surely would have faked his death by now. A few times over, most likely.

If tonight gets any worse, I might have to join him.

Beside me, Ivy is coiled tight with tension, her thigh clenched under my palm. Kyle is sneering across the table with so much intention it sets my blood on fire.

Then he clears his throat and stands, and I know, without a shadow of a doubt, my hens have come home to roost. "I know it's customary on the last night for the birthday boy to make a speech," he says, pasting on his gummy smile. "But I'm hoping you won't mind if I say a few words instead."

"I already said I don't need to bother with all that," Joe grumbles.

Kyle ignores him, victory in his eyes. "Trust me, you want to hear this."

There are a few wants I have that are nonnegotiable. Ivy, happy and by my side, preferably forever; that's number one. My family in good health is another. A single fish & chip shop in this damn country that can make a proper chippy; absolutely crucial.

But in this moment, I can't think of anything I want more than to not hear what Kyle says next.

"This weekend is supposed to be about commitment to this family, but someone here has done nothing but lie to every single one of us, and I'm here to set the record straight."

"Just get on with it," I growl, but I know he won't. He's enjoying this too much.

"Lincoln, something you want to add? Or maybe your girlfriend does?" His face contorts cruelly. "No, nothing? And you're normally so chatty." Screw family.

I'm going to kill him, and honestly? I'm not sure anyone would stop me.

"We've graciously opened up our home to you all because family was important to Pop," Kyle continues.

A few seats down, Judy lays down her spoon and rolls her eyes.

"You come here every year, pretending to get along, and we ignore what we know is being said behind our backs. But I've had enough of being treated like the asshole when I'm the only person in this room who isn't ashamed to be himself."

I fucking wish he would be and save us all.

He's aiming his words at Reed now, no smile to hide his malice anymore. "You don't even have the honor to take Deacon's name, but you'll take everything else? And then you sit there and act like you're better than us, talking about how family is important when you don't do shit for us. You took his money, and you kept it all for yourselves. You're worse than we are, because if Dad had gotten everything like he should have, we would have at least made sure you had something."

Kyle places both hands on the table, taking the time to glare at every person present. I was wrong. This isn't solely about money. The prick took his personal failures to make anything of himself and convinced himself it's our fault. No wonder Mr. Silver's popularity pissed him off. He's fucking jealous.

"But now it's time for you to get what you deserve," he continues. "Because guess what? Your family isn't perfect. Isn't even close. Well, guess what, dickheads? Your brother gets paid to whore his voice out for strangers. All that time you spent wondering how he paid for shit after you cut him off?" Kyle scoffs. "There's your answer. You're related to a digital prostitute."

Darcy is staring daggers at him. "The term is sex worker now, you uneducated twat."

"Fuck you, Darcy," Kyle replies.

She leans back and crosses her arms over her chest. "Yes, threatening me with incest is really making you look like less of a wanker."

The silence that descends is as bleak as I'd imagined it, and Kyle smiles, triumphant, despite the fact that his foot must be throbbing by now.

"I haven't called a sex line in years. Are they cheaper now?" Betty asks, and Art promptly chokes on his water, his shoulders racking with shakes that I can see are mostly laughter.

I don't know why I answer her. I blame the shock. "I couldn't tell you, Nan. I narrate intimate experiences for an online app. It's not quite the same thing."

"Not far off," Kyle sneers.

Betty is nodding. "Oh, that's nice. I spoke with a lovely young man on one after your grandfather died. He was very patient with me and even helped me change the Wi-Fi password. After that, the sex was a bonus."

There's a sharp intake of breath, but it's simply Darcy gasping for breath while she laughs behind her hand.

Meanwhile, Richard's gone dark red. He slams one hand on the table. "Mom, that is incredibly inappropriate." His voice bellows out. But there's no controlling us now. Kyle's little gamble just popped the pressure cork on this weekend, and there's no stuffing it back in.

"Where the hell did you even get the number from?" Judy asks Betty, leaning across the table. "And do you still have it?"

"This is disgusting." Richard throws his napkin onto this plate and stands, scolding us like children. "You should all be ashamed of yourselves for entertaining this. I'm going to bed." Helen follows him out, and for a second, I see Kyle debate leaving with them, but he must decide against it.

After all, my brother is yet to say a word.

Sally's husband stands, looking sheepish, mumbling something about an early night. He takes the kids with him. Dale waves off his family when they leave, undoing his tie and leaving it hung around his neck as he sprawls back in his chair. At the other end of the table, Judy fills her wineglass to the brim and tops Sally up when she gestures for more.

Ivy, my absolute rock, clutches my hand between hers, and I can't begin to say how grateful I am for her. No matter what happens here tonight, I know things will be okay.

I don't dare look at Reed.

"Well, if we're spilling secrets finally," Mum says, jolting me out of my stupor, "I should admit that I was the one who crashed Dad's Porsche."

Dale finishes chugging back his wine. "Of course it was you. You know Dad never forgave me for that."

Sally scoffs, pulling her hair out of its painful bun.

"As if you're any better, Dale. Or have you forgotten about buying Mason that scholarship when he failed to get accepted anywhere?"

"Jeez. Did everyone here bribe their kids' way into school?" Ivy asks quietly to herself.

Dale, for his part, almost looks wistful. I already mentioned my family was a shit show, right? "Loopholes used to be cheaper. You should see how much these lobbyists are asking for now."

"Oh my god, Dale. Would you shut up?" Judy gripes. She, too, has embraced the loosened atmosphere, shedding her rings and earrings in a small pile in front of her. "Unless you're going to tell us about having a juicy affair or a terminal disease, I don't want to hear it."

Chastised, he sits back.

For a moment, I think that'll be all, and I'm preparing to say something — possibly announce a move back to London at this rate — but then Sally bursts out with "I slept with your husband," which has every head turning.

There's barely enough time to wonder *who* and *what* before Aunt J laughs. "I already knew that, Sal. Neither of you were subtle."

Sally covers her eyes with one hand. "God, he was terrible in the sack."

"He really was, and so bony," Judy muses, and Christ, half her glass is empty already.

Sally nods. "Wasn't he just? It was like fucking a stick figure," she says, causing them both to raise their glasses in a toast to shitty ex-husbands. Darcy and I share a silent *what the fuck?* across the table.

Then Joe leans forward, because sure, why not? This circus is officially out of control. Let's just add my ninety-year-old great-uncle to the mix. He's even smiling, for Christ's sake. I don't think I've seen him smile in over a decade. I'm not sure what to do with myself. "You know, Art and I went to a sex club once. It wasn't bad. A tall man in a gimp mask brought me water and let me use him as a footstool. Do you remember that, honey?"

Art nods. "I do."

"Oh, fucking Christ. Not you too." Reed groans, the first words he's said since Kyle stood up, and beside him, Darcy is slipping off her chair, wheezing. Reed takes one look at her and finally cracks a smile.

I have no clue what is happening, but thank fuck I'm sitting down.

"That's it?" Kyle asks, leaning on the table more as he teeters on his good leg. "You're all just going to act like this isn't a disgusting insult to our family name?"

"Oh, put a pin in it, Kyle," Mum says. "You could stand to be half the man Lincoln is."

Ivy's hand is trembling, but her voice is venomous. "I think everyone here would be far more interested in hearing how you're currently being sued by four different people, or how you've been attempting to blackmail Lincoln for the past week."

He's breathing hard now. "Does he give you a discount every time you leap to his defense?" His gaze darts to mine. "Guess it makes sense you took the easy road, since you've never been smart enough to make it as anything else."

Everything stops when Reed stands, his chair screeching loudly along the floor, his face calm enough that I know he's truly angry. I ready myself for the onslaught, but it's not me he walks to.

No, he steps up to Kyle, politely says, "I owe you this," and punches him square in the nose.

CHAPTER 53
THE AFTERMATH (ISN'T WHAT YOU THINK)

LINCOLN

Things get chaotic after that. Reed disappears to ice his hand and Kyle storms off in a literal bloody rage. Ivy and I slip out of the room somewhere between Joe telling the filthiest joke I've ever heard and Judy confessing to flashing a cop to get out of a speeding ticket. "I had no idea it would work, but I was still breastfeeding Hayden back then, so they looked huge —" And that's when my brain shut down to save me the therapy bill.

Ivy has already returned to our bedroom alone, with a stern command to "talk to your brother," so that's what I'm doing.

I discover him in Deacon's old office, disheveled and ridiculous. "Good god, Reed. What are you wearing?"

He sighs, one hand on the door. "I see your eyesight is deteriorating in your old age. They're pyjamas, as you well know."

I know I'm smiling too much, especially considering all that's happened tonight, but I can't be blamed. "You look like a Christmas cracker. Is that a matching dressing gown? Does Felicity pull you at midnight for a prize?"

"As witty as ever. Are you done?"

"Not even close."

He steps back, a smile tugging at his mouth. Either he's taking everything remarkably well, or he's drunk. Or both. "Come in, then. It's freezing. Tea?"

"Stupid question."

He's holding an icepack to his knuckles, setting it down to pour a second cup as I settle into one of the armchairs by the bookcase. There's a large teak desk by the bank of windows, but Deacon never really worked in here, treating it more like a den than an office. There's even a wet bar hidden in the globe in the corner.

I'm glad to find Reed here. Depending on how this conversation goes, I might have to swap the tea for whiskey.

When he hands me the mug, I can't help a wince. His knuckles are red and raw. "First time punching anyone?" I guess.

His cup wiggles dangerously in his nondominant hand as he takes the seat opposite me. "And the last, hopefully. It's bloody painful."

I cup my hands around the mug, warming them while I decide where to start.

Reed beats me to it. "So," he starts, stretching the word out as he stares into his tea. "Erotica." Ignoring the fact that I will now live the rest of my life with the memory of my brother saying that, I nod. He levels a shrewd look over the rim of his mug. "I knew letting you have your David Hume phase at sixteen was going to bite me in the arse one day."

Christ, he's definitely drunk if he's making a joke right now.

"You could have told me," he adds quietly.

"Could I?" I challenge.

Reed crosses one leg over the other, brushes lint off his knee. "You really expected me to think less of you for it? That I give a toss about impressing those twats? I don't. For fuck's sake, Kyle's the one who tried to access the trust."

I sit forward. "You knew? You could have fucking told me." Would have saved me a lot of stress. At this rate, the tally of what we haven't told each other could rival a Hugo treatise on the Parisian sewer system.

"There was nothing to tell. Security handled it, and even if he had gotten in, he would have discovered there's no trust left."

That shocks me awake. "Excuse me?"

More casual than he's ever been, Reed shrugs a shoulder, like this is old news. Like I shouldn't be worried, because he isn't, and yes, I suppose if Reed — the chancellor of overthinking — isn't panicked at this fact, then I'm definitely missing the bigger picture, and I must be, because he looks as far from worried as anyone could be.

In fact, he looks proud.

"After the shit show of a fight we suffered over the estate, I wanted us to be free of them. I invested a small amount in the business and then donated the rest. Why do you think I'm working so hard?" There's a weighted pause, one that sucks any humor out of the room. "Or did you have so little faith in me that you thought I'd become worse than Deacon?"

The hit lands, and Reed's usually do. "How the hell was I supposed to know any of that? The only times I ever see you are when you're hauling me into your office to slap my wrist."

I'm expecting him to get mad. That's how this usually goes. I yell, he yells, we stop talking for a year to cool off. Clearly, I'm not the only one exhausted with that game, because Reed sets his cup down and sighs. "Because it's the only way I ever get to see you anymore."

"Well, fuck." I blow out a long breath, scrubbing at my face with both hands.

It's no coincidence I knew where to find Reed. He's probably spent more time in this room over the years than he has in his own bed. I always lost him to this room when we came here, but it wasn't until that night in Bruges that it hit me: I might never get him back.

It remains our biggest fight. Also, our longest, if you count the preceding years.

It would be nice to retire it.

He rubs his fingers under his eyes, hissing when it strains his hurt hand. There are bags under his eyes. I knew he wasn't sleeping, but it looks much more like the regret I've seen in my own reflection. "When you called me for bail, I almost had a heart attack. Started thinking I'd never see you again—"

"Don't be ridiculous," I say.

"Well, what was I supposed to think? I couldn't do anything from half a world away. I should've been there. Maybe then you wouldn't have—"

"Become such an asshole?" I offer, but there's no heat behind it. Not anymore.

"Are you going to finish all my sentences?" He sighs. "I reacted poorly. I never meant… I was trying to protect you, but if I'd known you'd cut me out of your life, I would have handled it differently."

I swallow past the lump in my throat. "You were right to be worried." Tonight's the night for honesty, it seems. "I was a prick back then. Couldn't tell my arse from my elbow, but what I needed from you," I stop. "What I needed was a brother, not a warden."

Reed nods slowly, giving me a small smile that feels like a good first step. "I can do that."

"Good. Now pull out that bottle of whiskey I know is hiding in here and pour me a real drink."

CHAPTER 54
I LIKE A LITTLE CHAOS
IN MY CALM

IVY

Overnight, it was decided that we'd cut the reunion short. All morning, cars have come and gone to collect the extended family, Kyle leaving the loudest. Richard and Helen sent word of mutual migraines this morning, and we're all glad for it.

"Did Sal and Judy get away okay?" Astrid asks.

"Yes," Art says, drowning his cut croissant in jelly. "And the minions rushed off in various carpools."

"Ride shares," Joe corrects.

And then there were eight. The dining hall is way too big to host us, but no one wanted to ask the kitchen staff to deal with any more of our bullshit, not after dinner, so we're making the most of it, squatting at one end like someone tipped the room over and we're the clinging remains.

It's probably the only reason we hear the knock at the front door.

While everyone else shares a confused look, the little string pull in my gut tightens, and I turn to Astrid, who

I'm shocked to find is blushing. I grab for Lincoln's hand.

This is it. The last mystery to be solved.

"Lincoln," I whisper as our guest breaches the room.

Darcy gasps. "Oh my god."

Lincoln is beaming. "Dad? What the hell are you doing here? I thought your flight wasn't for a few days." He stands to pull his father into a hug, and I shut my mouth, stuffing my realization back down.

Better to stay in the wings this time around, and from the way Simon can't take his eyes off Astrid, it's definitely not going to take very long.

"Actually, I've been in town for a few days," he says, pulling out of the hug and standing a little awkwardly by Lincoln's side, like he wants to move but can't quite work out whether he's allowed.

"You know it's interesting, Mum," Reed says to the room. He looks ready for the surprises to be over. I don't blame him. "I had a phone call last week, from the Ritz in London, saying that they'd found your bracelet and needed to arrange a courier to get it home. Which is funny, because you were meant to be staying in Paris."

"And I saw you sneaking back into the house before breakfast yesterday," Darcy adds.

Astrid leans back in her chair, placing both hands in her lap. Her smile has been hard-coded on her face since Simon walked in.

"Your mother and I met last month for coffee," Simon starts, but is quickly interrupted when all three kids talk at the same time.

"Last month?"

"And you never said anything?"

"Do you want to hear the rest or not?" Simon puts a purple and gold tin on the table in front of Darcy. All three of his kids look joyful at the sight of it, so it must be some British thing I don't understand.

Now free to walk over to Astrid, Simon says hello by bending down to kiss her.

Darcy rips open the pack, exposing what looks like a mountain of brightly wrapped chocolates inside. "We're going to need more tea."

"Don't hog all the green triangles," Reed says, pulling the tin across the table. "Or I'm only leaving the toffee pennies."

Lincoln steals the tin briefly to pick out a handful of orange and purple ones before it's back in Darcy's hands.

The rest of us watch in awe. "It's like watching a feeding at the zoo," Art says.

I snort into my coffee.

"Can I make a suggestion?" Joe asks over the din.

Reed swallows a chocolate whole. "If it's about breakfast, then no."

Joe carries on. "Next year we should do this somewhere else." Everyone looks to Art and Joe, who is smiling serenely. "Deacon had ninety years of attention. It's time. He was born four minutes older and he never let me forget it. Next year we celebrate my way."

Lincoln kisses my cheek. "Sounds great to me."

"As long as Ivy is there, I'm in," Darcy says.

Simon reaches over with a napkin. "Darcy, don't talk with your mouth full."

"I don't think your family can take any more of me," I joke. But honestly, as long as I never see this house again, I'll go wherever they want.

Wherever Lincoln is, is home now.

"I bet Lincoln is making a valiant effort on behalf of us all," Reed says.

My face heats so fast I'm glad I'm sitting down, because I'm pretty sure there's not enough blood to make any of my limbs work.

"But I'm hoping to see more of you," he adds. Of course he would know about the job offer.

I slip my fingers into Lincoln's, as solid and certain in my hand as my decision to say what I do next. "Then I guess I'll be seeing you in the office, boss."

After the congratulations die down, I open a text from Mom.

The Great and Powerful Mom: I love you always, my beautiful girl. I know I can be tough, but I'm always proud of you.

Me: Love you too. Call you tomorrow after we get back. Also, I want you to visit so I can introduce you to my boyfriend.

The Great and Powerful Mom: I'll need a photo first ;) He better treat you like a queen. You deserve nothing less. Talk to you soon. xoxox

Lincoln returns to the seat beside me, his arm draped around my shoulders. That's better. "Everything all right?"

"Better than all right," I say, kissing him.

"Now…" Reed stands. "If anyone else in this family has a secret, I'm going to need you to take it to the grave. Or wait until next year. Lincoln, you're not allowed another for at least three years."

Lincoln stares deeply into my eyes. "Then I guess I'll have to propose now."

My heart cuts out while I remember how to breathe.

"Don't even joke about that," Reed and I say at the same time, and then his brother adds, "Good god, man, at least do it properly."

I smile up at Lincoln and cup the growing stubble on his cheek. He looks sexy and messy in my favorite jeans and a loose white T-shirt. I want him this way, and every other way I can.

Everything goes kind of soft and fuzzy as I realize what we have ahead of us. More of this. Each other. "You heard your brother," I tell him as he kisses my palm. "If you're really going to ask, you better make it good. My last boyfriend once promised me an entire theater."

"What happened to the little things?" Lincoln asks, gray eyes sparkling.

"I guess I'm greedy." I reach up and twist a strand of his hair around my finger, knowing everyone in this room can see the way he lights me up. It's impossible to hide now that I know this is real. "I want everything you can give me, grand and small."

"Good." In his eyes is everything I'm feeling returned tenfold, and I know I don't want to be anyone, or anywhere, else.

DOWN ON MY KNEES

IVY

SHORTLY AFTER

"You've never sucked a man's cock before?"

I blink up, wide-eyed, from where I'm kneeling on the floor, then shake my head.

Lincoln and I love each other, but that doesn't stop us from finding new and exciting versions to fall for every day.

It absolutely doesn't stop us from slipping into the roles of someone new occasionally either.

What can I say? Lincoln likes to test ideas out before he records them, and he's *very good* at his job. It also happens to make me want to be very, very good in return.

He's sprawled back on the couch, legs splayed wide on each side of me, stretching the limits of his sweats. The hard line of his dick against his thigh is making my mouth water.

"It's perfectly natural. Let me show you."

He thumbs his waistband with one hand, reaching for me with the other. Warm fingers glide along my jaw, trace over my lips, slide onto my tongue.

I used to get in trouble for putting odd things in my mouth — chewing on the ends of pens, Barbies' hands, Legos. Was told it was a bad habit. *Dirty*. But I guess I never grew out of it.

There's so much hunger in his eyes that I have to press my palms flat against my thighs to stop myself from crawling into his lap. When I walked out of our bedroom in a sundress, I thought Lincoln would take me on the floor right then and there (don't worry, I'll be cashing in that raincheck in about forty minutes).

Getting dressed to suit the part is always worth it where he's concerned.

He pulls his fingers free, and they glisten in the overhead light. "You need to do as I say. Can you do that for me?" he asks, tone firm, and I can already feel how soaked my panties are.

I nod eagerly, ready for my lesson.

"Good girl."

He slides his hand into his pants, taking hold of his dick and giving it a few slow pulls. He's such a damn tease.

"We'll start slow," he says, and finally frees himself, pushing his waistband below his balls, and fuck, I can't wait to taste him. Holding himself at the base, his huge hand only emphasizes how big he is.

"Come here." His free hand slides around to my hair, massaging gently before pulling me toward his hard cock. "I want you to lick it." His voice is like charred gravel.

I swear I could come from the sound alone.

"Just your mouth for now, all right?"

Keeping my hands on my knees, I slide forward, leaning in until I can feel the heat coming off his skin, breathing in the thick scent of him, precum and body wash and a little sweat. My mouth is watering.

Guiding me by the back of my head, he presses the tip of his cock to my lips, and I lick around the head, pressing sloppy kisses down his shaft and back again, getting more confident as I go.

"Use your tongue. That's it. Good. Just like that. Get it nice and wet."

Fuck. If anything is wet, it's me. I clench my thighs together with a whine.

"God, you're so hungry for it," he says, and it's so incredibly rewarding to hear the strain in his voice already. "Look at you. You're salivating."

Positioning myself so I can look up through my lashes at him, I take the head of him in my mouth, swirl my tongue around the sensitive skin.

"Fuck, that's it. Right there. You're doing so well."

He pulls out of my mouth, fisting himself and spreading my saliva along his cock. "Are you ready for more?"

Oh my god, am I ready.

His smile is wicked when I nod. "Open up, then." I let my mouth fall open, pushing my tongue out. "We're going to start gentle. Careful of your teeth." He slides in, filling my mouth inch by inch, hot and heavy. I want to pack up and live here forever. "Perfect, there you go."

Jesus, my clit is throbbing. I'm dying to touch myself; it would probably only take ten seconds for me to come, but he hasn't given me permission, and I know from experience it'll be so much sweeter if I wait.

I trust him to take care of me.

"Keep going. You can take it."

When he pulls me off his cock, I have to gasp in a breath in the second before he pushes back into my mouth. Fuck, I need to touch myself so badly.

"You want it deep, don't you, dirty girl? Come on, Ivy. I'm doing all the work here."

He lets go of my head, placing his hand on his thigh, digging his fingers in like he needs to hold himself back from touching me.

I bob my head, taking him deeper and deeper, until he's hitting the back of my throat with each pass. Lincoln groans so deeply I feel it rumble under my skin. "Fuck, yes. Take me all the way. You're so fucking good to me."

And I love it, curling over him, both hands crushing the sundress in my grip, spit dripping over his cock and down my throat as I start moving faster, fucking my face on his cock. My breathing is crashing in my ears, burning through my nose, but it's worth it to watch him come undone when I hold myself down long enough to choke a little.

"Jesus fucking Christ, you're going to make me come so fucking hard."

I pull off with a cough, and fuck, my throat is going

to be raw tomorrow. But I can't get enough of him. My underwear is ruined, soaked through. I shift my heel underneath me for some much-needed friction as I dive back onto his dick.

He brushes his thumb tenderly across my cheek, so much love in that simple gesture I have to moan as I swallow around him. His fingers jolt, then he's cupping my cheek and coming down my throat with a rumble deep enough I feel it in my bones.

He's on his knees as soon as I pull off, framing my face in his hands and kissing me thoroughly.

"Christ, your mouth. Your beautiful fucking mouth," he says, kissing me again and again.

"Do I pass?" I croak, my throat aching just enough that I can't laugh, but I can still enjoy the breathy chuckle Lincoln lets out.

"With flying colors."

"Good," I breathe, clutching at him. "Usually, my mouth is getting me into trouble."

He presses his smile to my lips, my jaw, my neck. "I wouldn't have it any other way."

I AM ME

IVY

A WHILE LATER

I've spent a lot of time asking myself who I am. Trying to figure out if it was everything I liked as a kid, before I had to make my own doctor appointments or knew how to fill in a tax return.

Maybe it was who I became in college, when I started to finally feel like an adult, making grown-up choices about my future and discovering how big and broken the world really was.

Back then, leaving my childhood behind meant walking away from whimsy and daydreams and accepting that with responsibility came endless meetings and emails and saving to go to the dentist.

Are we who we wish we were? Who we could have been, if only we'd made different choices?

Which version do we count as the real us?

Or are we the sum of them all?

If we are all persistently shifting and changing and

becoming new again, will we ever really have one true version of ourselves?

I know better now.

I am me.

I am the choices I make and the causes I fight for and the way I treat the people I care about.

Lincoln says I'm too young to be getting existential. He eyes the nonfiction books that have begun congregating on my side table with a fond sort of amusement.

Yet he'll still lie beside me at night, curled around me like a parenthesis, and let me read to him.

Lincoln must be a mind reader.

He always knows when I need to be steadied, how to make me speechless when I'm talking too much or how to fill in the silence with what I can't say. Since the day I came down to the bar and found him there, he's made sure I know how he feels, poured it into every look, every touch, every word. Finds out what I want and then gives it, over and over and over.

He still makes me nervous in all the best ways, butterflies dancing around my heart like being hit with a fairy-tale wish.

My showers are concerts now, with candles flickering against the tiles while I serenade the room.

He's a soft bed at night, a shot of Jaeger on opening night, my favorite song on repeat.

It's too much. It's not enough. It's every fantasy brought to life.

SAY YES AGAIN
LINCOLN

MUCH LATER (until forever)

I swear London wasn't half as cold as this when I left. Thankfully, I have the most delicious body heater with me.

It's been years since I've woken up alone in a bed, and as usual, Ivy is curled tightly around me, her breathing slow and deep. Curls fan out around her head like a shield, as soft and wild as she is. I bury my nose in them, drinking my fill of the rose and citrus scent I've been addicted to since I met her.

I still remember her in that red dress, cut deathly low, her beautiful skin singing out to be devoured.

Fuck, I love this woman.

We're only here for a few days. It's not as long as most of our trips, but Ivy insisted we make time, since Mum will only turn seventy once.

Reed and Felicity and Darcy are here, which means

the trip is planned down to the second, and any time I'm not taking the piss out of Reed for his ridiculous clothing choices, Darcy is capturing it on film so we can rib him about them later.

I'm kissing my way along Ivy's shoulders as she wriggles awake. "Morning," she says, voice thick with sleep. With her head still tucked safely against my chest, there's no doubt she hears how my heart beats faster for her.

It's rare for me to wake before her, a sign she's been working too hard lately, but it's worth it to have the chance to watch her blink those beautiful brown eyes open, shining back at me with a depth of feeling that still rocks me to my core.

"Good morning, gorgeous."

I slide my hand under her shirt, enjoying the feel of her soft skin, until Ivy's soft smile is shining back at me.

"How do you manage to get more beautiful every day?" I ask, cupping her cheek. "If you keep taking my breath away like this, I'm going to need to see a doctor."

"Good idea," she says, her eyes not leaving mine as she turns to kiss my palm. "You can ask why your hands are always so cold."

"You love my hands."

Her eyes sparkle with mischief before she's taking my hand and turning it. My dick wakes up the instant she sucks on my index finger.

A quick look at the cheap plastic clock on the hotel side table informs me we have to be at breakfast in twenty minutes if we want to keep with Reed's schedule.

Which I absolutely don't plan on doing.

I brush my thumb across the tender skin under her eyes, where stress has been camping out for weeks.

In the years since she started working for my sister, the business has flourished in ways none of us could have expected. One offhanded suggestion from Ivy became her passion project, working with Felicity and the local shelters she paired with to provide training and job opportunities within the office and the factory.

She even engineered a positive hit piece about the company, highlighting the great working conditions and benefits, along with a personal challenge for their competition to do better.

Darcy says her candidness has made her a favorite in the company. I don't doubt it. I can't imagine any good person Ivy couldn't charm.

As her phone alarm beeps — it's honestly adorable how accommodating she is to Reed's absurd organizing — Ivy pulls away with a long-suffering sigh. No doubt rethinking how far her budding friendship with my brother extends.

Silencing her phone, she buries her face in her pillow and mumbles something I don't catch. Since Mum moved back to London, we've made visiting a habit, but the jet lag bowls Ivy over each time.

Plastering myself to her back, I begin to suck a fresh mark on her neck to replace the one that is slowly fading, groaning when she pushes back against my morning arousal.

"Forget my brother. Let me spend the day ravishing you."

Ivy sighs. "Oh god, that sounds amazing. But Astrid and I are grabbing lunch with Francis later, and Darcy promised to come shopping with me first."

With great reluctance, I let her go, watching as she shoots into the bathroom to freshen up.

I'm dressed and only mildly panicking by the time she exits again, looking fucking phenomenal in an over-sized lilac jumper tucked into a yellow leather miniskirt.

My breath hangs in my lungs as she walks past the gift I've placed on the floor, which is what I was hoping for. Francis's next show opens tomorrow night, and Ivy has no idea that our mystery date will include front-row seats.

"Oh," I say, pretending to pat down the pockets of my dress pants. "I think I've dropped the invitation Reed gave us; do you see it anywhere?"

"Let me look." Ivy turns around, searching, and yes, there, she bends down to get the tickets. "Is this it? Wait..."

Her face is already lit up with surprise when she stands and faces me, but her eyes go wide when she sees me on one knee.

"Ivy." I open the ring box, my heart pounding in my throat. "I'm going to need you to marry me."

"Be serious."

"I am."

She's clasping the tickets to her heart.

"I'm sure you were expecting something with far

more spectacle, and trust me, Mum will make enough of a ruckus to satisfy you later. She's been on me about this for months—"

"Lincoln," she says, breathless. "You're rambling."

I noticed. Damn nerves.

"In any case, I can't think of anything bigger than how much I utterly adore you, and short of pulling the stars from the sky, I may never find anything appropriately equal to your brilliance. So I humbly offer this: My complete devotion. For as long as life exists in the universe, it will be true that I love you."

Her eyes shine with unshed tears, and for as many words as I've said, in this moment, Ivy has none.

As the seconds tick by, we stay like that, eyes locked, my breathing loud in my ears. Waiting.

"Lincoln…"

"Yes?"

"I'm." She visibly swallows, then surprises me by falling to her knees, grabbing my face with both hands, and kissing me with force. "I'm so in love with you I'm a little sick about it. I want to love you every day for the rest of my life. It's time for the rest of the adventure."

Scooping her up in my arms, I get lost in her lips and hands and the way she lights up my future with a blinding magnificence I haven't yet found the words for. Though I'm sure Ivy could come up with something suitable.

Fuck, she's incredible.

"I don't mean to be pedantic," I say, finally pulling back. "But I haven't heard a yes yet."

The first tear hits her cheek as she laughs. "Yes, of course, yes. There's no other answer."

Well, thank the bloody heavens for that.

THE END (for real).

THANK YOU!

My first and largest thanks will always be to you, my wonderful readers.

I absolutely love to hear from you, so don't be afraid to send me a message! Every reaction DM, edit, unhinged ALL CAPS scream, and Dean Winchester gif makes my day.

If you loved the book and want to spread the word, please consider leaving a review wherever you hang out online. Your support means the world to me, and every little bit helps.

Dream big, live loud, create magic.

Dani xo

ABOUT THE AUTHOR

Dani McLean is Bi/NB Australian author who writes shamelessly fun contemporary romance with an open-door policy.

She loves coffee, karaoke, and stories that make you kick your feet up in the air.

If lost, she can be found on Ao3, or echo located through her kookaburra laugh.

To stay updated with new releases, giveaways, and more, sign up for her newsletter, or connect with her on social media.

Find Dani on TikTok and Instagram @danim-cleanwrites

ALSO BY DANI MCLEAN

The Out of Office Series:

Take It Offline

Take My Word

———

Mortgage of Convenience

———

The Movie Magic Novellas:

Midnight, Repeated

Not My Love Story

A Missing Connection

It Has To Be You

The Forces of Love

———

The Cocktail Series:

Love & Rum

Sex & Sours

Risks & Whiskey